LADY OF SEDUCTION

AMANDA MCCABE

Created with Vellum

PRAISE FOR AMANDA MCCABE

Praise for Laurel McKee's The Daughters of Erin Trilogy

Duchess of Sin

"4 Stars! Fascinating... readers will be eager to read the final story in McKee's trilogy."

—RT Book Reviews

"For a thrilling, sensuous trip to old Ireland, don't miss *Duchess of Sin*... I recommend reading the first book, and I look forward to *Lady of Seduction*."

—RomRevtoday.com

"A truly remarkable book that I could not turn away from... a one-of-a-kind read [with] a love to warm the heart and an adventure that never ended."

—FreshFiction.com

Countess of Scandal

"An unforgettable love story... captivating and poignant! Laurel McKee wields her pen with grace and magic."

—Lorraine Heath, New York Times bestselling author of *Midnight Pleasures with a Scoundrel*

"4 Stars! McKee sets the stage for a romantic adventure that captures the spirit of Ireland and a pair of star-crossed lovers to perfection."

—RT Book Reviews

"I am completely hooked on this series already—and I was from nearly the first page of this book! Ms. McKee tells a masterful story of love, rebellion, and beneath it all, devotion to a land and people... Elizabeth and Will's emotional attachment, as well as the obvious physical chemistry they share, leaps from the page."

—RomanceReaderatHeart.com

"Ms. Laurel McKee's magical pen captivates you instantaneously! She has fashioned blistering sensual romantic scenes and a love story that will be forever etched in your mind."

—TheRomanceReadersConnection.com

"Eliza's and Will's happy-ever-after, once reached, is both powerfully satisfying and forever engraved on the reader's mind and heart. Every word sings with unyielding intensity... Beautifully written, *Countess of Scandal* reads like a captivating love story of epic proportions. The ultimate page-turner."

—RomanceJunkies.com

"A hero to steal your heart!"

—Elizabeth Boyle, New York Times bestselling author

"An immensely satisfying and sophisticated blend of history and romance. I loved every gorgeous, breathtaking page!"

—Julianne MacLean, USA Today bestselling author of *When a Stranger Loves Me*

CHAPTER

ONE

OFF THE COAST OF IRELAND, LATE
SPRING 1803

This was not how Caroline Blacknall expected to die. Not that she had ever thought about it very much.

Living took up too much time and energy to think about dying. But she would have thought it would be quietly, in her bed, after a long life of scholarship and travel and family. Not drowning at the age of twenty on a crazy, ill-advised pursuit.

Caroline clung to the slippery mast as a cold wave washed over her and lightning pierced the black sky over her head. The little fishing boat rocked and twisted under the force of the howling wind. Waves crashed over its hull, higher and stronger each time, nearly swamping them completely.

She couldn't hear the shouts of the crew any longer, or even her own screams. All she could hear was deafening thunder and the crash of those encroaching waves. She squeezed her eyes shut and held even tighter to the mast. She dug her ragged, broken nails into the sodden wood. A splinter pierced her skin, but she didn't mind the pain, or the bitter cold wind that tore through her wet cloak. It told her she was still alive, though probably not for much longer.

Behind her closed eyes, she saw the faces of her sisters, Eliza and Anna, saw her mother's gentle smile. She felt the tiny hands of her niece and nephew wrapped around her shoulders, heard her step-daughter Mary's laughter. Were they all lost to her forever?

No! She had just begun to live again after her husband's death a year ago. She had just begun to find her own purpose in the world. That was what this voyage was about, putting the past to rest and moving into the future. She couldn't give up now. Blacknalls did not surrender!

She opened her eyes and twisted her head around to see the crew of the little boat scurrying and sliding over the deck as they desperately tried to save the vessel and themselves. They hadn't wanted to take on a passenger, especially a woman, but she had begged and bribed until they gave in. No one but fishermen ever went to the distant, forbidding Muirin Inish.

She wagered that they would never take a "cursed" woman aboard again, if they all made it through this.

Caroline tilted her head back to stare up into the boiling sky. It couldn't be much past noon, but that sky was black as pitch, dark as midnight. Only jagged flashes of lightning broke through the gloom, lighting up the thick clouds and the turbulent sea.

When they set out from the mainland that morning, it was gray and misty. One of the sailors muttered about the absence of sea birds, the silence of the water, but despite these supposed ill omens, they set sail. Birds couldn't stand in the way of commerce, and Caroline refused to be left behind. She had traveled too far to turn away now, when her destination was at last within her grasp.

She had even glimpsed the famous pink granite cliffs of Muirin Inish, so close, yet still so far, before those black clouds closed in. It was all much too fast.

Was he there somewhere, she wondered? Did he watch the storm from those very cliffs?

A crack sounded above her, loud as a whiplash, and she looked up to find that the mast, her one lifeline, had cracked. Horrified, she watched it slowly, oh so slowly, topple toward the deck.

Caroline felt paralyzed, captured, and she couldn't move. But somehow, she managed to throw herself backward, tearing her numb hands from the wood.

She moved just in time. The broken mast drove down into the beleaguered deck and cut a wound in the boat that swiftly bled more salt water. The boat twisted onto its side, and Caroline was thrown into the waiting sea.

She had thought it was cold before, but it was not. *This* was cold, a freezing knife-thrust into her very heart that stole her breath away. The waves closed over her head and dragged her down.

Somehow she ripped away the ties of her cloak and kicked free of its suffocating folds. She had learned to swim as a child, lovely summer days with her sisters at the lake at their home Killinan Castle. She blessed those days now as she summoned all her strength, pushed away the numb cold, and swam hard for the surface.

Her head broke through the water, and she sucked in a deep breath of air. The bulk of the floundering boat was far away, a pale slash in the inky sea. The rocky cliffs of the shore beckoned through the darkness, seemingly very far away.

Caroline kicked toward it anyway, moving painfully slowly through the waves. Her arms were sore and terribly weak; it took every ounce of her will to keep lifting them, to not give in to the restful allure of the deep. She knew that if she couldn't keep moving, she would be lost, and she couldn't give up.

A piece of wood drifted past her, a section of the broken mast. She grabbed on to it and hauled herself up onto its support. It floated toward shore, taking her with it, and all she could do was hang on tightly.

Once it had been fire that separated her from him, burning, scarring fire and the acrid sear of smoke. Now it was water, cold and just as burning. It felt like the primal wrath of the ancient Irish gods that she loved studying so much.

Caroline pressed her cheek to the wood of her little raft and closed her eyes. "This shouldn't be happening to me," she whispered. It was utterly absurd. She was a respectable widow, a bluestocking who preferred quiet hours in the library to anything else. She was not adventurous and bold like her sisters. How did she find herself caught in a perilous adventure straight out of one of Anna's beloved romantic novels?

But she knew why it was that she came here. Because of *him*, Grant Dunmore. A man she should have been happy never to see again. They seemed fated to brave the elements together through their own folly.

Caroline felt something brush against her legs, something surprisingly solid. She opened her eyes to find she was not far from the rocky shore of Muirin Inish. She tried to kick toward it, but her legs had become totally numb and refused to work.

She sobbed in terrible frustration. The tide was catching at her, trying to drag her back out to sea, even as land was so tantalizingly near!

Above the wind, she heard a shout. Now she was surely hallucinating. But it came again, a rough call. "Hold on, miss! I've got you."

Someone grabbed her aching arm and dragged her up and off the mast. She cried out at the loss of her one solid reality and tried to cling to it, yet her rescuer was relentless. He wrapped a hard, muscled arm around her waist and pulled her with him as he swam for the shore.

Caroline's chest ached, as if a great weight pressed down on her, and dark spots danced before her eyes. She couldn't lose consciousness, not now, so close to redemption! She struggled to stay awake, to hold on.

Her rescuer carried them to shore at last. He held her in his arms, tight against his chest. as he ran over the rough, stony beach. Caroline was vaguely aware that she was pressed to naked skin, warm on her cold cheek, like hot satin over iron strength. His heartbeat pounded in her ear, quick and powerful, alive. It made her feel alive, too, her heart stirring back into being.

He laid her down on a patch of wet sand and

gently rolled her onto her side. "*Diolain*, don't be dead," be shouted. "Don't you dare be dead!"

His voice was hoarse from the salt water, but she could hear the aristocratic English accent under that roughness. What was an Englishman doing on an isolated rock like Muirin Inish? What was she doing there? She couldn't even remember, not now.

He yanked at the tangled drawstring of her plain muslin gown, ripping it free to ease the ruined fabric from her shoulders. Through her chemise he pounded his fist between her shoulder blades, and she choked out the seawater that clogged her lungs. The pain in her chest eased, and she dragged in a deep breath.

"Thank God," her rescuer muttered.

Caroline turned slowly onto her back as she reached up to rub the salt water from her aching eyes. The man knelt beside her, and the first things she noticed were the stark blue-black tattoos etched on his sun-browned skin. A circle of twisted Celtic knotwork around his upper arm, a small Irish cross on his chest. Dark, wet hair lay heavy on his lean shoulders.

Dazed and fascinated, she reached up to trace the Celtic cross with her fingertip. The elaborate design blurred before her eyes.

He suddenly caught her hand tightly in his. "Caroline?" he said. "What the devil are you doing here?"

She slowly raised her gaze to his face, focusing on those extraordinary golden-brown eyes. She had seen those eyes in her dreams for four long years.

And now she remembered exactly why she had come to Muirin Inish.

"I'm here to see you, of course, Grant," she said. Then the world turned black.

CHAPTER
TWO

S ir Grant Dunmore carried Caroline gently in his arms as he climbed the steep, ancient stairs cut into the granite cliffs. The cold rain still pounded down from the dark sky, and thunder echoed off the stone. He had wrapped her in his discarded shirt, but that was quickly soaked through, and she trembled against him.

The sea might claim her yet, if he didn't get her warm and dry as quick as could be.

Her head lay heavy on his shoulder, her heart-shaped face pale as snow. Her dark hair clung to her skin like seaweed, and purple circles were like bruises under her eyes. She had always been slender, like an elegant willow, but now she seemed even smaller, a featherweight in his arms.

Caroline Blacknall. What was she doing here, at the ends of the Earth, after so long? After the terrible things he did to her, to so many people, he could not imagine why she would ever want to see him again. When he had glimpsed the hulk of the damned ship from his tower and ran down to try to save whom he could, he had never dreamed he would find Caroline in those waters.

She let out a deep sigh and twisted restlessly in his arms. He held on to her tighter, the soles of his sodden boots slipping on the wet steps. "Not much farther," he muttered against her ear, and she went still.

He had heard that she married a few years ago, and she wore a slim gold band on her finger. What sort of husband was he, to send his wife out into the middle of the sea on some wild, unknown errand? He obviously wasn't taking care of her as she deserved. The bastard.

Grant laughed ruefully at himself. He had no room to criticize anyone at all. He wasn't even able to take care of himself, let alone a bluestocking Blacknall woman.

At last, he reached the top of the cliffs and turned along the twisting, narrow path that led to his home. Muirin Castle was cold and forbidding, no place to nurse a woman back to health, but the small village was too far away. A freezing gray mist had wrapped around the whole island, closing them off from the world.

That was why he came here four years ago, wounded, scarred, trying to atone for his sins. If he hid here, he couldn't hurt anyone again. He should have known the past would catch up with him.

She said she came here to find him—and he had led her into danger once more.

Her fingers suddenly tightened on his shoulder, and her eyes fluttered open. Those eyes were the same as before, deep coffee-brown and fringed with

8

long, inky lashes. And they still seemed to look deep inside him, seeing every cursed shadow of his soul.

"We're almost there, Caroline," he said. "You'll be warm by the fire in no time."

She said nothing, just stared up at him. She slowly raised her hand to his cheek and brushed her cold fingers over the scarred left side of his face.

He recoiled, as if the fire that left those marks touched him again. Her hand fell away.

"It's been so long since I saw you, Grant," she whispered. Her hand dropped to his shoulder. "Yet it feels like it was only yesterday. How is that possible?"

Grant knew why that was for him—he thought of her every day of his lonely life here. But he said nothing, just held her tighter as he carried her through the gates of Muirin Castle.

His home was built of dark gray stone, nearly covered by thick skeins of overgrown vines. It blended into the mist, like an enchanted, cursed castle in some fairy tale. The tall, crenellated towers were shrouded in fog, and no light glowed in the narrow, old arrow-slit windows.

Grant pushed open the stout, iron-bound door with his shoulder and stumbled into the dim foyer. It was just as cold there as it was outside, with the cracked flagstone floor and stone walls. But his housekeeper, old Mrs. McCann from the village, stood at the top of the twisting stairs, staring down at him and his "guest" in open-mouthed astonishment

"Light a fire in one of the bedchambers, Mrs. McCann, quickly," Grant shouted. He ran up the steps two at a time; Caroline bad gone limp and silent in his arms again. "And send someone to the village for the doctor."

9

"He's gone to the mainland yesterday," she said. She scurried after him into the one upstairs chamber that was habitable besides his own.

"Then we'll have to nurse her as best we can," he muttered. He laid Caroline down carefully in the middle of the cavernous old bed and palled off her wet clothes before wrapping her in the heavy velvet counterpane. She sighed and slid deep under the haven of the covers.

"But—who is she?" Mrs. McCann said. She stood in the doorway, twisting her hands fretfully in her apron.

"A mermaid," Grant said. "We need a fire, hot water, and some soup. And clean clothes for her. Now!"

Mrs. McCann dashed away, and Caroline murmured in her sleep.

Grant leaned over the bed to tuck the blankets closer, not even noticing the cold on his own damp skin, the rivulets of rainwater that dripped from his long hair down his bare back. He only saw Caroline, so pale in the huge old bed. Caroline, flown suddenly back into his life.

He gently smoothed the tangled, seaweed-like hair back from her brow. Her skin felt slightly warmer under his touch, a faint trace of pink beneath the white marble of her cheeks. *Don't let her catch fever!* Her soft, pale lips parted on a breath, and be remembered how once, so long ago, he had tasted that mouth with his own. The merest, lightest brush of a kiss, and yet he remembered it so much more vividly than any night of lust with any other woman. "Caroline," he whispered. "Why were you out in that storm? Why does your husband not take better care of you?"

"Because he is dead," she whispered. Her eyes opened, and she stared up at him with an unfocused intensity. "I take care of myself."

He smiled at her. "Not doing a very good job of it, are you?"

"I was doing all right, until today. It doesn't seem *you* can take care of yourself, Grant. You'll surely catch a cold standing there with no clothes on."

He gave a startled laugh. Caroline Blacknall had not changed—she was still bossy, tart-tongued, and practical. But there was something new in her eyes as well, a flash of womanly awareness as her gaze swept over his bare chest.

Before he could answer, two of the footmen hurried in with buckets of coal for the fire. The maids followed with towels and hot water, and Mrs. McCann shooed him out of the room as they all set to work. He had never seen such efficiency in his quiet home before.

At the doorway, he glanced back to see that Caroline's eyes were closed again. She seemed to sink back into exhausted sleep even as the maids swathed her in towels and a clean nightdress.

"I'm so sorry, Caroline," he whispered, as he closed the door behind him. How he wished she had not come back to him again, reminding him of all he could never have. All that his sins had cost him.

11

CHAPTER
THREE

The flames scorched Caroline's skin, the thick smoke was acrid and bitter in her throat, even from a distance. She watched helplessly as the old warehouse collapsed in on itself—with Grant inside.

It was a dream, Caroline knew that very well. She had this dream so many times over the past few years, a vision of a frozen winter river embankment in Dublin, and watching the fires of Hell consume the night. But while it was happening, she could never rouse herself to reality. She was trapped, reliving that fire over and over.

And it felt so very real, that heat on her face, the ashes that stung her eyes. The tears for a man who was lost, in so many ways.

"*I haven't even started learning who I might be,*" he had told her, as they sat together in that freezing warehouse, kidnapper and captive bound together in the moments before the inferno. Bound together by an understanding that was strange and deep. "*Except for my evils, of course.*"

Caroline couldn't argue with the evils part. Grant

had wanted to marry her beautiful sister Anna, to make Anna part of his social and political ambitions, his perfect wife for his high place in society. When Anna preferred his cousin and enemy, the wild Irish Duke of Adair, Grant kidnapped Anna—and accidentally caught Caroline in that snare, too.

Yet in that moment, as Caroline stared up into his inhumanly beautiful face and saw the deep sadness of his eyes, she couldn't help but reach out to him. To try to touch the heart that he claimed he no longer had. She traced her fingertips over his cheek, and the feel of his skin, the harsh angles of his face, were more real to her than anything.

"*I think there is more to you than evils,*" she had whispered.

Those beautiful golden-brown eyes had narrowed as he watched her. Very slowly, as if he fought hard against something inside himself, be leaned toward her and his lips touched hers, lightly, tenderly. This was not how she imagined her first kiss would be, with a too-handsome, kidnapping villain, in a freezing old warehouse. Yet a sudden feeling of rightness shivered through her, as if this was what she had been waiting for her whole life. All her studies, all the tales of the fiery, forbidden passions of ancient Irish gods, could never have prepared her for the feelings of that kiss.

She reached out for him, desperately—and then the world exploded...

Caroline sat straight up in bed, gasping for breath. For an instant, she thought the smoke choked her again. She had no idea where she was, and a cold panic washed over her. What was happening to her? Was she going mad?

13

Then she felt the softness of old velvet under her hands and the gentle heat of the fire on her face. It was the comforting crackle of flames in the grate, not the consuming inferno of four years ago. It was just a dream. That was all over and done with. But she was still in trouble, for she was sleeping in Grant Dunmore's house.

Caroline slid back down against the pillows and stared up at the embroidered underside of the faded canopy. Everything came flooding back to her then—the storm that gathered so suddenly, overwhelming the little fishing boat. Being swallowed by the sea, and plucked out again by Grant.

He had carried her here, to this strange castle that looked like the dwelling of some magical ogre in an old myth. She was at his mercy again, miles and miles away from civilization.

She groaned and closed her eyes, listening to the crackle of the fire and the lash of freezing rain against the narrow old windows. This was what she wanted, wasn't it? Not the near drowning, of course, but to find Grant, to ask for his help. It seemed so easy, in her snug house back in Dublin. After all, that terrible drama was years ago, and she was a sensible widow.

Not so sensible now. Grant was not the sophisticated, aristocratic gentleman that he had once been, the man all the ladies swooned over. The most handsome man in Dublin. He was a wild, long-haired, tattooed islander now, his gorgeous face scarred by that fire, his eyes hard. Whatever she had once glimpsed in them, whatever connection she once imagined, was gone.

And she had no way off Muirin Inish.

Caroline eased back the bedclothes and carefully

14

slid her legs off the edge of the mattress. She felt battered and weak after fighting with the sea, her muscles sore, but she made herself climb down from the high bedstead to the floor. She wore a strange nightgown that was much too large for her, a voluminous tent of white flannel that flapped over her hands and pooled around her feet. Those feet were bare, the scarred wooden floor cold under her soles.

Her head spun with dizziness as she stood upright, and she clung to the carved bedpost until it passed. Her chamber was large and dim, lit only by the fire in the stone grate, and it was full of old, heavy, dark wood furniture. It smelled slightly dusty and stale, as if it was not much used. She carefully moved across the floor, holding on to chairs and chests when she became dizzy again, until she came to the window. She pushed back the green velvet draperies and unlatched the old-fashioned mullioned glass casement to throw it open. A blast of cold, salty air washed over her face and blew away the last clinging vestige of her dream.

She found herself looking down over a cliff face into the lashing, roiling sea far below. It crashed against the rocks as if it would carry the castle away, but the old stones stood firm.

She shivered as she remembered the cold waves closing over her head. Where was the poor crew of the boat? Had they been rescued, too? Or was she alone?

The chamber door flew open behind her, and she spun around to find Grant standing there. He held a lamp in one hand, and its flickering golden light cast shadows over his lean, ruined face and the tangled waves of his brown hair. He was more fully dressed now than he had been before, in a loose white shirt and doeskin breeches, but that wildness still clung to him. It was a part of him now; it was him.

He had changed. He was a stranger to her. A frightening, primitively attractive stranger.

"*Diolain*, Caroline," he growled. "Are you trying to kill yourself with the ague?"

He plunked the lamp down on a table and crossed the room in four long strides to catch her up in his arms. He swept her high against his chest and carried her back to her abandoned bed.

"I wanted to see if the storm had passed," she murmured, as he tugged the blankets up around her again.

"It hasn't," he said. "And it won't, not for a few days anyway. It's a very foolish time of year to try and cross from the mainland."

Caroline noticed that he carefully kept the scarred left side of his face turned from her. From the right, he was as beautiful as ever, his profile all sharp, clean, elegant angles, high cheekbone and arched brow. Yet she wanted to see all of him, the real him, as he was now. Not as he had lived in her dreams all those years.

"The captain of the boat said the weather would stay clear long enough to reach Muirin," she said.

"Then he was a fool," Grant said harshly. "Both because of the weather and because of the French. Haven't you heard they patrol these waters?"

"I thought that was just hysterical gossip. There's been so much of that since the Uprising. And since the Peace of Amiens, we have a truce with the French, do we not?"

The corner of his sensual lips quirked, almost but

not quite, as if he would smile. "You never did heed gossip, did you?"

"No. I have better things to do with my time."

"You would have done well to listen this time, and stayed away from Muirin Inish."

"Would I?" Probably she would, if she were as sensible as she thought. But she didn't feel sensible right now, when he was so close to her.

"You put your life at risk, Caroline." Grant dropped a necklace onto her blanket-covered lap. It was the locket she always wore, a gold oval, etched with a shamrock and set with tiny emeralds and seed pearls. Inside was a portrait of her namesake, Anna's new baby Caroline, called Lina.

"Your child would have missed you," Grant said quietly.

Caroline opened the locket to stare down at Lina's painted blue eyes and soft blond curls. The tight gold lid had protected the image. "I only have stepchildren, who are all grown and married now. Lina is my niece, Anna and Conlan's baby."

Grant's shoulders stiffened at the mention of their names. Anna, whom he had once hoped to marry.

"Did you not know about their children?" Caroline asked him gently. "They have two now, Daniel and Lina."

"We are very isolated here. I know nothing of anyone now, and that is the way I prefer it."

His tone was cold, abrupt, yet some imp living deep inside Caroline made her argue. That imp always did get her into trouble. "But don't you even want to know..."

Suddenly his hands were hard on her shoulders,

AMANDA MCCABE

pressing her back down onto the bed. He was strong now, his body all lean muscle and heated power. His face was hidden in deepest shadow, but his eyes burned into her.

"I want to know nothing," he said fiercely. "I came here so I could be alone and forget. Why have you come here, Caroline? Why do you torment me?"

She couldn't breathe. Her heart pounded, louder than the stormy thunder outside. His nearness sizzled through her, and all she knew was him. The hard heat of him, the clean, smoky-brandy smell of him. It felt more intimate than any of those hurried encounters with her husband in the darkness of their marriage bed.

He seemed to feel something of that heat, too. His hands turned gentle on her shoulders, sliding down her arms to take her hands. His fingers, rough and callused now, but still long and elegant, twisted with hers. He held her against the bed as he slowly lowered his forehead to rest against her shoulder.

His hair was soft on her throat, his breath cool against her bare skin. She kissed his temple and felt the vital pounding of his life's blood against her lips.

"Why, Caroline?" he whispered, his voice filled with rough torment. "Why are you here?"

"Because I had to see you again," she said simply. "I just had to. That's all."

18

CHAPTER
FOUR

G rant stared down at her in silence for a long, tense moment. Caroline suddenly felt nervous. What had she really gotten herself into, coming here to Muirin Inish? She was so far from everyone she knew, anyone who could help her, and any number of dangers could lurk here.

She had to remember why it was so necessary to come here. Why she couldn't stay away.

"I think you should get some sleep now," he said. His voice was gentle, which only made her feel more nervous. His hands slid away from her, and he started to turn away, but Caroline reached out and grabbed his hand. She didn't know why she kept him there. She had so much to think about, plans to make now that she was trapped here on the island. And she definitely couldn't think with him standing so close, clouding her senses, making everything so topsy-turvy.

"Grant, wait," Caroline said. "I didn't mean to trespass on your hospitality. I was only going to come here, ask you what I needed to ask, and leave on the next tide. I never meant..."

A crooked smile touched his sensual lips, and for an instant, he seemed like the old Grant Dunmore. Handsome, charming, careless. But then it vanished, and he was that hard, wild stranger again.

"You didn't mean to use your Blacknall witch-woman powers to summon the storm?" he said. "I'm surprised to hear that."

He glanced down at her hand on his, and she suddenly realized that she still held it tightly. Flustered. she let go, and he stepped back from the bed. He crossed his arms over his chest, still watching her warily, as if he didn't know what she might do next.

Caroline wasn't sure what she would do, either. Ever since she had decided to come to Muirin Inish, she hadn't been quite herself.

"I do study ancient tales of magic," she said. "But I haven't yet mastered the spells for myself."

"Only a matter of time, I'm sure."

Caroline pleated the edge of the sheet between her fingers. "That's why I came here."

"I don't know any magic to teach you."

She laughed. She feared that he had far too much he could teach her—about sex, need, the rawness of life. All the things she had always tried to keep at bay by living in her mind, in a historical world that had vanished except for the stories. It was safer that way. But to get what she needed from her work now, she had to face Grant.

"I want to see *The Chronicle of Kildare*," she said.

Grant gave a surprised bark of laughter. "And you had to brave the stormy seas for that? A letter would have sufficed."

"Would you have answered a letter I sent? Would

you even have read it? Our last meeting was not a very congenial one."

"I suppose it was not, considering I had just kidnapped you and locked you up in a cold warehouse."

"So you do remember."

A muscle tightened along his square jaw, the only sign of any emotion. "Every day. And you are right—I probably would not have answered a letter. I don't exactly maintain a correspondence here."

"Then perhaps you remember another time? That dinner party at your house in Dublin, when you showed me *The Chronicle* in your library."

"You are surely the only lady in Dublin who could have appreciated it. You seemed awestruck, as if someone had handed you a jeweled crown."

Caroline closed her eyes and pictured that night, felt again the soft leather of the book's cover as Grant placed it in her bands. *The Chronicle of Kildare*, a history of the land written and illuminated by Brother Michael of the monastery right here on Muirin Inish in the 900s, carefully protected over the centuries from Vikings, Cromwell's soldiers, and enemies of all sorts who would use its beautiful words for ill. She had half-thought its existence must be a legend, for few scholars had ever seen it and even fewer had read it.

There were only three copies in existence. One had belonged to a French nobleman who died in the Revolution, and his book disappeared. The other was only a partial copy and was locked up and jealously guarded at Trinity College, with only a privileged few allowed to see it. They had constantly refused Caroline's many requests, despite her husband's reputation as a scholar and position as a graduate of the college.

The third copy was Grant's, which she had glimpsed all too briefly that night in Dublin. She desperately needed to study *The Chronicle* to complete her own work. He was her only hope.

She opened her eyes to look at him. He still stood there in the shadows, his cool expression unchanged.

"It was more beautiful than any jewel could be," she said. And she had been foolish enough to think that any man who owned and loved such a book could not be bad. He could not be the cold, ambitious man that rumor claimed. A man who cared only for wealth and position, who used and discarded dozens of women—or so they said.

She thought she glimpsed a tenderness in him that night, a yearning for beauty and truth that matched hers. But she had been proven horribly wrong. She knew better than to trust him again.

Yet she needed *The Chronicle*, and he was the only way to get it. If she could only banish the weak spot she still had for him.

"I need to study it closer," she said. "I have been working on writing a history of Ireland through the old legends for many months now. *The Chronicle* is such a vital source that my work can't be complete without it."

"It must be for you to come so far. To face me again."

"Yes. I also have research to do in the islands, old sites to visit and study. But I would not have come here if the book wasn't so important."

"I'm very sorry to disappoint you then."

Caroline's heart sank. She was so close! Could he possibly turn her away now? "Disappoint?"

"*The Chronicle of Kildare* can't be seen by anyone now."

"What?" she cried. "Has it been destroyed?"

"It can't be seen," he said again, and she could see by the hard look in his eyes that was all he would say. And he would not be moved. "You can study the other books in my library; there are a great many of them there. There's little else to do until the weather clears and you can leave Muirin Inish."

Caroline sank back against the pillows. Her head pounded, and the room whirled around her. Everything suddenly seemed far too much.

"Will the weather clear soon?" she whispered.

"I hope so. I'm expecting visitors any day now."

"Visitors?" Caroline said in sharp surprise. What sort of visitors could such a recluse have, besides unwelcome ones like her?

"And you don't want to be here when they arrive." Grant abruptly turned away from her and strode to the door. "You need to sleep now. You're still ill. Tomorrow Mrs. McCann can show you the library."

"Grant," she called as he opened the door. "I haven't come this far just to give up now. We will speak of this again, and again, and again, until you see things my way."

The old smile appeared again, fleeting and heartpounding. It made her shiver. How could he still affect her that way, after all that happened and all the time that lay between them?

"I would expect nothing less from a famously stubborn Blacknall woman," he said. "But surely you have learned by now, Caroline, that I am just as tenacious when I want something. Believe me—not seeing *The Chronicle* and being gone from here as quickly as possible is for your own good."

Caroline slammed her fist down on the mattress in sudden fury. She had been told all her life things were "for her own good," by her parents, her sisters, her husband. It was always things that she did not want, things that went against her own will, her own nature. She was sick of it, and she wouldn't take it from Grant Dunmore.

"Grant, come back here and listen to me!" she cried.

"Good night, Caroline," he said, and closed the door firmly behind him. To her shock, she heard a key turn in the lock, and her anger flared even hotter. The villain had trapped her in this chamber, just as he had in that warehouse.

She threw back the blankets and swung her legs off the side of the bed. When her feet touched the floor, another wave of dizziness hit her, and she staggered back. He was right; she was still too ill and weak to fight him. She needed a good night's sleep. But tomorrow would be a different story. Tomorrow she would get her strength back, and she would fight him with everything she had.

For now, she contented herself with throwing a pillow as hard as she could at the door. She crawled back onto the mattress and curled up on her side as sleep crept in to claim her.

"This is not over, Grant," she whispered. "I promise you that."

GRANT HEARD THE DULL THUD OF SOMETHING HITTING THE door just above his head. Nothing shattered or exploded, and there were no shouts or screams. Tantrums didn't seem to be Caroline's style. But he could still feel the blistering heat of her anger even through the thick wood.

Good. He wanted her anger. It was better than her pity.

He leaned his forehead against the door and listened for any more sounds from the room beyond. There was the rustle of the bedclothes, a few incoherent murmurs, then silence.

He closed his eyes and imagined Caroline lying there in the center of the big bed, her dark mermaid's hair spread out in waves over the pillows, the pale skin of her throat and shoulders against the white gown and the dusky coverlet. In his vision, she was neither angry nor pitying. She smiled, a joyous, glorious smile, and held out her arms to him in welcome. He slid into the haven of her embrace and inhaled deeply of her sweet perfume as she kissed him. All forgiven, the past forgotten.

He opened his eyes and stared blankly at the locked door. The old wood might as well be vast thickets of thorny forests and fire-breathing dragons for all that lay between him and Caroline Blacknall. That vision would never in a thousand years come true. She would never forgive him, and he didn't deserve it.

Now she was a woman, the promise of her almond-shaped dark eyes, high cheekbones, and her wide, sensual mouth grown into real beauty. Not the fashionable blonde perfection of her sister Anna, but something elegant and unique. And her mind seemed as cool and determined as ever, despite what she had suffered on the sea.

She wanted *The Chronicle*. As much as he wanted to give her anything she asked for, anything to make her leave Muirin Inish and never return, he couldn't give her the book. He just had to distract her until she could get off the island. And if he remembered correctly, the best way to distract Caroline Blacknall was with a library.

He smiled reluctantly when he remembered that party at his Dublin house, where he found Caroline hiding in the library. Her face glowed as he showed her his treasures, the things he shared with few people—especially when he placed *The Chronicle* in her hands. None of his mistresses had ever been so excited when he gave them diamonds and expensive carriages as Caroline was to hold that book.

So he would pile volumes and volumes in front of her until she could see nothing else of what was happening on Muirin Inish. He had work to do, and she had to be gone before it all came together.

He pushed away from the door and hurried down the twisting, worn stone stairs to the library below. The room was a vast space, full of shifting shadows that curled around the corners and twisted up to the beamed ceiling. The fire had gone out, and the place was bone-chilling cold. Grant quickly lit the lamp on his desk near the tall, narrow windows and went to work.

He cleared all his papers and letters from the locked drawer. Surely nothing so flimsy as a lock would keep Caroline out. She was probably only still in her locked chamber because she was utterly exhausted. He would have to take care to hide the documents very well, especially those in French.

He piled them up along with a few books he would rather she didn't see, but one paper wasn't where it should be.

"Damn it all," Grant muttered, as he knelt down to dig into the recesses of the drawer. It was not there. He turned out the other drawers, dumping out sticks of wax, bottles of ink, and ledger books onto the faded carpet.

"Blast!" He pounded his fist on the floor, only to see it flutter from the drawer before him. How could he be so careless, after everything? He wasn't paying attention to his business.

"Sir?" a tiny, frightened voice said. "Is that you?"

And he was careless again. Usually no one could creep upon him at all. He was too distracted.

Grant rose from behind the desk to see that it was the young housemaid Maeve who hovered in the doorway. She held a candle high in one hand, its flame casting an amber glow over her round face. Her skin was pale beneath the copious freckles, her eyes wide and startled.

It had been thus ever since the terrible tragedy of Bessie, the maid who took a tumble from the tower—or was pushed from it. One more black sin to his name. Now everyone was even more frightened of him than before.

"Yes, Maeve, what is it?" he said, more brusquely than he intended.

Her eyes widened even more. "I just,,, Mrs. Mc-Cann said I should light a fire in here, in case you wanted to read later. It's been even damper than usual."

"I'm almost done for the evening. You can go now."

"Yes, sir."

She started to turn away, but froze when Grant called out, "Has anyone been cleaning around my desk of late?"

"Oh, no, sir," the maid answered in a trembling voice. "You said we shouldn't. I just dusted the tables and some of the shelves, sir, like Mrs. McCann told me."

"Did you happen to move any papers while you were dusting?"

"No, sir. Did I do something wrong?"

Feeling like an utter bully, Grant shook his head. "Not at all, Maeve. You can go now."

She scurried away, and Grant kicked at the desk leg in frustration. One false step and they could all tumble down into disaster.

He thought of poor Bessie falling from the tower, and for a terrible instant, it was Caroline's face he saw, her dark hair streaming behind her as she fell to the sea. Her scream he heard.

"I will protect you, Caroline," he said. "This time I will protect you. Whether you like it or not"

T he sound of someone singing out of tune pulled Caroline from her dark sleep. At first she thought it was just another strange dream, like all the others that had plagued her through the long, restless night, dreams of drowning and lightning and Irish gods with bronze-brown hair. Maybe it was a siren singing on the rocks below?

Caroline pried her eyes open and rolled over to find no such thing. It was only a housemaid in a plain brown dress and white mobcap, who knelt by the grate raking up the ashes and singing.

"And who are you, me fair pretty maid, and who are you, me honey? I am me mother's darling!" she warbled softly along to the scrape of her brush on the hearth stones, oblivious to the room around her.

It was the most wonderfully ordinary thing Caroline had seen since she arrived in this unreal, spooky place. There were real people here, not just ghosts! Not just Grant Dunmore with his hard, haunted eyes.

She stretched out on her back to listen to the maid's tune, one of her own favorite Irish folk songs, and stared up at the canopy above her head. A pale gray morning light was beginning to creep in at the window, heralding the end of the long night, but there was still the staccato patter of the rain against the glass and the rumble of the thunder in the distance. The storm was not yet over.

The green velvet canopy and bed hangings were old and faded, yet Caroline could make out the patterns of the gold embroidery, the entwined forms of dragons and flowering vines. If she stared too long, she feared their twisting shapes would creep down to wrap around her and trap her there forever.

She had to escape from Muirin Inish, which she started to fear was cursed, just as the villagers in the mainland inn had told her when they heard her destination. *You can't go there, miss,* they protested in horror. There are demons and evil spirits!

Caroline laughed them away. Evil spirits only lived in the old tales that she loved to study. Muirin Inish was only an island, a lump of rock where once there was a monastery and a church, a great pilgrimage site. Now—well, now, she feared she should have listened a little closer to their warnings.

The maid's song ended, and Caroline turned her head to see the girl had laid fresh fuel in the clean fireplace and was gathering up her bucket. Surely she wouldn't leave Caroline alone just yet!

"Are you already finished?" Caroline asked. She sat up in bed, gathering the rumpled blankets around her.

"Oh, miss, you startled me! I thought you were sleeping," the girl cried. She dropped her bucket with a clatter, and powdery gray ash spilled out. "Now Mrs. McCann will box my ears for sure."

"I'm so sorry. I didn't mean to frighten you." Caroline jumped down from the bed and hurried over to kneel beside the maid and inspect the damage. "Surely we can clean it up so no one will know?"

As the maid watched with wide eyes, Caroline caught up the brush and tried to sweep the spilled ashes into a pile. She only seemed to scrub them deeper into the threadbare old hearth rug.

"Obviously I am hopeless at this," Caroline said. She pushed her tangled brown hair back from her eyes and stared down ruefully at the mess. "I certainly don't want to be the cause of trouble for you."

The maid laughed and took the brush away to start sweeping herself. Caroline saw that she was quite young, surely no more than fifteen, with a very freckled nose, blue eyes, and dark red curls escaping from under her crooked cap. A dark smudge marred her cheek, and her apron was dusty.

The efficient housekeeper at Caroline's girlhood home at Killinan Castle would never let a maid like that out of the kitchens, but she had a nice smile and seemed so normal. After the shipwreck and meeting Grant again, Caroline craved a bit of normal.

The girl shook her head. "There's not many who'll come work here at the castle, miss. They're all scared of the master, of the ghosts. Mrs. McCann has to take what she can get, even if it's only me."

"Have you seen any ghosts here, Miss...?"

"I'm Maeve, miss, Maeve Kinley, and I haven't seen any such thing." Maeve seemed rather disappointed about that. "I've heard things, though, especially since poor Bessie died."

"Bessie?"

Maeve frowned, and for the first time, a shadow

31

flickered over her open expression. "I shouldn't have said anything about that."

Caroline was most intrigued. This place seemed so full of mysteries and tales, even more than one of the romantic books Anna loved, which boasted dark foreign villains, ruthless smugglers, virtuous heroines, and crumbling ruins by the dozens.

"You can tell me," Caroline whispered. "I won't tell a soul. Surely if I'm to be trapped here until the storm clears, I should know of any ghosts to beware?"

Maeve glanced at her uncertainly. "I don't think it's ghosts you need to beware—not *just* ghosts, anyway. And if Bessie's spirit is here, I'm sure she wouldn't hurt anyone. She'd just be sad, miss."

"Who is, or was, Bessie then?"

"She was housemaid here before me. She was the daughter of a farmer from the mainland, and she was lonely when she came here to work. She would come into my mum's tavern in the village on the other side of the island, and we got to talking. She was nice, but quiet-like. Sad, like I said. And then..."

It *was* like one of Anna's novels. Sad heroines in black castles. Somehow Caroline was sure that she wouldn't like the end to this tale, but she felt compelled to hear it nonetheless. "And then?"

"She died, miss," Maeve whispered. "During a storm just like this one. She fell from the tower down onto the cliffs. Or at least they say she fell."

Caroline shivered in a sudden rush of trepidation. "You mean she was—pushed?"

"Mick, who was a footman here and Bessie's beau, he got to drinking at my mum's one night, and he said she wouldn't have jumped like that. Not being a good, religious girl like she was. He said..." Maeve glanced over her shoulder, as if to be sure no one listened, and then hurriedly whispered, "He said Bessie was afraid of something."

"Like what?" Caroline whispered back.

"He didn't know. But he thought it had to be the master. There have been such wild tales, miss, ever since he came here all those years ago, all scarred like that. And he prowls the beaches in the middle of the night like he's watching for something."

Caroline closed her eyes, and a sudden vision flashed in her mind. Grant stalking along the ramparts of a tower, lightning sizzling in the sky above him, a dark cloud whipping around him as he came near a girl who shrank back against the stones. He reached for her, and she cried out...

Just as Caroline had when the warehouse caught fire.

She opened her eyes and curled her trembling hands into tight fists. "Do you believe such tales, Maeve?"

Maeve shook her head, but Caroline could see the shadow of doubt still lingering in her eyes. "Mick was drunk, miss, and grieving. He went away to work on the mainland, and Bessie was buried in the churchyard. The vicar said it was all an accident, and no one else has proved anything else."

"And that's why you came to work here? Because you don't believe the stories?"

Maeve shrugged. "My mum didn't want me to take the job, but there's no others to be had on the island and we need the money. I have brothers and sisters, my da was a fisherman who died at sea, and the master pays very well. I'll say that much for him."

"But you see... Bessie sometimes?"

33

"Oh, no, miss. I just hear things sometimes, like voices behind the walls. And once I saw a flash of light on the tower walkway..."

"Maeve!" a stern voice said. Startled, Caroline twisted around to see a tall, hard-faced older lady clad in a black silk gown standing in the doorway with a tray in her bands. It had to be the ear-boxer, the housekeeper Mrs. McCann.

"There is no time for gossip, Maeve. You still have the fire to do in the library and the drawing room to dust," Mrs. McCann said.

"I'm sorry, Mrs. McCann," Maeve stammered, stuffing her brushes and rags back into her bucket "I'll see to it right away."

Caroline slowly rose to her feet. She was still dazed from hearing Maeve's dramatic tale, but she tried to be as dignified as possible in her oversized, borrowed nightgown.

"It was my fault," Caroline said. "I asked Maeve about the history of the castle and distracted her from her work."

Mrs. McCann's flinty eyes narrowed as she plopped her tray down on a table. "You can read about all that in the library, my lady, where I am to take you once you have finished your breakfast. The books will tell you a great deal more than some silly housemaid."

Maeve bobbed a hasty curtsy and dashed from the room. Caroline's curiosity still burned about Bessie and all the island tales about Grant and his life here. She had the feeling Mrs. McCann would not be nearly as forthcoming as Maeve. Whatever her reasons for taking a position here, she was obviously a well-trained housekeeper.

"So I'm to be allowed to see the library?" Caroline said. She sat down at the table as Mrs. McCann poured out a cup of tea and uncovered bowls of porridge and racks of toast.

"As soon as you eat and I send up some clothes for you, my lady," the housekeeper answered. "You're to be allowed to go anywhere you like, within reason."

'That's very generous of Sir Grant," Caroline murmured, thinking of the way he locked her in last night. Perhaps she was not meant to be a complete prisoner after all.

"I wouldn't recommend going beyond the main rooms, my lady," Mrs. McCann said. As Caroline set about buttering her toast, the housekeeper inspected the fire and the dressing table where Caroline's borrowed brushes were laid out. "The library and drawing room should be fine, once Maeve does her duty and airs them out, and I'll have the dining room set to rights. But little else is fit to be seen. We simply haven't the staff to keep this place presentable for surprise guests."

And yet Grant had said he was expecting company. Very odd. "What about the tower?"

Mrs. McCann gave her a sharp, frowning glance. "The tower, my lady?"

"It looks most intriguing."

"It's quite derelict, my lady. No one goes there, not even Sir Grant."

"I see. And where is my host today?"

"Sir Grant has gone to the village. He probably won't return until evening, if then. He never informs us as to his plans."

Caroline looked at the window, where the rain still pelted the glass. It had to be past midmorning now, but all she could see was steely-gray sky. "He went out in this?"

"If one waited for the rain to stop before one went out on Muirin Inish, my lady, everyone would stay inside all the time." Mrs. McCann strode back to the door, the keys at her sash jangling. "If that is all, I will leave you to your breakfast while I arrange for bath-water and clothing to be sent up. Maeve can change the bed linens while you're in the library so she won't annoy you with her prattle."

Once she was gone, Caroline took her teacup with her to the window and peered out. There were still the jagged rocks and wild froth of the ocean far below, even more stark and cold in the light of day. She could see nothing of the horizon through the mist. It was as if the world had vanished, leaving only the enchanted land of Muirin Inish.

She twisted her head to the side and glimpsed the tower at the edge of the house. Its ramparts were also wrapped in the mist, like bits of ragged gray silk caught on the old, crumbling stones. It seemed the ideal place for a sad ghost to haunt

Caroline trembled and turned away from the tower. She had always been drawn in by a dramatic tale, beginning with her nanny's childhood stories of ancient Irish heroes, gods, fairies, and witches, the more blood and tears the better. She'd never been able to escape that fascination with tragedy and grandeur, so different from her own quiet, studious life.

It was that fascination that led her to working on her book. and to Muirin Inish, and back to Grant Dunmore. But she had to remember her work now, *The Chronicle*. It was her reason to be here, not ghost stories. And definitely not Grant Dunmore's golden-brown eyes.

"And here is the library." Mrs. McCann threw open the double doors. "No one comes here except Sir Grant, so I fear it is a bit musty."

Her tone said that she was quite suspicious of anyone who would want to spend their time in such a place, but Caroline barely even heard. She drifted past the housekeeper into the vast, enticing room.

The library was dark and full of drifting shadows. The heavy, brown velvet drapes at the windows were drawn back, but very little light filtered through the grimy glass. The fire in the grate drove away some of the chill, and cast a small circle of brightness over the worn chairs and settees gathered close to it. The carpet underfoot was so faded that the colors couldn't be deciphered, and there were no paintings on the paneled walls, only a seascape over the fireplace.

Caroline remembered Grant's elegant library in Dublin, where glass cases were filled with glorious ancient treasures. That was where she first saw *The Chronicle of Kildare*, nestled among the sheen of gold and amber *objets d'art*.

There were no cases of treasures here. Only books. Shelf upon shelf of wonderful books, so high that there were ladders and stools to reach them. Caroline ran her finger over the leather binding of one volume, feeling the softness of it under her touch, the supple pliability that said it was well read.

"Are you sure you won't work in the drawing room, my lady?" Mrs. McCann said. "The footman can fetch whatever you need from in here."

Caroline wasn't sure yet what she needed, or

where Grant might be hiding *The Chronicle*. The fact that he kept it away from her made her even more eager to see it. "No, I will work in here."

Mrs. McCann sniffed. "As you wish, my lady. I will send in some tea, and more lamps if they can be found."

"Thank you." Caroline waited until the door clicked shut behind the housekeeper before she pulled the volume from the shelf. It was a French text on astronomy. Interesting perhaps, but not much use for her project. She replaced it and moved on to the next and the next.

The farther she went from the fire, the colder it became. The dark shadows seemed to wrap around her like a chilling wind from the storm outside. She drew her borrowed shawl closer over her shoulders. She couldn't imagine how Grant Dunmore, whose palatial town house had been the envy of all Society, had lived so long in a crumbling, damp castle on an island in the middle of the sea. The glitter and gossip, the battle for power and wealth, the life of the city had been such a part of him. Yet here he lived like a hermit, or a demon locked up in an enchanted cell.

"Oh, don't be silly," Caroline whispered to herself. She was a somber widow, a bluestocking who everyone said must be immune to fanciful romance. Grant had come here to nurse his wounds, and if he found he preferred solitary study to the clamor of city life-well, she could understand that. She just wouldn't have thought it of Grant Dunmore.

And the tragic tale of Bessie the housemaid—it was just a sad accident. Wasn't it?

A loud bang of thunder rattled the windows, and Caroline jumped at the sudden boom.

"Surely anyone would become a little strange living in such a place," Caroline said. She would just have to leave before it affected her any more than it already had. She had to get away from Grant before he affected her anymore. She was already talking to herself.

She stared at the row of books in front of her, but she could only see his face, gilded by the candlelight as he laid her on the bed. She again felt his hands on her skin, so warm and strong. He had always been so handsome, almost otherworldly, but the scars made him more human. They also reminded her of how ruthless he could be, how she always had to be careful of him.

Caroline pushed away the thought of Grant, yet she couldn't entirely push away the strange, almost frightening hold he had over her still. She should not have come here. She came seeking *The Chronicle*, which she needed so much. But was it the only thing she sought on Muirin Inish? "Of course it is," she said firmly. She drew several thick volumes of Celtic mythology from the shelf and took them to the table set up by the fire. She didn't want to sit at the desk near the windows, which was surely Grant's own. She wanted distance from him, even when he was not there in person.

She managed to lose herself in the old, familiar tales of the Tuatha de Danann for a few hours, only pausing when Maeve brought her tea, and later a tray of sandwiches. The maid seemed embarrassed by her earlier confidences and scurried away as fast as she could.

Caroline was still reading when the clock on the mantel struck the hour. She looked up, startled, and realized how much time had passed. And Grant had not returned.

She stood and stretched her shoulders, stiff from bending over the books so long. The rain still poured down outside the windows, and the sky looked even darker past the wavy old glass. What could he be doing out in such weather all day? Perhaps he was as eager to avoid Caroline as she was to avoid him. But that didn't mean he needed to catch a chill. The castle was so vast, surely they didn't have to see each other at all.

But Caroline knew that if Grant was in the house somewhere, she would be drawn to see what he was doing. To see that he was really and truly there after all these years. She drifted to the window to stare out at the rain. The library didn't face the sea as her chamber did. It looked out over a tangled, windswept garden. Gnarled vines were twisted over narrow pathways, and flower beds spilled out from their borders in sodden profusion. In the distance, through the mist, she glimpsed a little stone cottage. Pale light glowed from one of the windows like a beacon.

Who was out there? Caroline determined that once the storm eased, she would go find out. The island seemed full of mysteries, both great and small, just waiting to be discovered. The cottage, the tower, the ancient monastic ruins that she longed to see...

Well, maybe she would not go up in that tower. It seemed too frightening even for her.

Caroline turned away from the window and went back to the bookshelves. Grant certainly had eclectic tastes in reading matter. There were texts of ancient Greece and Rome, agricultural pamphlets, astronomy and chemistry, myths and legends, Elizabethan poetry and plays. French novels. All the same books he had kept in his library in Dublin.

As she drew out one of those slim volumes, Caroline noticed a strange thing, a crack between two of the bookcases wider than usual. She peered closer, and cold air drifted over her face. The shelf stood out from the wall an inch or so.

A secret door? There were mysteries on Muirin Inish, more every minute it seemed. Caroline grasped the edge of the shelf and carefully tugged. It was very heavy, but it did slide toward her a few inches. She pulled harder, putting all her strength into it, and with a rusty groan, it opened a full foot.

"By Jove," Caroline whispered as she peered into the inky darkness of a secret passageway. Cold, damp air washed over her, and she smelled the richness of wet earth.

She had read of such things, of course. Priest holes, ingeniously built into English manor houses and smuggler's caves under coastal roads. When they were children, she and her sisters had explored Killinan Castle in search of just such a thing, but they never found it. Killinan was much newer than this place, with only one medieval tower remaining near the Palladian-style mansion that her grandfather built. They had been terribly disappointed.

And now here was a secret passageway right before her eyes.

She glanced back over her shoulder to the empty library. She had work to do—she should stay here where it was safe. But that old sense of adventure was so very tempting.

"I'll just go a little way," Caroline said. Perhaps it would give her some clue to where Grant had hidden

The Chronicle, or if she was really lucky, lead her right to it.

She took one of the lamps and carefully used a table to hold the door open. Then, drawing in a deep breath, she plunged into the unknown.

"Oh, what am I doing?" Caroline whispered, as something skittered over the toe of her boot. The passage was narrow and dank, with stone walls that dripped with water and a dirt floor that was probably home to all manner of crawly little creatures. It smelled of earth and rottenness, and faintly of the salty tang of sea. She could see little beyond the circle of her lamplight, and what she could see was not promising.

There were a few broken, empty crates piled along the walls, but no ancient Irish ruins or anything that could hide treasures and books. Nothing that could justify venturing into such a place. Caroline usually read about adventures. She didn't often embark on them herself. Not since the terrible Rebellion of 1798, when she and her mother and sisters had to flee their home. She had seen enough adventure, bloodshed, and battle then to last her whole life. Battles in history books, tucked safely away at a distance of hundreds of years, were more her pastime now.

But she felt a little thrill as she made her way along the secret passage. The whole world was turned upside-down ever since she had decided to come to Muirin Inish. Finding a dark passageway and deciding to explore it, against every grain of prudent sense, just seemed to be an extension of all that impulse.

Maybe she was a true Blacknall woman after all. Caroline laughed and walked faster along the corridor, suddenly very eager to see what happened next. Until a shrill scream pierced the darkness ahead of her. A black, winged demon-creature suddenly swooped out of the shadows and flew toward her head.

She shrieked and dove to the ground. The lamp fell from her hand and rolled across the dirt as the bird flew away.

"Don't go out. Please don't go out!" she whispered frantically, crawling toward the flickering light. She carefully set it upright and listened for the return of the screaming bird—and probably dozens of its cohorts.

The lamp stayed lit, and the passage was blessedly silent again. Her heart slowly ceased its frantic pounding. "Don't be ridiculous," Caroline said. "It was just a crow or something commonplace like that."

Or maybe it was a bat? She peeked cautiously behind her to make sure it—whatever it was—was quite gone before she slowly rose to her feet. Surely the presence of birds must mean that she was close to an entranceway. And maybe even closer to some of Grant's secrets.

Caroline shook away the lingering chill of sudden fright and plunged ahead. She had come much too far to turn back now.

She turned a bend in the corridor and felt a brush of colder air on her skin. The salty tang of the sea was heavier now. Then the passage widened out into a small cave.

More crates were stacked along the walls. She rattled a few of them, but they all seemed empty. What had they once held? Brandy and silks smuggled from France, destined for the homes of the Dublin Ascendancy? Or something worse?

She kicked at a crate in frustration. She wasn't sure what she had expected to find here, but surely something more than piles of old rubbish! There had to be other caves along the island's shore, other places where things could be hidden. She would just have to find them before the storm abated and Grant's mysterious guests arrived, and he tossed her off Muirin Inish.

For now though, she had quite enough of caves and secrets. She had to see if there was an easier way back to the castle than retracing her steps.

Caroline hurried toward the faint, grayish-yellow light that she could see just ahead. The cave finally ended in a narrow entranceway, barely tall enough for her to duck through. She could glimpse the steady sheets of rain beyond and the charcoal-colored sky. She extinguished the lamp and left it on the dirt floor before she pressed past the doorway—and almost tumbled down into the sea. Caroline let out a scream and threw herself back tight against the rock. There was only a very slim pathway outside the cave, wide enough for one person to traverse. It wound its steep way down the side of the cliff to the rocky beach below.

She cautiously peered down past the sheer

granite ledge. It seemed to be a sheltered cove, but even there the waters crashed and boiled in a fury. No boats could possibly put in there today. Her hair and clothes were soaked in an instant by the blowing rain, and she ducked back into the mouth of the cave. Was she feeling bold enough to make her way down that path, wherever it might lead? Or should she go back the way she came?

Caroline shook her head. She couldn't face the bird-plagued passageway again just yet. She would take the daylight, even though it meant another dousing. She took a deep breath and swung out onto the path.

Strong hands seized her by the arms, holding her in an iron grip before she could take a step. Terrified, Caroline screamed and kicked out. twisting hard against her captor's hold.

"Caroline!" he shouted hoarsely over the rush of the waves. "Damn it all, you cursed woman, hold still."

Grant. It was Grant who held her prisoner, who seemingly appeared out of nowhere. Caroline peered up at him through the wet tangle of her hair. Her throat was so tight with panic that she could hardly breathe.

He was soaked, too, his white linen shirt clinging to the muscled contours of his chest, his black wool coat sodden. His hair was tied back, and rain ran in diamond-like rivulets over the angles of his face. His jaw was tight with fury. Caroline went very still, but he did not let her go. His clasp tightened on her arms, and he pressed her back farther into the cave. He held her against the stone wall, his body so close to hers that she could feel the heat of him on her skin, the raw strength of him. Whatever he did on this island, it was obviously not just sedentary study.

She stared up into his golden-brown eyes, which blazed with anger. She knew she should try to break away, to run. But she was caught by those eyes, mesmerized like helpless prey under the gaze of a gorgeous but poisonous snake. She couldn't turn away.

He seemed to feel that strange pull as well. His body was drawn taut with tension, his breath harsh.

The storm outside was nothing to the one in her own heart. She stared at his mouth, the sensual curve of those lips, and remembered how they had felt on hers when he kissed her so long ago. The way he tasted and the blurry, hot confusion that came over her, so different from anything she had ever known. So intoxicating.

But she had been an innocent, virginal girl then. She was a woman now, a widow. Surely if he kissed her now, it would not be so very overwhelming. She knew herself better, knew how disappointing the physical side of marriage really was.

Yet her skin burned where he touched her, and she ached to feel those lips on hers again. She swayed toward him against her will, and his hands turned gentle on her arms. They slid down to take her hands in his, his fingers twisting with hers as he held her against the wall.

His lips parted as his head tilted toward hers. Caroline shivered and arched against him. But he did not kiss her. "*Mollaght,*" he said harshly, as he pushed her back even tighter to the wall. He spun away from her, rubbing his hands hard over his face.

Caroline bit her lip to hold back a sob. She pressed herself tight to the cold stone to keep from falling.

What a fool she was, she thought bitterly. To be lured in once again by Grant Dunmore's handsome face was beyond foolish. Had she truly learned nothing in all these years? She had seen what he was capable of.

Yet still she wanted his kiss, wanted to feel that press of his body against hers. "What the hell are you doing here, Caroline?" he said. His back was still turned to her, his shoulders stiff. "How did you even find this place?"

"I was working in the library, and I found the doorway behind the shelf."

"So of course, you had to walk through it," he said. "You didn't even know what was in there or where it would lead."

Well, no, she hadn't. And that was not like her in the least. Caroline curled her fists against the stone wall in chagrin. "There must be a spell on this island that makes people act like bedlamites."

Grant whirled back toward her, so fast that she didn't even see him move until he had her pushed against the wall again. His palms were flat to the rock, his arms holding her prisoner. She was tall for a woman, but he was much taller, and she couldn't breathe or think as she tilted her head back to stare at him. There was not even an inch between them. She could feel every bit of his body against hers.

"There is a spell on this house, an evil one," he said. Somehow the words in his calm, cultured voice seemed all the more frightening. All the earlier roughness was gone, and he just seemed cold. "It's not safe for you here, Caroline. That's why you should stay in your room and not go wandering around. Who knows what wickedness you might find."

"That's true enough," she said. Caroline stiffened her spine with a courage she didn't completely feel. Not when he looked down at her so steadily with those chilly, blank dark eyes. "I found you."

"And you're lucky you did." His hands slid over her shoulders, and she trembled at the heat of his touch through her wet dress. "You could have been hurt, and no one would know where to find you."

The truth of those words made her feel even more foolish. "So I should stay hidden in my room?"

"Yes, until I can get you off the island." His gaze moved over her shoulders, to the way the wet fabric clung to her bosom. Those chilly eyes heated to a dark chocolate intensity. She thought of the old tower, of Maeve's wild tale of the dead housemaid. "And I definitely shouldn't go to the tower?"

His stare snapped back up to her face, and his hands tightened on her upper arms. "Why would you want to go to the tower? There's nothing there."

"Nothing at all?"

"It's practically a shell, and it's not safe there, either." He suddenly pulled her up against him, her body pressed to his as he drew her onto tiptoe. She could feel every hard angle of him against her softness, the strength of his lean body—his erection through her wet skirts. Whatever this insanity was, he felt it, too.

He leaned his head down to whisper in her ear, his hot breath stirring her hair. "Don't make me lock you in again, Caroline."

"Do you lock all your guests in their rooms?" she murmured. She laid her hands on his chest, curling her fingers into the damp shirt to try to find her balance. The feel of his smooth skin and the strong

49

beat of his heart under her touch only made her dizzier.

"Only the troublesome ones," he said, and for the first time a smile touched the corner of his lips.

"Am I a troublesome prisoner, then?"

"Most assuredly you are." He kissed the soft, sensitive spot just below her ear and touched her there with the tip of his tongue.

Caroline gasped at the rush of lightning-hot sensation. Her fists closed convulsively on his shirt, and her eyes closed. His lips slid slowly along her neck. open and warm. He bit lightly at the curve of her shoulder, and her knees collapsed under her.

His arms came hard around her waist, lifting her up high. He braced her between his body and the wall, and Caroline instinctively wrapped her legs around his waist to keep herself from falling. She had never felt so weak, so strange. Something primal and instinctive grew from deep inside her, overwhelming all her senses.

His lips met hers roughly, urgently. She felt the sweep of his tongue against her lips, and she opened to him. He tasted of the rain, and of something dark and secret that she craved so much. She tangled her fingers in his hair, loosening it from its tie until it spilled over her hands like silk.

He moaned deep in his throat as her tongue tangled with his, and the sound drove her to even dizzier heights of maddening desire. She pushed his shirt out of her way so she could touch his naked skin and feel the hot, vivid life of him under her hands. The roughness of the old scars abraded her palms. The lacy pattern of them traced from his face, along the side of his neck, all the way to just below his breastbone, marring his otherworldly perfection.

She remembered the flames and the terrible crash of the warehouse roof as it caved in. The way Grant lay so still on the icy pavement after Conlan dragged him from the inferno, barely breathing, his skin blackened.

Somehow all that horror, which had been so vivid to her for years, seemed the distant dream now. For here Grant was, in her arms, the most alive person she had ever known. He made her feel alive, too, as if she had been asleep all her life, trapped in some kind of gray stasis, and now she was free.

He moved her hand roughly away from the scars, like he couldn't bear her touch on them, and his kiss deepened. There was no seductive art to it, as she would have expected from a man who was once the most notorious seducer in Dublin. There was only a hungry, desperate need that matched her own. She fell deeper and deeper into him, drowning in him.

But he suddenly tore his mouth from hers. Caroline gasped and tried blindly to pull him back to her, to seek more of these new, intoxicating feelings. He resisted her, all his muscles tense, and she opened her eyes to stare at him in hazy confusion.

He looked back at her with horror in his eyes, as if he had never seen her before until she landed here in his arms. Caroline felt like a freezing wind suddenly washed over her, chilling the heated passion into terrible, sick shock.

He lowered her to her feet and stepped away from her. As she stared at him, aghast, he held his hands up as if in mute apology. Those scars, so pale and faded, seemed to stand out against his skin in a stark reminder of who he really was and all that had ever happened between them.

"I told you that you should stay in your chamber," he said hoarsely.

Caroline nodded. She couldn't find her voice to answer him, and what was there to say? This place was making her truly mad.

"Come with me; I'll take you back to the house," he said. He turned away from her toward the cave's entrance, drawing his shirt back into place. But she knew the scars were still there, always.

"It's still raining," she said.

He glanced back at her over his shoulder. That old mask was back in place, the passion, anger, and confusion hidden behind cold blankness.

Caroline had to learn to hide her turbulent emotions as well. Who knew how long she would have to stay on this island with him?

"Do you really want to stay here in this cave?" he said. For one crazy instant, she did want to stay there. She wanted to drag him back into her arms and make him kiss her again, so she could see if those emotions were real. To see if she, the Dowager Lady Hartley, could actually feel that way. But then she wasn't sure if she really wanted to feel that way at all. It was too foreign, too frightening.

She had to retreat and do what she did best—study the problem and come to a rational solution.

"No," she said. "I want to go back to the house."

"Very sensible." Grant held out his hand to her. "Stay close to me. The path can be rather treacherous."

Just like everything else on this island, Caroline thought.

CHAPTER
SEVEN

G rant held on to Caroline's hand as they made their way down the path, but he did not glance back at her.

He felt like Orpheus, allowed to take his love Euridice out of the underworld and back to life, as long as he didn't look at her until they emerged into the sun. Yet Orpheus had been weak and given in to temptation, just as Grant had when he kissed Caroline. Orpheus watched as Euridice, and all his hopes and dreams, faded back into oblivion. Grant didn't even remember if he had hopes and dreams. None that didn't involve ambition or revenge anyway. Long ago, in those few moments he spent with Caroline, he could feel the soft, bright warmth of her youthful enthusiasm and her joy in his books. For an instant then, he had glimpsed what it must be like to feel free and to find true, pure pleasure in the world.

All that vanished in a flash, and he was left only with the tantalizing wisp of a memory. And with the knowledge that he had hurt one more person—the last person he ever wanted to see wounded.

Like Orpheus, Grant couldn't help but glance back

AMANDA MCCABE

at Caroline. She had drawn her wet shawl up over her head in a futile attempt to keep some of the rain away. Her dark hair clung to her shoulders and across her forehead, and her face was so pale that a few golden freckles stood out across her nose. She looked back at him steadily, her large brown eyes calm.

Her lips were ripe and red, as if crushed by his kisses. He could still taste the sweetness of her, feel how soft and yielding her mouth was under his. She was so startled and eager when they touched, and she wrapped her legs around him to pull him close, as if she had imagined such a moment just as he had.

He couldn't lose control like that ever again. He had hurt her once, and that was enough.

"Not far now," he shouted over the roar of the wind and rain. It battered against the rock cliffs and whipped at the ocean far below. No boats could put in there for a few days yet, until the storm subsided and the waters calmed. Caroline was trapped on Muirin Inish, and he was trapped with his lust for her.

Caroline nodded, and her fingers tightened on his. She glanced uncertainly down over the ledge of their narrow path. Surely there was nothing like this in her safe life of Dublin libraries. He would see that she was returned in one piece to her life as soon as possible.

They turned a sharp corner, and Caroline's boot suddenly slipped on the wet gravel. Her hand slid from his as she tumbled toward the edge of the path, and the sea below.

Panic seized Grant, cold and furious, and he lunged forward to seize her around the waist.

For an instant, they both hung suspended over the roiling abyss, halfway between life and death.

54

Then he pulled them back to the precarious safety of the path. He pressed his back to the cliff and held Caroline close against him. She wrapped her arms around his neck, and he could hear the frightened catch of her breath.

I won't hurt you again, Caroline, he thought. She was the one drop of goodness he had seen in his life, and he didn't want to lose that. Even if she was far from him, she had to be there in the world.

"Are you well?" he said against her ear. She nodded but still held on to him.

"Let's get back to the castle then," he said. "You'll catch a cold."

"Better that than falling into the sea again," she said. They quickly made their way down to the rocky beach.

Grant led Caroline around the path that led back to the steps of the castle. They didn't speak again until they stepped into the empty foyer.

The echoing silence of the house was deafening after the howl of the storm. Grant shook back his wet hair and slumped against the wall. Caroline wrapped her arms around her waist, shivering. She looked exhausted, and self-loathing rose up in Grant again.

"Have you had enough of adventure yet, Caroline?" he said.

She laughed and reached behind her to ring out the sodden braid of her hair. The movement pulled the wet fabric of her bodice close to her breasts, outlining their soft shape and the darkness of her erect nipples. Grant tore his stare away from them.

"I have had enough of being cold and soaked to the skin," she said. "But adventures—I don't know. I

55

think I could get used to them. It's certainly a change from having adventures only in books."

"Books are a great deal safer."

"Oh, I don't know," she said. Grant glanced back at her to find her bright, avid gaze focused on him. "There must be something very dangerous indeed in one book—*The Chronicle of Kildare*."

Before he could answer her, Mrs. McCann came bustling in with her keys jangling. She took in their pitiful, soaked state with astonishment.

"Sir Grant?" she said. "I thought you were in the Library, my lady."

Grant pushed himself away from the wall and gave the housekeeper a warning look. "It seems our houseguest was not being looked after and decided to go wandering, Mrs. McCann."

Mrs. McCann flushed. "Her ladyship said she did not require anything else, and Maeve has many duties to see to."

"Well, now I think I require a hot bath and a copious number of towels," Caroline said. "I'm sorry for the trouble I caused. I will just go back up to my chamber now."

She hurried to the stairs and dashed up them, leaving behind a small puddle of rainwater from her hem at every step. At the landing, she stopped and looked back down at him.

"Thank you for saving me, Grant," she said. "Again." Then she disappeared, her footsteps fading until he heard the faraway slam of her bedroom door.

Grant turned back to Mrs. McCann, who watched him with a stern but worried frown. "She can't be allowed to wander around," he said.

"There are very few servants here, Sir Grant, as

you know," she said. "None of us has the time or training to be a guard, especially to a fine lady."

Grant saw her message—if he wanted Caroline kept close and safe he would have to do it himself.

"Go and see to her now," he said. "Perhaps she will join me for dinner, and we can come to an understanding for her visit."

He followed Caroline up the stairs, taking the steps two at a time as he turned at the landings and went to his own turret chamber on the floor above Caroline's. He shed his wet clothes and tossed them away as he caught up a towel from the washstand. Roughly toweling his hair, he went to peer out the window at the gray sea and sky beyond.

Night was coming, creeping toward Muirin Inish with its black, smothering cloak. He usually welcomed the night. He could hide inside of it, from everything but himself. Now Caroline was there, her presence close to him even when she was in another room, and he suspected he couldn't hide from her. Not for long.

He looked at the wooden floor under his feet and imagined Caroline just below. He envisioned her slowly lowering herself into a steaming bath, her tall, slender, pale body naked. He saw her long neck, bared by her upswept hair, the delicacy of her shoulders, the softness of her breasts. She glanced back over her shoulder at him, an inviting smile on her lips...

"*Mac an donais*!" Grant growled. He brought his fist down hard on the stone window ledge, obliterating her sensual image.

If only he could lock her away in the dungeon until this was all over. But he suspected she would find a way to escape that as well.

Grant threw the towel to the floor and turned to grab a clean shirt and breeches from the wardrobe. He caught a sudden glimpse of himself in the one looking glass he allowed in the room, the small shaving mirror over the washstand.

With his hair slicked back, the fading gray daylight was stark on his ruined face. The burn scars traced a spider web over the left side of his face and neck, all the way down his torso. They made a mockery of his old nickname among certain ladies of Dublin Society—"Apollo the ever-bright." Once his looks had brought him a great deal in life. But now they also made a mockery of his erotic daydreams of Caroline. She could do so much better.

58

CHAPTER
EIGHT

C aroline sat down heavily on her
bedchamber chaise. Her whole body
ached, and her mind felt weighed down
with exhaustion after her adventures of the day. Yet
she was still oddly restless, unable to sit down for
long or make any sensible plans at all.

This island, with its secret passages and treacherous paths, its caves and dead housemaids, was getting to her. It was pushing the real, practical world
farther and farther away, until this windswept rock
was the everyday reality, and Dublin the fantastical
dream.

And Grant's kiss felt like the most real thing of all.

Caroline reached inside the neckline of her dress
and drew out her locket. The tiny emeralds set in the
engraved shamrock twinkled in the candlelight, glim-
mering despite the scratches of the ordeal it had gone
through. But the tightly closed hinges protected what
was within. She opened it and gazed down at her
niece's little painted face. She tried to remember
Lina's and Daniel's childish laughter. Her mother and
sisters. She had to focus on getting back to them.

She snapped the locket shut. What were they all doing now? Before she left Dublin, the city was abuzz with rumors of a planned French invasion. It was said that Robert Emmet himself was returning from his long sojourn in Paris with new allies, and old ones ready to rally around him again, as well as a French army at his back.

Caroline had scoffed at those rumors and dismissed them as mere hysterical gossip. Even though the Rebellion was years ago now, and Ireland's official Union with England had happened two years ago, the old fears of war and chaos lingered, as did the distrust between the Ascendancy and their Irish tenants and servants. There was always simmering panic that could bubble to the surface and explode at any moment.

Ireland was constantly in danger, of course, but from its own population and overlords. An occupied nation was never safe. But Caroline was quite sure France must have better things to do than waste their Grande Armee invading Ireland.

A knock suddenly sounded at the door, loud and insistent. "Come in," Caroline called. She half feared, or hoped, it was Grant.

But it was Mrs. McCann, looking even sterner and more disapproving than usual after Caroline's "escape." She wondered how the housekeeper came to be employed here at such a ramshackle old castle in the first place. "I hope you're feeling quite well, my lady, and that you have not caught a chill from the rain."

"I am very well, thank you, Mrs. McCann," Caroline answered. "The hot bath was a great improvement."

"Then if you please, Sir Grant has asked that you join him for dinner in the dining room."

CAROLINE SIPPED AT HER WINE AS SHE STUDIED THE ROOM. It seemed all stone—rough stone walls, flagstone floor covered with a faded old carpet, a carved fireplace that was big enough to roast an ox. The only furniture was the old table and x-back chairs, and a sideboard that held only dusty bottles of wine and no silver plate. She remembered again his fashionable Dublin dining room, with its graceful French furniture, delicate Murano glass chandeliers, and yellow satin draperies and cushions.

Oddly, she much preferred this room, with all its antique mystery. It had an austere elegance that suited this new Grant, the Grant who sat beside her at the head of the massive table.

"It's very interesting in here," she said. "I almost expect a row of chanting monks to walk through at any moment."

Grant laughed. "It's not very *a la mode*."

"Neither am I, I'm afraid. I prefer something with more substance, more interest to it than what is fashionable. Something that speaks of the past."

"Muirin Inish is full of the past. It's also cold and damp."

"And haunted?" she asked.

He glanced at her, his eyes hooded. "So they say. But isn't every old house and grove in Ireland said to be haunted?"

"Do you believe in ghosts, Grant?"

"Not in the spirits of the dead." He paused to pour more wine into their glasses. "At least I don't believe they walk the corridors at night, moaning and clanking chains. They stay with us in ways that are far more subtle and insidious."

Who haunted Grant like that? Caroline wanted very much to know. Who lingered in his heart and his memory, giving those terrible sad shadows to his eyes? But he said nothing more, and she didn't know how to ask without driving him away. She had never been as adroit with emotional matters as she wanted to be, as her sister Anna was.

"I'd like to see more of the island's history," she said. "I read about the monastery before I left Dublin, and I heard there was an ancient Celtic ring fort."

"There is, though there's not much to see there now. The stones were used to make a new fort in Cromwell's time, and that was destroyed soon after. The monastery is much more extensive in its remains, but it's not safe for you to go there alone. I can take you tomorrow, if the rain ceases for a time."

Caroline looked at him in surprise. "You would go with me?"

"Someone obviously has to keep you from falling into a hidden pit or stumbling over ledges," he said. "Someone has to see to your safety."

Caroline laughed. She never felt less safe than when she was with him. She never felt less like herself, less in control. "And you have appointed yourself my keeper?"

He leaned toward her over the corner of the table. His gaze was suddenly quite serious and intense. "I don't see anyone else here to do it. And you Blacknall women seem to bring trouble in your wake wherever you go."

Caroline thought of how he once wanted to marry a Blacknall woman—Anna. She sat back in her chair, away from the warm lure of his body, and took another gulp of wine. "The wine is very good."

"Unlike the food?" Grant slumped back in his own chair and pushed away his untouched plate. "It should be good, it's French." He rose from his chair to restlessly prowl the room.

"French? How did it come to be here at Muirin Inish? Are you not in the blockade?" It had to be smuggled. Brought in at the secret cove? Along with what other contraband?

"I must have some comforts here in my monkish life, Caroline."

She couldn't quite picture him as entirely monkish, despite the austere castle and his reclusive ways. She had glimpsed the old, rakish Grant in that charming grin, the man who loved the sensual pleasures of life like wine, fine clothes, fast horses, and pretty women. She felt her cheeks flush hotly as she remembered the desperate, hungry passion of his kiss, and her equally hungry response to him. She could feel that hunger rising up in her now as she looked at him across the table.

Caroline turned her head away from the sight of him, from her vision of him as a fierce warlord of old Celtic tales, who would ravish her, his captive maiden, in front of the fire. Her stare caught on a pair of portraits hanging on the wall over the sideboard.

They seemed out of place in these medieval surroundings. They were far more modern images of a man with long, powdered hair and a bright blue satin coat, and a young woman in a white, billowing gown with a bunch of roses in her hand. She looked so very much like Grant, with the same sharp cheekbones and bronze-colored hair falling in curls over one shoulder.

"Is that your mother?" she asked, gesturing to the painting with her glass.

"Yes. In her younger, happier days before she met my father," Grant said. "You remember her story?"

Caroline studied the lady's painted face and thought of her tale. How she was the daughter of the last Duke of Adair. How she was the pampered, beautiful daughter of a proud, well-to-do, staunchly Irish Catholic family. When she married Grant's father, a handsome wastrel, and worse, an Anglo Ascendancy Protestant, she was cast out of her family. So when her husband turned out to be a penniless gambler, who had counted on her family's money and grew cruel when he did not get it, she didn't know what to do.

When Grant's father's debauchery caught up with him and he died young, Grant and his mother were alone. She was turned away by her brother when she took her young son to Adair Court to beg for help, and Grant's hatred for his mother's family took hold of his heart and turned it hard and bitter.

Caroline felt a pang of sadness as she studied the woman's pretty, youthful smile and her hopeful expression. No one could see the future or the heartbreak that awaited. No one knew what fate their choices would bring. Maybe that was a blessing.

"She was beautiful," Caroline said "You look a great deal like her."

A bitter smile twisted Grant's lips. "So people

used to say. But I fear my heart was never tender like hers. It is more like my father's."

Caroline went to stand beside Grant under the gaze of his self-deceived and ill-fated parents.

"I don't think you are like either of them," she said. "You are much stronger than them. You knew you could change the direction of your life, that you could make yourself better."

He stared down at her with those fathomless eyes, almost black now in the firelight. "Do you really think I have changed?"

The darkness around them, the crackling fire, the never-ending rhythm of the rain, and the wine all combined to make her feel light-headed and not at all herself. The past seemed so close and yet so far away, like a half remembered dream.

Surely he would vanish again, this new Grant, this stranger who so disturbed her.

Caroline gently laid her hand on his chest, and her gaze moved to his face, to the tracery of scars that stood out pale over his elegant bones. He was still the most handsome man she had ever seen, so handsome he surely could not be part of the human world. This place did suit him far better than the city's theaters and assembly rooms ever could.

She couldn't stop herself from touching those scars. When her fingertips caressed the long, crooked lines that snaked over his jaw, he drew in his breath with a hiss and jerked his head back. But she would not be deterred. She stretched up on her toes and kissed the scar. It was rough under her lips, and he tasted of soap and salt and wine. She wanted more of him, more and more.

"Caroline, you were surely sent here to drive me to madness," Grant groaned.

"Then we are both mad." Caroline rested her forehead on the curve where his neck met his shoulder. She closed her eyes and inhaled deeply of his clean, spicy-dark scent, drawing it down into herself. A bittersweet longing swept over her, overwhelming. She longed for him, and also for something deep and desperate she couldn't quite grasp. Yet she sensed it was something of vital importance. She curled her fingers into the front of his shirt and kissed the pulse that beat at the base of his throat. She parted her lips and spread a line of kisses along his throat, his jawline, the spot just below his ear. His skin was hot and smooth, and the slight roughness of his whiskers abraded her lips.

She tore open the lacings of his shirt and at last touched his naked chest. How had she gone without this for so long?

She pressed her mouth to that heartbeat and felt the rhythm of it on her lips. She traced her tongue around his flat, hard nipple and reveled in the moan of his response. He wanted her, too, she knew that. She wasn't alone in this madness.

His fingers twined in her hair and pressed her against him. "Caroline," he said, and his voice sounded rough and desperate, the fine English accent and cool distance gone. "I tried to fight against this, whatever this is between us..."

"I know," she whispered. "Oh, I do know!"

"I've never known a woman like you," he said. "It's as if, when I'm with you, I see only you, as if you've cast a spell over me, over this whole island."

Caroline looped her arms around his neck and

stretched on tiptoe until her body was pressed flush to his, hip to hip, breast to hard chest. "You are the sorcerer, I fear." He was sent to beguile her away from her purpose, to trap her in this heated pleasure until she could see nothing else. She didn't want to see anything else. If this was to be her downfall, then she welcomed it.

For tonight anyway. Tonight was part of the spell, and tomorrow was very far away.

His hands closed hard on her waist, and he bent his head to capture her lips in a hard, hungry kiss. She opened her mouth to him in eager welcome, and his tongue touched and twined with hers. He tasted of wine, and of that darkness she craved so much.

His kiss was full of desperation, and it made her desperate, too, made her fall deeper and deeper into the humid, hot abyss of longing. She needed him; she needed to be closer and closer to him until she could no longer tell where she ended and he began.

His clasp tightened on her waist and drew her down with him to the floor. He landed hard on the old carpet over the flagstones and dragged her over his lap until she straddled him. Her hands braced on his shoulders as they slid back into the hard rhythm of their kiss.

She felt his open palm slide roughly over her hip until he grasped the hem of her dress. Slowly, enticingly, he pulled her skirt up until her right leg was bare. The heat of the fire and the cold draft washed over her naked thigh at the top of her stocking, and she shivered.

Their kiss deepened, wet and hot and full of raw need, and his elegant, skillful fingers slid under her garter to caress her bare skin. His touch was rough—

he had obviously been laboring at more than reading on Muirin Inish. It felt wonderful, and the fire of need flamed even hotter inside her.

Caroline couldn't breathe or think. She could only feel, and the rawness of it felt foreign and frightening —and glorious. She was free in this one perfect moment.

She tightened her thighs against his hips, and the cloth of his breeches felt abrasive on her soft, bare skin. His lips slid from hers and along the arched line of her throat. Her head fell back as she gave herself over to him. She held on to him tightly, twining her fingers in his hair as she tugged it loose from its tie. It fell over her hands, binding her to him.

His tongue traced the line of her low, square neckline and dipped into the hollow between her breasts. His teeth nipped lightly at the sensitive flesh, and then he soothed it with a sweet kiss. Her nipples ached, and a heaviness expanded low in her abdomen. Her whole body strained for his touch, and she arched herself against him.

His fingers curled into the edge of her too-large bodice and tugged it lower, releasing one pale, small breast from its confinement She had always been rueful about her thin body, her small bosom, so different from the soft, plump creaminess that was so fashionable and looked so good in stylish gowns.

But now, as Grant stared down at her in avid hunger, she forgot all of that. She felt... beautiful.

"So perfect," he whispered. And he leaned down to capture her pouting nipple between his lips, rolling it, biting it lightly before he drew her deep into his mouth.

Caroline cried out at the startling rush of pleasure

that roared through her. She twisted her fingers into his hair again to hold him against her. Between her spread legs, through the fabric of their clothes, she felt his penis grow even harder. She was falling...

Then there was a sudden sound in the corridor outside, a crash, as if someone dropped a tray and footsteps rushing away back to the kitchen. Shocked, Caroline tumbled off Grant's lap onto the cold floor.

"*Mollaght*," Grant cursed. He grabbed her arm and dragged them both to their feet. She was shaking so hard that her hands couldn't grasp her muslin bodice to tug it back over her breasts.

Grant did it for her, smoothing her dress into place and her tumbled hair back from her shoulders. She saw that his hands trembled, too, and his eyes were nearly black.

"Come with me to my chamber," he whispered urgently into her ear. "Please, Caroline. Nothing will happen that you don't want to, but—come with me now."

CHAPTER
NINE

Grant's bedroom was in darkness except for one candle set on the bedside table. The old, massive, dark wood furniture loomed, and shadows flickered through the uncovered windows with their medieval panes of diamond-shaped glass.

He had led Caroline up a narrow, twisting staircase to the floor above her own room, and the tapestry-covered walls were gently curved, so Caroline was sure they must be in a turret. Surely it was not the fatal tower, for everyone said that was merely a shell, but this space seemed quite fearsome enough. It was like a chamber for a wizard or an alchemist, with its hulking furniture and faint scent of burned sandalwood.

But she had no time to think about her surroundings. Grant pulled her into his arms and pressed her back against the door. He bent his head to kiss her neck, his loose hair trailing over her skin. His mouth was open and hot, tasting her greedily as if he was starving for her.

An answering hunger, raging and insatiable, rose

up inside her. She wanted to lose herself in him, forget everything but emotion and sensation, the way she felt when he kissed her like that. To hell with being sensible.

She pushed herself against him and tilted her hips to press against the hardness of his erection. His kiss trailed lower, enticingly, until she cried out in longing. His tongue traced along the edge of her bodice and on the bare, soft skin of her breast before he left her.

"Grant!" Caroline cried. She braced her head against the door and stared up at him in the shadows. His eyes glowed like dark stars.

"I'm here," he said. "I've always been here, even when you didn't know it."

His arms slid around her and pulled her tight to his body. Her eyes closed as he kissed her temple, the edge of her cheekbone, the corner of her mouth, as if he would consume her. Yet she wanted to be consumed until there was nothing left except the feeling of it all.

He lightly caught her earlobe between his teeth. His breath was hot in her ear, making her gasp in a shuddering rush of response. She grasped handfuls of his long hair and drew his lips back to hers. If he didn't kiss her now, she would surely scream!

But he seemed happy to oblige. Grant groaned and swept the tip of his tongue over her eager lips before he plunged deep inside.

Not breaking their kiss, his embrace tightened around her, and he turned her toward the waiting bed. She was barely aware of the softness of the feather mattress and the cool linen sheets against her back. She only felt him, the weight of his lean, hard-muscled body pressing her down onto the soft mattress.

She reached out with hands made clumsy with desperation to push his coat off his shoulders and throw it to the floor. The thin, fine fabric of his shirt clung damply to his chest, outlining every angle of his body. Moving from pure instinct, she slid her mouth from his to taste his neck with her tongue. The smell of his skin made her head spin.

She touched him through his shirt, lightly scraping the edge of her thumbnail over his flat, puckered nipple.

Grant groaned and pulled back from her touch. She whimpered and reached out for him, but he evaded her. He grasped the hem of her dress and dragged it up. In the flickering candlelight, she could see his gaze, heavy and hooded, following the line of her leg as he bared it. The naked white skin of her thigh above the stocking, the curve of her hip, her bare womanhood.

As he stared down at her, Caroline watched him, panting with need, trembling. She had never imagined such a moment, not in her wildest dreams. But here they were, and at the very point of no turning back, and somehow it seemed inevitable that they would come to this. Ever since that night in his Dublin library, they had been moving toward this one moment.

And it suddenly struck her that no one had ever seen her like this before. Hartley had done his marital duty in the dark, under the covers, raising her gown just enough. He hadn't seen her, and he had definitely never looked at her the way Grant was doing now, as if he were a starving wolf and she was a banquet laid out just for him.

It made her feel powerful. Feminine. As if she was more than her sensible, scholarly self. She laughed and reached down for the fastenings of his breeches. She wanted to see him, too. She freed his erect, heavy manhood into her hand. It was soft and hard at the same time, velvet stretched taut over hot iron, veined and throbbing. It tightened under her touch, and he shuddered deeply as she traced its length in fascination. Its tip was damp.

"Caroline, you're killing me," Grant groaned. His body lowered onto hers, and he pressed his open mouth to the soft hollow between her neck and shoulder. Her legs parted to cradle him against her body, and he tugged down her bodice to bare her breasts again.

Her nipples felt heavy and aching as he rolled one of them between his fingers. He caught the other deep in his mouth. Caroline couldn't breathe. She held him against her and closed her eyes tightly to absorb every single feeling. His hand roughly caressed the bare skin of her upper thigh, and his thumb searched out the wet center of her womanhood. She cried out as it slid inside her and traced the softness with an enticing friction.

"Yes," she whispered. "Now."

And then she couldn't speak at all. She spread her legs wider, and he gently reached between them to part her with his fingers as he sought entry. Her head arched back against the bed as he slid home, their bodies joined as one. Caroline tensed, and he went still against her. It had been a long time since she had coupled with a man, and her body had to adjust to the sensation of fullness and pressure again, the friction of his flesh against hers.

Slowly, the discomfort faded away, and the warm pleasure built up again, hot and heavy, deep inside her.

"Did I hurt you?" Grant said hoarsely.

"No," she whispered. She wrapped her legs around him and arched her hips to draw him deeper.

He drew back one slow, alluring inch at a time, almost sliding out of her before plunging back inside, deeper and deeper.

Caroline cried out at the rush of pleasure, like a shower of sparkling, burning stars scattered over her skin. His movements grew fast and desperate, deeper with every thrust. Her world grew darker at the edges, and she heard a humming in her ears, louder, a chorus of pleasure. She definitely never felt like this before.

Then her climax broke over her, fragmenting like a great explosion that sent her soaring upward into the very sky.

Above her, she felt Grant's body arch taut as a drawn bowstring, and he shouted out incoherent words. His muscles tensed under her touch, and his head was thrown back in primitive exultation.

Then he fell to the bed beside her, their legs entangled. His breath on her bare shoulder was hot and uneven, and she found that she couldn't remember anything but him. She felt like she was sinking back to Earth from those glittering stars. She was weighed down with delicious, aching exhaustion.

She opened her eyes to stare up at the darkness above her, the folds of the velvet bed curtains. Grant's breath grew slower, as if he slid into sleep. Sleep tugged at her as well, but she couldn't give in to it yet. Her head was whirling with mingled pleasure and confusion.

She rolled onto her side to look at him. The candle was sputtering low, and its light flickered over his face. He looked young and relaxed in the warm after-glow of pleasure, not the hardened recluse she had found here on Muirin Inish. His hair spilled over one shoulder, the linen shirt ripped away to reveal his glistening skin. Had she done that? Torn away his clothes in her passion? How very unlike her.

She reached out to smooth the jagged linen edges together. He suddenly grabbed her hand in his and kissed her palm without opening his eyes.

"I should go back to my own room," she whispered.

"Don't go yet," he answered. "I know I have no right to ask it of you but stay with me just a little while longer."

Caroline nodded. She laid her head on his shoulder and watched as he twined his fingers with hers and pressed her hand to his chest

Even as they lay there wrapped in each other's arms, she couldn't quite believe what she had done. Ever since the terror and peril of the Rebellion, she had spent her life making herself and her family safe, living her life in a practical, quiet way. Now she had thrown all that away and made love with the most dangerous man she had ever met. A man who still carried so many secrets inside him. She had rushed out and thrown herself into the whirlpool She had brought the danger into her very bed, knowing the dangers of it. What would become of her now?

She traced her free hand over Grant's chest and

remembered his touch, his kiss, the way he moved against her, as if he had been making love to her for years and knew just what would please her. At least when she did meet her downfall, she would remember how truly glorious it was.

TEN

C aroline climbed up the steep hill behind Grant. The thick mud sucked at her boots, but she would not be held back. Who knew how long the rain would stay away, or how long Grant would stay with her?

She had been surprised to get his note on her breakfast tray that morning, inviting her to see the ruins. She wasn't sure what he would think or say to her after last night, which was why she had crept from his bed in the predawn darkness before he could wake up. She didn't want to see regret in his eyes or hear any apologies. It was too late between them for polite words. It was too late for so many things.

And she had no regrets. Last night was a great revelation. Now she understood the terrible pull of desire, the way passion could drive people to do insane things. The way it caused so much havoc in the old myths, even starting wars and crusades. She had completely lost herself in Grant's arms. For one night, she forgot all the mystery and distrust that lay between them.

AMANDA MCCABE

But today was a new start. She had to step very carefully. She hurried up the hill to Grant's side. Since today's walk was a long one in rough weather, she had left behind her dresses and petticoats and borrowed some old breeches and boots from one of the younger footmen, along with a shirt of Grant's. She thought she might wear such clothes all the time since there was such a marvelous freedom about them. She could walk faster and move easier.

And the look on Grant's face when he first glimpsed her in the foyer, dark and intense, was most gratifying. He hadn't forgotten last night any more than she had. Not a single moment was lost in a wine haze; every touch, every kiss, every hot movement of his body against hers was vividly remembered.

But all he had said was, "We need to go before it starts to rain again."

"Are we almost there?" she asked now. Caroline had to lengthen her strides to keep up with his fast pace.

He glanced down at her, his brows arched as if he was surprised to see her still there. Surely, he knew by now that she would never give up so easily. Or perhaps he was preoccupied by other matters.

"Not far," Grant said. He kept walking quickly, but he reached out and caught her hand in his.

"This path seems like a well-trodden one," she said, glancing back at the narrow trail behind them. "Not overgrown like the others."

"It was a pilgrimage site for many years," Grant answered. "People would land their boats on the main beach and come up this path to the monastery. It boasted a reliquary containing the little finger of St. Ceolach, who helped the souls of those who died at sea, since he himself drowned at the hands of his English enemies. The relic was said to cure—well, many things."

"Things like what?" Caroline asked curiously. "It seems like he'd be no help with seasickness or shipwrecks if he himself drowned."

Grant laughed ruefully. "It was said to be an excellent cure for infertility or, er, sexual deficiencies. Things of that sort. He was very popular among pilgrims."

"I would imagine so." Caroline felt her cheeks grow hot, even in the cool breeze, and she turned her face away so he couldn't see her silly blush. It was ridiculous after the things she had done with him last night.

And it seemed that St. Ceolach's influence lingered on the island, if Grant's performance was any indication. She only hoped the fertility would not take hold. Not that it was very likely—she had never conceived at all during her marriage, even though Hartley had three healthy children with his first wife. That at least was one thing she didn't have to worry about now.

"Do people still come here on pilgrimage?" she asked.

"Not really. The monastery was disbanded by the men of Henry the Eighth, and mostly destroyed in the sixteenth century, and St. Ceolach's finger disappeared. What they didn't accomplish, Cromwell's soldiers did a hundred years later, when they used the castle and the ruins to watch for Royalist ships from France. Many of the islanders were unable to find work after that, as they mostly served at the monastery or ran shops and inns

AMANDA MCCABE

catering to the pilgrims. They say a few people, stubbornly faithful, sneaked onto the island to pray over the years. They probably take this path sometimes."

"And you don't mind?"

"Mind? Why would I?"

"Well," Caroline said carefully. "St. Ceolach is an Irish saint, yes? His shrine would be important to Irish Catholics. And I remember they said you invoked the old Penal Laws against Catholics, to try and take Adair Court from Conlan."

Grant snorted. "I didn't hate my cousin for his religion. I have no real faith myself any longer, but I don't care if anyone else does. That was only a convenient excuse. And I'm sure you also remember it didn't work."

"Yes, I do remember."

"I don't care if someone wants to come all this way to say a prayer. I own only the castle, not the monastery. I only hope they put a few coins in the villagers' pockets while they're at it." Grant stepped on the crest of the hill and pointed. "There it is, the monastery of St. Ceolach. What's left of it, anyway."

Caroline shielded her eyes from the gray glare of the sky and peered down into the valley. The ruins were sheltered in the bowl-like space, scattered across the green meadow like an old, insistent whisper that would not completely fade away. She could see the two standing walls of the church, including the nave with its blank geometric pattern where once there must have been an elaborate stained-glass window. Trees towered over it now, their branches tangled on the jagged, broken stones of the walls. Thick grass, matted down by the rains, lay over the old aisles. Moss carpeted the standing tombs.

She could see the lines of the old outbuildings, the cloister with its long gallery walks, the chapter house, the kitchens and enclosed gardens. Once this place had been its own world, self-sufficient and bustling with people and activity. For an instant, she could see it as it once was, whole and new, with monks making their serene way about their tasks and pilgrims filing into the church. She could hear their voices and the tolling of the bells.

In a strange way, it reminded her of Grant himself, still handsome despite the vast changes and the vanishing of the past.

"I told you there was not much left," he said.

"It's beautiful," Caroline answered. She hurried down the winding path into the valley. She climbed over the remains of the outer wall and went past the tangled old kitchen gardens. A few herb plants remained there. The scents of mint and rosemary, crushed by the rains, were sweet in the fresh air.

She passed the arched colonnades of the cloister and the old well, now a deep, echoing pit in the center of the courtyard. She had a glimpse beyond of the roofless chapter house, where once monks had illuminated manuscripts like *The Chronicle*. She peered inside and thought of the knowledge their hours of labor helped preserve, knowledge she treasured now, so many years later.

She tried to step up on a low wall to get a better view, but the crumbling rock gave way beneath her. She tumbled toward the ground, her stomach lurching in panic, but Grant caught her around the waist and held her high up off the ground.

"I told you that you needed someone to keep you safe here," he said, his voice low and deep, echoing through her. He held on to her easily, as if she weighed no more than a feather.

Caroline braced her hands on his shoulders and stared down at him, entranced by his austere face in the hazy light. "You always seem to catch me when I need you."

He lowered her back to the grass and stepped back. "I won't always be able to catch you, Caroline."

Reminded that this moment was only a fleeting one, this island an enchanted place out of time, Caroline felt cold again. Soon she would leave Muirin Inish and probably never again see Grant Dunmore. She had somehow thought that if she came here to find *The Chronicle*, she would also find Grant again and put the past to rest. But she had only made things more complicated.

How could matters between them ever be put to rest now? Especially when they had so little time together, and she didn't even know what she really wanted to say to him.

"We should stop by the village before we return to the castle," he said abruptly. "I have some errands there. And then you can see life here is not so entirely solitary."

Caroline nodded. It seemed she would get no more confidences out of Grant today. They climbed out of the sacred valley and back to the crest of the hill on the other side. A wider road, rutted with mud and straw, led to the shoreline, where a tiny village waited.

It was only one lane, lined with whitewashed cottages with thatched roofs and green-painted shutters, as well as a few larger stone structures. There were two or three shops and a tavern, where a sign painted with the words "The Blue Mermaid" and the image of a crude, fish-tailed woman with long hair, swung in the breeze. Even at that afternoon hour, the tavern looked full. Caroline could hear laughter spilling from its open door.

"That must be the tavern of Maeve's mother," she said.

"Maeve?"

"Your housemaid, of course. She said her mother owned the tavern in the village." She gave it a wistful glance. It would be nice to see someone besides Grant with all his complexities, and the castle's dour servants, for a few minutes. "Shall we go in for a quick ale? I never get to visit such places at home."

Grant frowned as he studied the doorway. "I don't usually go there."

"Then surely it's about time you did. Just for a moment, before we walk back?"

He gave her a stern look as if he was about to refuse her, but then he nodded. "Just for a moment."

When they stepped through the open door, Caroline had to pause to let her eyes adjust to the sudden dimness after the daylight. She heard the low hum of talk and laughter fade away as they saw Grant standing there. It seemed he was right; he didn't visit the tavern very often. But one of the men stopped him to ask a question about the harvest, and Caroline went to sit at the polished wooden bar where Maeve's mother, the proprietor Mrs. Kinley, was serving. It seemed Maeve had already told her all about Grant's new visitor.

"I imagine you'll be going back to the mainland as

soon as you're able," Mrs. Kinley said as she placed a beaker of ale before Caroline. "This is a rough sort of place for a lady to land in."

Caroline glanced over at Grant where he talked with the men. He was listening to them carefully, nodding, with a solemn expression on his face. She thought of their touch among the ruins, and the way he held on to her as if he was hungry for her. As if he needed her.

"It has its own charms," Caroline said. "I like to study Irish history, and there is much of that to be found on Muirin Inish."

"A history of death and battle," Mrs. Kinley said with a shiver. She tucked a lock of graying red hair back into her cap. "I never go out to the ruins myself, and I always warned my children to stay away from them, too. They're cursed."

Caroline sipped at her ale. She often had such feelings when she visited old sites. It was one of the reasons she liked them. "You are Maeve's mother, are you not?" Caroline said.

"Aye. She's my oldest, or next to. My first-born died as a wee one. I hope she's not given you trouble."

"On the contrary, she's an excellent maid. She's helped me a great deal." Caroline lowered her voice. "She's told me such interesting tales of the castle, that it is haunted, too."

Mrs. Kinley glanced at Grant, who was still conversing with the men at the other end of the room. "The castle's always been a strange place. No one lived there for years before Sir Grant came. It was left to the birds and the rot. But the fishermen always said they could see lights in the tower windows when they brought in their boats at night, despite the fact that it's been deserted for years."

"Maeve told me about poor Bessie. I think Maeve believes her ghost is still there, searching for the truth of what happened to her."

Mrs. Kinley went very still. Then her lips tightened, and she turned away to wipe at some glasses on the scarred wooden counter. "My Maeve was always a fanciful girl. What happened to Bessie was a terrible accident, nothing more. I didn't want Maeve to take the job, but we needed the money. I warned her to stay with her duties and not go wandering about. You should do the same, my lady."

Caroline nodded thoughtfully. It was too late for her, she had already succumbed to curiosity and gone tumbling down into the depths. But maybe there was still hope for Maeve. "Perhaps when I leave here, Maeve could go with me, and I could find her a position in Dublin or at my sister's estate. If she would like to try a new place."

A smile lit Mrs. Kinley's weathered face. "Would you do that, my lady? That would be a real blessing for my girl! God knows, there's no prospects here. No real work or anything else."

"No suitors? Maeve said Bessie had a beau."

A shadow flickered over Mrs. Kinley's smile. "Aye, Mick O'Shea. For what he's worth. I heard tell he's come back to Muirin Inish after losing his job on the mainland. I just hope he ceases his drunken ravings. I refused to serve him here anymore after Bessie died. It's not safe to say such things, not here on this island."

Caroline was intrigued. Dublin gossip had

nothing on the tales of Muirin Inish. "What did he say?" she whispered.

At first Mrs. Kinley looked like she wouldn't answer. But she shook her head and went on wiping the glasses. "He was just grieving, the poor young sot. He was sure Bessie was killed there in the castle, but no one listened."

"Killed by who?"

Mrs. Kinley shook her head harder. "I don't repeat drunken gossip, not even in this tavern." She hurried away to tend to another customer.

Caroline finished her ale, thinking of ghosts and murders. She couldn't help but imagine poor Bessie atop that rainswept tower, running in terror, her feet slipping on the wet, worn stairs as something bore down on her...

"Are you ready to leave?" Grant suddenly said behind her. Caroline jumped, startled, and spun around to face him. "Grant!"

He frowned. "I didn't mean to frighten you."

"You didn't. I was just daydreaming I suppose. I didn't hear you."

"Have you finished your ale? I have work to do at the castle, and it's a long walk back."

"Yes, of course." Caroline glanced past his shoulder to see the men he had been talking to, clustered now at their table in the corner. "Have you finished your conversation?"

"It was hardly that. I had only to listen while they talked. I'm not much of a farmer." Grant took her arm to help her down from the stool. "We should go now."

Before they could take another step, a young man appeared in the doorway. He had obviously been running because his face was red and he was panting for breath. He waved his hands over his head and the room fell silent. "There's a boat approaching!" he shouted. "From the east."

"What sort of damnable fool would try to make the harbor now?" Mrs. Kinley said.

"The rocks'll tear them apart," one of the men muttered. The messenger spun around and ran off again, followed by everyone else. The tavern emptied as they all hurried to catch a glimpse of the boat.

Grant's hand tightened on Caroline's arm. She thought of her own storm-tossed vessel, the cold waters closing over her, and she felt a surge of fear for those people. It was a miracle that she had survived, for no one else had.

"They're early," Grant said low under his breath.

"Who is early?" Caroline asked in bewilderment.

"Come with me," he said. He held on to her arm as he led her from the tavern. They didn't follow the others to the cliffs to peer down at the sea, but instead turned back toward the path to the castle. He walked so fast that she practically had to run to keep up.

"What is happening?" Caroline cried. "Who are those people?"

Grant shook his head. "When we get to the castle, you have to stay in your room, Caroline. It's safer that way."

"My room? But..."

His grasp tightened, and he gave her arm a little shake. "For God's sake, Caroline, for once in your life don't argue with me! Just listen and do as I say."

"As you say?"

"As I ask, then." He stopped in the middle of the road and turned to look into her eyes. The lines of his face were taut and stark. "Please. Just stay there until I come for you."

Caroline slowly nodded. "I will stay above stairs."

Upstairs—but perhaps not necessarily in her room...

CHAPTER
ELEVEN

G rant paced the ramparts of the old tower, his spyglass trained on the sea far below. It was a much clearer day than the one that brought him Caroline, the rainfall steady and soft, and he could see to the far horizon.

He could also see the vessel making its way to shore. It was pounded back by the waves, but then it would surge forward again, plowing fiercely against the water. Clearly the occupants were very determined to reach Muirin Inish. He still couldn't quite make out the figures huddled on the deck. They were blurry masses at this distance, wrapped up in oilskin coats and wide-brimmed hats. He knew who they were, though. No one else would be out there today.

"*Donais*," he growled. He snapped the spyglass shut and tapped it against his palm as he watched the vessel bob and weave among the foaming waves. They were not supposed to arrive for several days yet; that was the agreed plan.

Grant stared down to the winding trail to the beach. They would not land there, but at the hidden cave below the passageway so as to meet with no one. The villagers would know someone was on the island, but they wouldn't know who. It would be easy enough for them to conclude their business and be gone with no one the wiser as to what had really happened. It would be just one more wild, speculative piece of gossip about Grant and the strange events at the castle.

But Caroline—she was too smart and too curious for her own good. And she was a distraction he did not need now. His task had to go perfectly if all was to work as planned. He had to be focused and cold-blooded. He cared not for his own safety now, but he feared he cared all too much for Caroline's.

He braced his hands against the wet stone and watched as the boat vanished around the cliffs to the other edge of the island. They would be here soon, and the game would begin.

He turned to look up at Caroline's window. The light glinted on the glass, and the wind caught at a bit of drapery and pulled it out like a fluttering banner. She had opened the casement and was also studying the sea, but at least she stayed in her room as he had ordered. How long would that last? Not long, he would wager.

Grant had not asked Caroline to come to Muirin Inish. He had thought that he'd never see her again, except in his memories or dreams. She would never know what he did to atone for the hurt that he had caused her in Dublin. But he had chosen to make love to her, to selfishly grab on to her light and goodness like a damned man reaching out for redemption as he fell to Hell. He had chosen to draw her to him when he should have pushed her away.

He wouldn't be selfish now. She deserved so much better. He had to make sure she was untouched by what happened here, and that she made it safely back to her life in Dublin.

With one more look to her window, he turned away and ran down the winding stairs to the foot of the old tower. His boots echoed on the stone walls that stretched down into emptiness. Once the tower had had floors and chambers, where warlords of Muirin Inish planned their raids and battles. Now there was just a shell and the stairs that twisted past blank walls, with an ancient dungeon hidden behind a trap door at the bottom.

He went into the library and lit a lamp before opening the entranceway to the passage. His steps were sure and swift as be hurried toward the cave. He had to forget Caroline now and focus only on what was ahead. It was the only way to protect her now.

At the entranceway, he paused to study the little cove below. The boat had just landed there, and Grant could see it moored out beyond the rocks, bobbing like a child's toy. A smaller boat was making its way to the beach, with two burly sailors pulling the oars with all their might to fight the strong current. Four other people huddled in between, still muffled in their coats and hats.

It landed at last, the figures stumbling unsteadily onto the pebbled shore. One of them ducked behind a boulder and bent over to be sick. Grant made his way down the slippery, winding path to greet them. It was time for the first move on the chess board.

By the time he reached the beach, the sailors were already rowing back to their ship. Obviously they had had quite enough of their "cargo," and would not return until summoned to bear them away again. The seasick one still crouched behind the boulder, while another person knelt beside him proffering a handkerchief. The other two milled about on the sand as they studied the cliffs.

"Ah, Sir Grant! *Monsieur*, we meet at last," one of them called, as he saw Grant approaching. The man's oilskin coat flapped open to show a fine, dark-brown wool jacket with gold buttons, an impeccably tied white cravat, and a wide leather belt holding a short sword and two pistols. He swept off his hat to reveal cropped golden hair and a surprisingly youthful, handsome face.

"I am Captain LaPlace," he continued. His English was impeccable, only lightly touched with the lilt of a French accent. "It is a pleasure to meet you in person at last. Monsieur Emmet has told us a great deal about you."

Grant was sure he had. Robert Emmet had told them exactly what Grant wanted him to say. "So you are my contact, Captain LaPlace?"

"Of course. Here are my letters of introduction, all in order I assure you."

Captain LaPlace drew out an oilskin-wrapped packet from his coat and handed it to Grant. As Grant scanned the lines and the signatures and seals, the other three people moved closer. Caution hung heavy in the air, a tense wariness that felt like walking delicately on the edge of a sharp sword. Everything could explode at any instant.

"*Merci*, Captain," Grant said, refolding the letters. "Welcome to Muirin Inish."

A sunny smile broke across LaPlace's face. He looked as if he should be performing in a schoolboy cathedral choir rather than leading a covert mission. Very clever of Emmet and his allies to choose such an innocent-seeming emissary. "*C'est bon*! And may I present my cousin, Monsieur Michel, as well as the Vicomte d'Allay. You are most aware of the Vicomte's errand here, I am sure."

The Vicomte was the man who had been ill behind the boulder, a thin, frail-looking figure of middle years, with a pale face and graying hair tied back at the nape of his neck. He gave a nod as he pressed his handkerchief to his lips. "Sir Grant."

"*Monsieur le Vicomte*," Grant said. "I am glad you were able to make the journey."

"Ah, *oui*, the sea does not agree with me," answered the Vicomte. "But I would have gone much further to accomplish this goal, *monsieur*."

LaPlace's cousin, Monsieur Michel, bowed, but said nothing. He looked to be an older, harder version of LaPlace, and he also had several weapons strapped to his hips. He held a tightly padlocked case under his arm.

The fourth person drew closer, and the Vicomte held out his hand. "And this, Sir Grant, is my daughter, Mademoiselle Victorine Muret. As my health is not good, she must accompany me when I travel."

The mademoiselle swept back her hood, and lush auburn curls tumbled over her shoulders. Her bright green eyes, set in a creamy oval face, sparkled as she gave a little curtsy. Her full, pink lips curved in a flirtatious smile. She seemed to carry no weapons. Yet Grant was sure that of all the members of this mission, Mademoiselle Victorine was the most dangerous.

But even as her smile widened and she stepped

closer to him, giving him the complete effect of her immense beauty, he felt coldly emotionless. She could not disturb him as much with all her lush beauty as one tiny glance from Caroline Blacknall could.

"I hope you do not mind my uninvited intrusion, Sir Grant." she said in a husky, lightly accented voice. "I must accompany my father as he said, to make sure of his comfort."

"I do not mind at all, *mademoiselle*," Grant answered. He gave her a flirtatious smile of his own, one he had not used in a very long time, and raised her gloved hands to his lips. "You are most welcome indeed to Muirin Inish. I only wish I could offer you more luxurious accommodation, as you deserve. I fear my home is rather rough."

"On the contrary," she murmured. "I think I will enjoy my time here very much."

Grant offered her his arm and said, "Come, let me show you to the castle. I fear it will rain again soon, and you must be tired after your journey."

"Thank you, Sir Grant." said Captain LaPlace. "'We are certainly eager to discuss our business here."

CAROLINE PEERED CAUTIOUSLY OVER THE EDGE OF THE balustrade to the foyer far below. She couldn't see anything interesting at all, but she could hear the echo of voices and she could feel the tension in the air. Even though it seemed that outwardly nothing had changed, the whole feeling of the castle was transformed.

Something was definitely afoot. Grant's "guests" had arrived. But who were they? What drove them to this bleak place in the middle of a storm? Perhaps they were just mad, as she was.

She pressed closer to the carved wood of the railing and craned her neck to try to see more as she thought of the walk back from the village. Grant had said little, and she had also kept silent when she sensed that he would tell her nothing. Grant had always been a mystery to her, completely outside her experience of all other people, giving her only quick, enticing glimpses of the man behind his careful, handsome mask. Even their raw, passionate night of lovemaking, so desperate, so out of their control, had left him more hidden from her than ever.

And that mask was even more firmly in place as they hurried back to the castle. Only the grasp of his hand on her arm, so tight and close, revealed any tension.

So far there was nothing she could see, just that enticing echo of conversation from somewhere down there. Once in a while there was a burst of laughter that seemed incongruous with the solemn place.

Caroline heard a door slam somewhere along the corridor and the clatter of hurrying footsteps. She quickly ducked down below the balustrade to kneel in the shadows. Maeve appeared in the corridor, the servants' door at the end of the hall swinging shut behind her. She held a large, covered tray in her hands, and her cheeks were flushed as if she had been working hard that evening. She turned at the landing and went away from the direction of Caroline's chamber and along another corridor into the depths of the house.

Caroline bit her lip as she peered down into the foyer again. She shouldn't care in the least what kind of trouble Grant was in. He had certainly caused her enough trouble in her life. But she couldn't seem to stay well away from him. And she also couldn't seem to stop caring what he did or whether he was safe.

She didn't want to explore those feelings right now. It seemed far less dangerous to find out what was happening in the castle, rather than what was happening in her own heart. She turned and hurried toward the servants' door before Maeve could come back.

The back stairway was steep and narrow, lit by a few sconces that showed a faded carpet underfoot and peeling green paint on the walls. Caroline ran down the steps, listening closely for any noise as she went. It would be most embarrassing to be caught sneaking around belowstairs. But she wasn't going to learn anything hiding in her room. At Killinan Castle, she had learned that the servants always knew everything that went on.

At the bottom of the stairs, two hallways went off to the right and left. One was dark, but from the other, she could hear voices and the clatter of china and silverware. She tiptoed along that one, ready to duck into one of the open, darkened doorways at any approach. She passed the empty dining room, pantries, offices, and wine closet. But the voices were all from the cavernous kitchen at the end of the hall.

Caroline slid behind a tall cupboard to watch as footmen rushed around with trays, a small, plump lady in a stained apron stirred at a steaming pot, and Mrs. McCann stood at the center of it all waving her hands.

"No, Jimmy, don't take that yet! You don't have the claret," Mrs. McCann shouted to one of the hapless footmen. "Is that soup nearly finished, Mrs. O'Rourke? They'll be going into the dining room soon."

"I'm working as fast as I can," the cook muttered. "We had to find extra vegetables to stretch it, and at this time of year, too. No one told me we had to feed four extra mouths tonight, as well as the master and her fine ladyship. And what am I supposed to do for pudding?"

"I don't know, Mrs. O'Rourke," Mrs. McCann cried. "I wasn't told there would be four of them, either, or that they would arrive today of all days. I knew that I never should have taken this job. No, not that bottle!"

"My lady! Whatever are you doing there?" Maeve suddenly said.

Caroline spun around to find the maid standing just beyond her hiding space. Maeve certainly walked quietly without her clattering tray. Caroline grabbed her hand and tugged her into an empty closet.

"What is happening here, Maeve?" she asked.

Maeve shook her head in a bewildered gesture. "The master has guests."

"So I gathered. But who are they? What are they doing here?"

"I don't know, my lady. I've only seen one of them, and she's not very talkative. Not to a maid like me."

She? Caroline felt a twinge of something like jealousy at this bit of news. But there was no time for such silliness now. She pushed it away and said, "So it's a lady?"

97

"Oh, yes, and one who seems to think herself quite fine. The bathwater I took up at first wasn't hot enough, and now my hands are too rough to fasten her fine silk gown. I'm to send Mrs. McCann to her right away." Maeve's sniff said what she thought of such haughty behavior.

Had one of Grant's elegant mistresses come back to him? "Did you hear this lady's name?"

"No, my lady. But she's not Irish. Not even English, I'd say. Now I have to go fetch Mrs. McCann or I'll be in trouble!"

"Yes, of course." Caroline let go of Maeve, still puzzling over her words. A silk-clad, non-English lady at Muirin Inish?

Oh, Grant, she thought. *What trouble are you making here?*

Maeve hesitated at the door. "My lady, I would stay in my chamber if I were you. I don't know who these people are, but I don't have a good feeling."

Caroline thought of poor Bessie, dead on the cliffs. "I will be careful, Maeve, I promise. If you will do the same."

Maeve grinned. "Oh, don't worry about me, my lady!"

She hurried away on her errand, and Caroline slipped back up the servants' stairs and into the castle.

Barely had the door swung shut behind her, when her arm was seized in a rough, steel-strong grasp. A hand covered her mouth, and she was shoved back hard against the wall. Caroline screamed against the hand and kicked out in a rush of cold fear and fighting instinct.

Her borrowed bedroom slippers made scarcely an impact, and her skirts wrapped around her legs, but still she fought on. All she could see of her captor in the dim light was a deceptively slim figure, not as tall as Grant, and a cap of glowing gold hair. He wrapped his other arm around her waist, as tight and suffocating as iron chains, and lifted her up.

She felt the unyielding wall at her back, and she couldn't breathe. She remembered the Rebellion, when she was on the run across the countryside with her family amid battles and destruction—and the soldier who tried to rape her sister. The memories made her fight even harder, kicking and twisting against him. She managed to open her mouth enough to bite down on the soft spot just below his thumb. She tasted the salty tang of blood.

"*Foutre!*" her captor cursed in French. For an instant, a malicious glint lit his eyes, but then to Caroline's surprise, he laughed. "They do say Irish women have much spirit. I had no idea how correct they are."

His hand slid away from her mouth as be examined the wound that she left behind. Caroline took advantage of his flash of distraction to lunge her knee toward his crotch, but he dodged away from her. He laughed even harder.

He leaned closer. His lips lightly skimmed over her jaw, making her shiver. His caressing touch was somehow even more frightening than when he had roughly grabbed her.

"I think I may enjoy my visit to this barbaric place far more than I anticipated," he murmured.

Caroline thought swiftly. Her every instinct screamed at her to get away from this man. She was frightened, confused. and angry all at the same time, in one dizzying jumble.

"Only if you want to duel with Sir Grant," she said, in a far more stern and cold voice than she could have hoped for. She remembered whispered rumors of duels that Grant fought in Dublin over various scandalous women. Duels that he usually won quite handily. "He is the greatest shot in all of western Ireland. And he is very jealous indeed."

The man drew back to look at her with narrowed eyes. They were a celestial blue color, like angel's eyes. "Jealous, is he? And who are you that he should be jealous of, *mademoiselle*?"

Caroline swallowed hard. Her throat felt very dry and tight. "I am his mistress, of course. Who are you?"

He laughed and lowered her to her feet, but he still held tight to her waist so she could not escape. "How very unkind of our host to keep such beauty hidden away. I see we were misled by tales of his isolated, monkish existence on this island."

"He does not care to share—anything."

He leaned close again, and she could smell the sweetness of his cologne. "We shall see about that, *ma belle*."

Caroline felt a flash of temper and tried to twist away from him. His hold seemed to be casual now, yet she couldn't break away no matter how hard she tried. "Let me go!"

"Perhaps not just yet, *mademoiselle*. Tell me, why are you skulking around up here all alone? Are you in hiding?"

"I don't have to answer to you."

"Oh, I think you should."

Suddenly Grant shouted, "LaPlace! What is the meaning of this?"

The man's grasp loosened on Caroline's waist, and she yanked herself away from him. She ran to Grant, who took her arm and pushed her behind him.

The man, LaPlace, turned to Grant with a light-hearted smile. A ray of lamplight fell across him, and Caroline saw that be was angelically good-looking, with a cap of golden hair and a face that was all high cheekbones and blue eyes. He was as handsome as Grant once was, and probably just as deceptive behind that fine façade.

"I was returning to my chamber to change for dinner when I found this lovely little morsel tiptoeing around," LaPlace said. "It was most unfair of you to hide her away, *monsieur*. A ray of beauty in this tedious gray place."

"She is no part of this business," Grant said tightly.

"Ah, so she is here solely for your pleasure then?" LaPlace said affably. "She did say you were very jealous."

Grant gave her a quick glance. Even though his hand was still hard on hers, she thought that she glimpsed a glint of amusement deep in his eyes. But it was gone in an instant, replaced by his usual chilly remoteness.

"I am certainly jealous where she is concerned," he said.

"But surely, *monsieur*, that does not mean she must be shut away as if this were a Turkish harem," LaPlace said. "She must join us for dinner. I assure you, she need fear no improper advances, now that we know the state of the *affaires d'amour*."

"I am not dressed for dinner," Caroline said quickly, thinking of the fine lady in silk that Maeve had waited on.

"We can wait for you," LaPlace answered cheerfully. "I am sure Mademoiselle Victorine is not finished with her toilette yet, either."

"Come with me," Grant said abruptly. He pulled Caroline with him down the corridor toward her chamber, his touch implacable on her arm. She felt a frisson of fear, as if she had jumped from one dangerous captor to another.

"I look forward to seeing you again, *mademoiselle*," LaPlace called after them. "I am sure we have a great deal to learn about one another."

"Like hell," Grant growled. He kicked open Caroline's door and pushed her inside.

Infuriated by such treatment, and by all the secrets he was keeping in this house, Caroline whirled around on him as he slammed the door shut. She could barely see him in the sputtering candlelight. He was just a looming figure leaning against the door. He radiated a simmering anger to match her own. The air crackled around them.

"What is the meaning of this?" she cried. "Who is that man, and how dare you..."

He answered by catching her in his arms and covering her mouth with his. His kiss was hard, merciless, surrounding her with blistering heat. She fell into it headlong, passion and anger boiling up inside of her.

She curled her fists into the front of his shirt, her mouth opening as his tongue plunged inside to taste deeply. He spun her around to press her back against the wall. Her knees collapsed with the storm of emotion breaking over her, and he caught her up in his arms.

He tilted his head away from her, and Caroline slowly opened her eyes to stare up at him in a daze. He smiled at her, an echo of that old rakish grin that wreaked havoc on the ladies of Dublin.

"So I'm jealous, am I?"

CHAPTER
TWELVE

Caroline shoved him away. He stumbled back, his smile widening. She paced across the room, as far from the infuriating Grant as she could get.

"What else could I say?" she said. "I wasn't expecting to be grabbed by an amorous Frenchman as soon as I stepped out of this room. I didn't have a clever tale prepared."

That smile vanished, and the hardness crept back into Grant's eyes. "I'll kill him for assaulting a woman in my home. For touching you."

"But who is he?" Caroline cried. "Why is he here? What trouble are you in, Grant?"

"He is no one." Grant moved toward her slowly, as if he thought she might slap him or maybe cry, and he carefully took her hand in his. "And I am in no trouble. I merely have some business to transact with these people; then they will be gone."

"What nature of business? He is French."

"And you have no doubt heard wild rumors of imminent invasion, rumors that have been going around for years."

Of course she had. She remembered that Grant had involved himself in complicated and dangerous politics before. And it seemed that even if he hid from such complexities here, they had come to him.

Just as she had.

His grasp tightened on her hand, and he drew her slowly toward him. He gave her time to run away, but she went into his arms instead. She rested her forehead on his chest and closed her eyes. The world was raging around her, and he was the only rock she could cling to.

She felt his cheek against her temple, the brush of his hair on her skin. "Oh, Caro, I know I have never given you a reason to trust me. Quite the opposite. But for now, I ask you to. Don't go wandering the castle without me. They will be gone soon, but until then..."

Caroline gave a rough little laugh. "You are very jealous, remember? I wouldn't want to cause any duels of passion."

"Thank you," he said. Those two words sounded cautious, as if he seldom used them. "Just stay close to me and try to say as little as possible to LaPlace and his friends."

Caroline pulled back and looked up at him. "You will tell me nothing more about them?"

He just looked back at her, his jaw set in that hard line she had come to dislike so much, and she sighed. Trust surely had to go both ways, and it seemed he could not yet trust her. But they had to rely on each other now, even if it must be blindly.

"I actually have nothing to change into for dinner," she said.

105

"Perhaps I can find something," he answered. "Wait here for a moment, and for God's sake don't..."

"I know." Caroline laughed. "Don't go wandering around alone. I have learned my lesson this time."

His lips twitched. "Somehow, Caroline, I doubt that."

GRANT SHUT THE LIBRARY DOOR WITH A FIRM CLICK AND turned the lock. Caroline should be safely alone in her room now. It was time to finish this business.

"Let's make this meeting short," he said tersely as he crossed the room to sit behind his desk. If he had to look at LaPlace very long, he would surely beat the man to a bloody pulp for what he had done to Caroline. And then the whole painstaking plan would fall apart.

LaPlace sat back in his chair with a lazy smile. "*Quelle dommage*, where is the famous Irish hospitality?"

"You are not my guest. You are merely here for one purpose. So let's get on with it, shall we?"

LaPlace's smile faded, and his eyes took on the cold cast of winter ice. "Quite right. Time does grow very short. These documents must be delivered in Dublin by the end of the month, if our little alliance is to hold. And we all want that *n'est-ce pas?*"

He drew out a sealed packet of papers from the case at his feet and leaned forward to place them on Grant's desk. Grant examined them carefully. This was it then, the culmination of all the careful planning, the lies and plots. His salvation and his atonement were at hand. He watched LaPlace closely over the edge of the papers. It felt as if time stood still for one tense moment. It could all fall either way.

"If anyone asks here on this godforsaken island," LaPlace said, "I was merely the Vicomte's escort, a man who appreciates fine literature. Just as you are, *monsieur*. No one will know of these papers."

"Of course not."

"Not even the oh-so-pretty *mademoiselle*."

Grant threw down the papers with a growl. "She has nothing to do with any of this. I have my own reasons for taking part in your scheme."

"Just be sure those reasons don't cause you to double-cross us." LaPlace gave a deceptively affable smile. "I fear you would certainly regret it, as would so many of your countrymen."

He took out another paper, folded very small and sealed, and tossed it across the desk. "This is the address in Dublin where the documents must be delivered. If they don't reach our contact by the agreed-on day, we will assume the alliance is broken, and we will be forced to take our own measures. They may not be very pleasant."

Grant said nothing, merely watched LaPlace with a hard, stony stare. He had known that the double scheme would be tricky and perilous. He had nothing to lose by taking on this role. But that was before Caroline arrived. Now he had to protect her.

"I have chosen my path," Grant said. "I will do as I said I would, you and your cohorts can be assured of that."

LaPlace smiled again. "We cherish our bond with our Irish allies and hope we can be of much use to each other in the future. If we find we cannot..."

"All will be well, LaPlace. If we keep this strictly business. No more harassing my guests." Or Grant would kill him.

"Certainly not! A Frenchman never poaches on another man's preserve. If I had known she was your plaything..." LaPlace shrugged. "I have copies of all the documents, of course, and I always carry them. Just to be certain."

Grant watched as LaPlace rose to his feet, as lazy as a jungle cat. "Yes," Grant said brusquely.

"Then we are agreed," LaPlace said. "I shall see you at dinner, yes? Perhaps then some of that hospitality will be evident."

After he left, closing the door behind him, Grant finished examining the papers. It was as he expected —treasonous agreements, a prelude to revolution, to be delivered to traitors in Dublin. And he had to play the traitor right along with them.

As he reached for the wax to reseal the packet, he heard a sudden noise in the corridor outside. A clatter and the patter of footsteps. He quickly locked the papers in a drawer and ran out of the library.

It all looked deserted and silent, but then he heard steps running up the staircase. And he smelled a trace of sweet perfume in the air.

He dashed up the stairs two at a time and along the corridor to the bedchambers. Caroline's door was closed. Was he imagining things? Perhaps all the plotting had driven him mad. He saw spies around every corner.

But then there was the sound of a lock turning. She hadn't been in there long, if she was just now locking the door.

Grant braced his palm on the wall beside her door

and listened closely. He could almost imagine that he heard her breathing in there, quick and panicked after a run.

The little eavesdropper. He should lock her in her chamber and not let her out until this was all over.

He pounded on the door. It was a long moment before she called out softly, "Who-who is it?"

"It's Grant," he answered. "I've come to take you down to dinner, if you're ready."

After another moment, the door slowly swung open, and Caroline stood there. Her cheeks were pink, but she met his eyes steadily. If she had been listening, surely she could not have heard much. She didn't know what he was doing. But if she suspected, if she tried to find out, he would have to stop her. For her own safety.

"I'm ready," she said.

"Then let's go. Everyone is waiting."

G rant watched Caroline closely as she sat with the Vicomte d'Allay at the other end of the table. They spoke to each other quietly, their heads bent together over the soup as they talked and laughed with every sign of easy enjoyment. They seemed to have much in common, and Caroline gave no sign of suspicion or disquiet, no sign of what she might have overheard earlier.

But every once in a while, Grant caught her glancing at him from the comer of her eye, and her fingers clutched at the stem of her glass. She was trying to play it cool and calm, yet Grant was sure she would demand answers later. He would have to see that she did not find the answers.

Mademoiselle Muret laid her hand lightly on his arm to draw his attention to her. When he looked, she gave him a flirtatious smile and leaned closer so that he could smell the spice of her expensive French perfume. She was exactly the sort of woman he was accustomed to in his life before Muirin Inish—beautiful, sophisticated, elegant, adept at the games of flirtation and fully cognizant of their rules.

With her, Grant could feel himself slipping back into his old ways. He forgot his sins and all the hard-won lessons of the years since then—almost. He could never entirely forget with Caroline Blacknall's voice in his ears.

"Sir Grant, your home is so very charming," Mademoiselle Muret said. "Like something in a romantic novel!"

"And you are a most charming liar, *mademoiselle*," Grant answered with a laugh. He gestured to the footman to refill their glasses.

"*Non!*" she said. Her own laughter trilled like crystal bells, her eyes sparkling with mirth, yet Grant saw the hardness beneath, the glint of careful calculation behind her charm. He remembered something else about the women of his past, something beyond their beauty and grace. He remembered that they were as dishonest and artificial as he was himself. Every word and smile was part of a careful plot. Only the object had changed since his days in Dublin. Grant could handle women like Victorine Muret. He had played their game for a long time, and he understood them. But Caroline Blacknall he didn't understand at all. She played no games, at least none he understood. She didn't hide behind sophisticated artifice. She was an intelligent woman who felt no need to conceal who she was.

An intelligent woman with a streak of wild curiosity that was proving to be dangerous to both of them.

Grant took a long drink of his wine and turned away from Caroline's study. She baffled him, turning his careful world upside down. He wanted her body with a burning lust he had never felt for his elegant

111

mistresses, and that was bad enough. But he also wanted to know her mind, her thoughts and opinions, her feelings. He wanted to lose himself in that calm brightness of hers, and be clean again. And he hated that feeling; he resisted it with all his strength. Grant Dunmore was not accustomed to needing another person. He had vowed when he and his mother were turned away from Adair Court that he would care only for himself, look out for his own interests, and be utterly ruthless in fulfilling them. He would never be vulnerable again.

He lived his life in that way, cold and selfish, for years, until it all ended in that fiery warehouse. Now he had a different goal, and once again Caroline Blacknall was in his way.

She was the most damnable, confounding woman he had ever met.

"Monsieur, I fear you are not paying attention to me," Victorine said, breaking into his brooding thoughts.

Grant turned back to find her pouting prettily up at him. She tapped his wrist with one manicured finger. It was soft and white, not stained with ink as Caroline's was. He smiled at her in return with his old, practiced smile of seduction. It had always worked on the females of Dublin and London, actresses and duchesses alike, and it seemed to work on Victorine Muret. A pretty pink blush stained her cheeks, and Monsieur Michel glowered at them.

"Do forgive me, *mademoiselle*," he said in a low, intimate voice. "I could not possibly neglect you for even a moment. It is so rare to have such lovely company on Muirin Inish."

Her pout deepened. "And yet you seem so distracted, *monsieur*. Does the tall *mademoiselle* so occupy your thoughts?"

Grant glanced at Caroline, but she was lost in conversation with the Vicomte again. She was tall, and slender, her long neck like a graceful swan's above the low bodice of her pale-yellow muslin gown. She had her very own sort of elegance.

"It is better than being alone here, I suppose," he said.

"Ah, *pauvre* Sir Grant!" Victorine murmured. She laid her hand on his arm again, light but inviting. "How very lonely you must be, even here in your charming castle. You should come to Paris and really live your life again. There is no place more exciting in all the world, I am sure."

Grant laughed. "I doubt an Englishman would be welcome in Paris right now, *mademoiselle*."

"You are Irish, are you not? There are many Irishmen in Paris now. The charming Monsieur Emmet and his friends, for instance. I meet with them everywhere, at the theater, riding in the parks, even at the Tuileries. We are united in one cause now, *non*? To defeat the stuffy, ridiculous English."

"And that is why you and your friends are here, is it not, *mademoiselle*?"

For the first time, Grant saw a hint of doubt in her eyes. She glanced at LaPlace, who had joined in the conversation with Caroline and the Vicomte, and paid Victorine no heed, and at Monsieur Michel, who stared at her in stony silence at the end of the table.

"I am not sure about Captain LaPlace and Monsieur Michel," she said. "They do not talk to a silly girl like me. But you know my father and I are here on our own errand. One I hope will conclude to my father's satisfaction."

"I hope that as well, *mademoiselle*."

Her hand softly caressed his arm, and her smile brightened. "It would mean so very much to him, Sir Grant, to see his dream fulfilled at long last. His health has been so frail, and I am sure this will make him feel stronger."

Grant shifted in his chair. "We will have to see what the terms are, Mademoiselle Muret."

"Will you not call me Victorine?" She leaned closer, revealing even more of her lovely bosom in her ribbon-trimmed bodice. "If I can add to the offer in any way..."

He laughed and drew away from her. Her pout returned. "We cannot discuss business at the dinner table, *mademoiselle*. I am utterly unable to think of such things in your charming company."

"You are quite right, Sir Grant," Captain LaPlace said. "We can't bore these lovely ladies with such dull talk. Perhaps we may retire to your library shortly and leave the English lady and Mademoiselle Muret to chat about bonnets and such."

Caroline's lips tightened, but Grant sensed that it was not entirely out of anger. She seemed to be trying not to laugh.

"How kind of you, Captain LaPlace," Caroline finally said. "It is true I am sorely ill-informed on Paris fashions this season."

"Poor *mademoiselle*!" cried Victorine. "I see that so clearly. But I am most happy to give you any advice I can."

Caroline's eyes narrowed, and she gave a tiny

little smile. Grant suddenly felt rather sorry for Mademoiselle Muret.

"SHE DOES NOT UNDERSTAND WHY WE ARE HERE, I'M afraid," the Vicomte said.

Caroline looked at him in surprise. She had been lost in her own thoughts, half-listening as Mademoiselle Muret played on the rusty old harpsichord someone had unearthed for her and set in the corner of the drawing room. Her thoughts kept turning on the snatches of talk she had heard earlier between Grant and LaPlace, the hints of treason.

The question now was, what was she going to do about it?

"I beg your pardon, *monsieur*?" she said.

He nodded toward his daughter. Mademoiselle Muret's pretty auburn head was bent over the keyboard, a discontented pout on her lips. No doubt because no one of the male persuasion was there to admire her performance.

"She doesn't understand why we're here, not really," the Vicomte repeated. "On a bleak, cold island in the middle of the Paris social season."

"Hmm." Caroline took a slow sip of her tea. The music, the crackle of the fire in the grate, and the patter of the rain on the windows combined to make a cozy scene. It could almost appear normal.

"Why *are* we here again, *monsieur*?" she said. As the days passed, the daily world of her Dublin life receded farther and farther away, and the strangeness of Muirin Inish became the reality. She had to be very careful not to lose herself completely. "I seem to need reminding sometimes."

"Oh, I think you and I are here for a very similar reason, Mademoiselle Black," he answered. "For love —in our own ways."

That caught her attention. She turned to him, and he gave her a little smile. "Love?"

"Come now, *ma chere mademoiselle*. Why else would an intelligent, pretty young woman such as yourself bury herself on such a bleak island? Why would I come so far at my age, when my wanderings should be long over? It would have to be something very powerful indeed."

"I am not in love," Caroline protested strongly. She had loved Hartley, in her own way, which was not the overwhelming, soul-bound way her sisters loved their husbands, the way her mother loved her stepfather. It was quiet and calm and safe, but it was love nonetheless. That was surely how she loved. What she felt for Grant was nothing like that.

"*Non?*" said the Vicomte. "Well, desire can be very strong as well. I remember that from my own youth. Victorine's mother was an extraordinary beauty."

"But what sort of love has brought you here?"

"Why, the love of learning, of course. That you understand, I think?"

"Yes, I do understand the love of learning." Caroline sat back in her chair, deeply disquieted. "I am writing a volume of Irish history and mythology, though I fear it's far from finished."

"Then we are kindred spirits, *mademoiselle*. I enjoy studies of many kinds. Greece and Rome, *naturellement*, the Renaissance, art and mythology. My father owned one of the most renowned libraries in all of

France, and I was allowed to read anything I liked from it when I was young." He gave her a wink. "Even the more risqué items he kept hidden from my maman."

Caroline laughed. She rather liked the Vicomte. He didn't seem to fit with LaPlace and Michel, though surely he, too, had some hidden errand here on Muirin Inish.

"It sounds marvelous," she said.

"So it was. But alas my father perished in the Terror, along with so many others, and his chateau was sacked. So much was lost. I have recovered some, but many of his treasures have eluded me, or been sadly destroyed."

Caroline felt terrible for the Vicomte and for the loss of any library. The loss of so much learning and beauty was surely a tragedy. "I am very sorry for your losses, *monsieur*. My mother's husband lost his family in Paris, too. And I am sorry for my own loss. I would have loved to see such a treasure."

"Once the sad conflicts between our countries are ended, you must come to Paris, *mademoiselle*. I will be proud to show you what I have recovered. My own daughter is terribly bored by it all." He glanced at LaPlace and Michel. "She cares only for romance. And who knows? Perhaps our nations will be on amiable terms once more. The Peace of Amiens is a hopeful sign. You will visit Paris one day."

Did he know something about the political situation then? Caroline studied him carefully, wondering what information she could get from him, but he just gave her one of his placid smiles and held out his glass to be refilled.

"Tell me more about this book you are writing, *mademoiselle*," he said. "It sounds most intriguing."

Caroline outlined her work for him, and what she hoped to accomplish with it in the future. She wanted it to be a comprehensive source for Ireland's dramatic and important history and old tales, a source of dignity and pride for Irish families. She seldom spoke of it, except to her scholarly friends in the Hibernian Society, but the Vicomte seemed very interested and had many questions.

Caroline was able to lose herself in talking about the project, until the drawing room door opened and Grant reappeared with LaPlace and Michel behind him.

She searched his face for any hint of what might have transpired in the library, but he looked as cold and expressionless as ever. Truly he could have been a famous actor at the Crow Street Theater. She could never decipher him.

"Ah, Sir Grant, there you are at last!" Victorine cried. "How you neglect your guests. It is most shocking."

With one last glance at Caroline, Grant turned toward the harpsichord. "Forgive me, *chere mademoiselle*," he said. "You must know I thought of only one guest in particular at every moment."

"ONLY ONE GUEST IN PARTICULAR AT EVERY MOMENT?" Caroline cried the instant Grant closed the bedroom door behind them and they were alone. She let out the burst of laughter she was holding inside. "Did you learn that in a Minerva Press novel?"

Grant leaned back against the door, his arms crossed over his chest. He laughed ruefully, and she saw the first hint of a real expression on his face for the only time that evening. "She seemed to like it," he said.

"Of course she did. You were obviously most admiring of her large—eyes as you said it."

He grinned at her, and it was as if the sun suddenly broke from behind the dour clouds. "Are you jealous, Caro?"

Caroline let out her breath in a huff. "Of such patently false compliments? Certainly not!"

"I think you are. Most astonishing." He reached out and caught her around the waist to draw her closer to him. "You shouldn't be, you know. You have very pretty—eyes of your own."

Caroline beat her fists against his chest, trying not to laugh. She tried to remember her terrible suspicions, her fears, tried to remember that he was a possible traitor to Ireland, consorting with French spies. But when he looked at her like that, the deep rumble of his laughter warm against her, it was hard to remember anything at all. "Very pretty indeed," he whispered as he nuzzled his lips against her neck. "You taste so sweet. Like sugared roses."

Caroline tried to laugh, but her breath caught on a gasp as his mouth opened on her skin. His kiss was hot and wet and eager, and it made her tremble. "S-sugared roses?"

"I always did have a terrible craving for sweets."

Her head fell back against the door as he traced a line

of kisses along her collarbone to the curve of her shoulder. He pulled her gown away from her body as he went, baring her skin inch by inch. He caressed her naked breasts gently, tracing his long, rough fingers over their curves, closer and closer to her aching nipples, teasing and retreating. Caroline couldn't breathe with the force of her need for him to touch her, really touch her.

"Oh," she sighed as he finally caught one of the pink, erect crests between his thumb and forefinger, lightly pinching and rolling, sending waves of pleasure through her. She strained up on her toes, her whole body arching toward him. "Oh!"

"These," he said hoarsely, "are the most beautiful breasts in all the world."

Caroline laughed weakly. She knew they were no such thing, but when he said it, and when he looked at her with those intense dark eyes, she could almost believe it. "More beautiful than Mademoiselle Muret?"

He kissed the soft upper slope of her breast, and she felt his smile on her skin. "You *are* jealous. How gratifying."

She seized handfuls of his hair and pulled him up to face her. She stopped his laughter with a fierce, hard kiss. Her tongue pressed into his mouth to twine with his, to taste the wine and darkness of him. He made her feel drunk, dizzy, giddy with this terrible, primal need she had never imagined before.

And he seemed to feel the same. He lifted her up and pulled her tight against him. His hands were hard on the curve of her backside, tilting her toward him so she could feel the iron length of his erection through their clothing. She wrapped her legs around his waist and held him close to her.

When they kissed like this, when they fell head-first into this roiling maelstrom of lust, she felt closer to him than she ever had to anyone in her life. Her body and soul were open to his, connected to his, in ways she thought only existed in myths. It was all an illusion, of course. In the cold light of day, those fiery bonds snapped, and there was only old suspicion and chilly distance.

But now, when he kissed her with such hunger—they were like one.

Suddenly desperate to hold on to that strange, almost mystical connection, Caroline deepened the kiss even more. She tilted her hips against his and rubbed along the length of his penis, making him groan.

Grant swung around toward the bed, and they fell onto its softness in a tangle of limbs and cloth. He kissed the soft curve of her shoulder, the tip of his tongue tasting the hollow of her throat. Caroline closed her eyes tightly to absorb every lightning-hot sensation.

He slowly drew her gown and chemise away, down the length of her body, dragging the soft fabric over her sensitive skin. As the muslin slid away, his mouth followed its path. He kissed the soft white skin between her breasts, the curve of her waist, the flare of her hip. He lightly bit at the top of her thigh as he drew off her stocking, making her gasp, before he kissed the underside of her knee.

"These," he said, "are the most beautiful legs in the world."

According to his vast experience? Caroline knew that was not true, any more than the beauty of her bosom. But she bent her leg around his hip and cradled him against her. When he looked at her like that, she felt beautiful, and powerful, in ways she never had.

He reached for her other leg and slowly stripped away its stocking, kissing every newly bare inch as he went. He cast the flimsy silk away and kissed the arch of her foot, her ankle, her toe. He gently nipped at its tip, and she laughed at the shivery, tickling sensation.

"And the most beautiful foot, too," he muttered. To her shock, he drew her toe between his lips. The pleasure of it was too much. She pulled away from him and sat up against the pillows.

"You, Sir Grant Dunmore, are entirely overdressed for this occasion," she said. She had wanted the words to sound alluring, tempting, but they came out all breathless and eager. Her head felt light and whirling, and her skin flushed hot.

Caroline reached out to push his coat away from his shoulders and tossed it to the floor to join her gown and chemise. He went very still, watching her with narrowed eyes. She set her trembling fingers to his cravat. The loops of starched muslin were simply tied, but she kept getting distracted by the heat of his skin, the roughness of the whiskers along his jaw, and the way his breath stirred her hair as he leaned close.

At last, she tugged it free and dropped it onto the rumpled bed. He still did not move; he just let her do what she would. Whatever she wanted. It was a heady feeling.

She unlaced his shirt and drew it over his head. His bare chest gleamed with a light sheen of sweat, hot and damp under her exploring touch. She traced the looping patterns of his tattoo and lightly scraped the edge of her nail over his flat nipple. It puckered into a hard disc, and his breath sucked in hard, but he still didn't move.

Caroline bent her head to kiss him. The tip of her tongue tasted the tiny, salty drop of sweat at the base of his neck. She inhaled deeply of his scent, the clean greenness of his soap, the dark hint of male desire, and it made her feel even more lost. She kissed the hard angle of his shoulder and drew that nipple between her lips to bite and taste it.

"*Mollaght!*" he shouted, and his rigid control snapped. His arms swept around her, and he bore her down to the bed. His mouth claimed hers in a hard, merciless kiss.

Caroline kissed him back and let herself tumble entirely into that new, topsy-turvy world she found only in his embrace. Nothing else mattered now but the two of them together.

She traced her caress down his hard-muscled chest until she reached the band of his breeches. She quickly unfastened them and touched the hot velvet of his erect penis.

"You'll be the death of me, Caroline Blacknall," he muttered against her lips. His kiss slid along her jaw to the soft spot just below her ear, and he lightly bit at it.

"And you of me," she gasped. "But it's not a terrible way to go."

He laughed and kissed her lips again, deep and possessive, until she moaned and could think no more. She could only feel. He eased his breeches over his hips and gently spread her legs until he was cradled against her body.

She felt the press of him as he slid inside, all hot, damp friction. She knew the feeling of him now, knew their rhythm and how they fit together so per-fectly. She wrapped her legs around his waist and arched up to meet him. He pushed forward until he was sheathed completely, and it was the most perfect feeling Caroline had ever known.

He drew back and plunged forward again, and she met him with every movement, faster and faster. She caught his groans with her kiss and echoed them with her own. Outside her window, thunder ex-ploded, but she was sure it was her own shouts as pressure built up inside her. It sparkled and sizzled, just beyond her reach, the ultimate pleasure.

Suddenly that pressure exploded into a million shining pieces. Everything seemed bigger, grander, every sound and sensation amplified. His touch, his kiss, the soft sheets at her back, the rain outside, it was all more vivid and intense than she could ever have imagined.

She felt as if she had leaped off the cliffs and gone soaring into the sky.

"Caro!" Grant shouted above her. Within her arms, she felt his whole body stiffen and tighten, his head thrown back. "*Mac an donais.*"

Then he collapsed to the bed next to her. She closed her eyes and tried to breathe slowly, to bring herself back down from the stars into her own body. His harsh breath blended with the sound of the rain and the pounding surf far below.

She felt him bury his face in her shoulder, and she held on to him to try to pull herself up. She had lost herself completely there for a moment, and it was a frightening sensation. Would she ever really find her-self and be whole again without him?

CHAPTER
FOURTEEN

Caroline sat up against the pillows as she watched Grant sleeping beside her. There in the silent shelter of the bed, in the still aftermath of the storm of passion, he should be at peace. But the lines of his face were strained and his fists tightly furled, as if he fought demons even in his dreams.

"Why can you not tell me what torments you so?" she whispered. She traced a soft caress over the scars on his face, the hard line of his jaw, and smoothed back a strand of hair from his brow. Once he had confided in her, and she had felt close to him for that one fleeting moment. She had felt that she glimpsed the real man behind all the glitter and beauty.

But that was long ago, and so much had changed. What if the bitterness of losing his fine Dublin life had hardened that last little bit of his soul and driven him to something terrible? To treason?

Caroline wanted to know what he was doing and why this French group was really here. Yet what would she do if she knew? What *could* she do?

She suddenly felt terribly alone. She knew she had

to dig deep and find her own strength, the strength of the Blacknalls, and help herself. Perhaps she could help Grant, too, if he would let her. The man she had glimpsed so long ago. the loving, protective, strong, Irish man, had to be in there somewhere.

Grant stirred in his sleep, and her hand fell away from his hair. His eyes opened to stare up at her, and for an instant, his fist tightened as if he didn't recognize her. But then he relaxed and smiled.

"So you *are* here," he said. His hand lazily drifted through a loose lock of her hair, twisting it around one of his fingers.

"Of course I am," Caroline answered. "This is my bed. I wouldn't go anywhere."

"It was just a dream, then." Grant tugged at her hair and brought her down to meet his kiss. Unlike the hard desperation of last night. this kiss was gentle, questioning. Caroline kissed him back. She laid her hands on his chest, feeling the leashed power of his body under her touch. He was calm now, lazy, sensual, but she remembered the wild strength when he made love to her. The memory made her draw in a sharp breath and lean back from him before her own lust could overtake her again. She needed a cooler head now if she was to gain his confidence.

"What did you dream?" she said.

He trailed his fingertips in a whisper-soft caress over her shoulder and along the sensitive inside of her arm. His gaze followed his touch, growing more heated as he saw her bare breast. Caroline drew the rumpled sheet around herself.

"I can't remember," he said, toying with her hair again. He wrapped it around his wrist like a rope and drew her down to lie across his chest. "It's fading away. It seems as if I was searching for you, that there was some terribly important reason I had to find you, but you were gone."

Caroline closed her eyes and listened to his heartbeat against her ear. It was strong and true, as elemental and full of life as the rain outside. "I am here," she said.

She heard the rumble of his laughter deep in his chest. "In your own bed. But there is an ancient law on Muirin Inish that says everything on the island belongs to the lord of the castle. Every stone of every house, every morsel of food, every stick of furniture..."

"Every person who sits on that furniture?" Caroline suddenly sat up and shook free of his hold. He grinned up at her and stretched his arms lazily above his head, the very picture of the arrogant lord he once was. That old Grant did indeed seem to think that everything in sight belonged to him, his for the taking. Seats in Parliament, houses, carriages, estates in the possession of his cousin. And women, too. Was that the way of the new Grant as well?

"It would not be so bad to belong to me, would it, Caro?" he said, still so deceptively lazy and teasing. He reached out one hand to touch the soft underside of her breast, caressing it as if he knew just where she liked to be touched—and he did know, damn him. His caress drifted over her ribcage, along her waist, lower and lower...

"You seemed to like it last night," he whispered. "If this were a hundred years ago, you would be on your knees swearing fealty to your lord right about now."

"How dare you?" Caroline burst out, and he laughed. Her Blacknall temper fully roused up now,

127

she threw aside his hand and straddled him. "A Blacknall woman belongs to no man."

"*They* belong to *her*, is that it?" he said. He still smiled at her, teasing, goading. He seemed as if he looked forward to what she might do next.

Caroline herself had no idea what she would do. She had never felt as she did now as she looked down at Grant lying beneath her. It was like a growing sense of power and freedom, and she liked it.

But she didn't like him, not just then. He played some dangerous game here on this island, and with her, and she wanted to know what it was.

She seized his wrists in her hands and pressed his arms to the bed above his head. Holding him as her captive, she bent her head and kissed first one corner of his lips then the other. She flicked her tongue against the dimple in his cheek and felt his smile fade.

As she slid her kiss over his cheek and bit at his earlobe, she felt the side of her hand brush against something soft—her discarded silk stocking. Still kissing him, she leaned forward, her hair falling around them in a curtain, and looped the stocking around his wrists. She pulled it into a tight knot.

Grant stiffened, and his head tilted back from her. "What are you doing?"

Caroline smiled at him sweetly. "It would not be so bad to belong to me, would it, Grant?" she echoed his words. "It might even be fun."

She found her other stocking and used it to tie his bound hands to the bedpost. He watched her warily, his body tense, but he didn't pull away from her. And she saw his erection growing beneath the sheet.

She pulled the cloth away to leave him naked beneath her. In the rush and heat of their passion, she hadn't been able to fully appreciate him, but now she saw he was quite magnificent. His muscles were lean and strong beneath the satin of his skin, his torso sculpted into hard planes like one of the classical statues at Killinan Castle. His arms strained against her bonds, powerfully defined, circled by the tattooed band of knot work. His long, bronze-brown hair fell over his shoulder.

She traced her fingertips over the pattern of scars on his left side. They were faded now to a pale pink on the smooth olive of his skin, but they only seemed to increase his allure. They made him more human, more warrior-like. They reminded her of their complicated past, and even more complicated present.

She carefully kissed his scars, one after the other, feeling their roughness under her lips. She forgot her anger as she wished she could take away all that pain. If only they could begin all over again, fresh and clean, only Caroline and Grant. But that was impossible. The past was always there, a wisp of shadowy darkness hanging close to them.

She slid down his body, kissing, tasting, exploring. She had never seen or felt a man like this before, and it was a wondrous thing. Her teeth lightly scraped over his hip bone, the taut line that traced along his upper thigh, and her tongue circled his navel.

"Caroline!" he said tightly, his body twisting under her caress.

She pressed him back down. She knew he could break his bonds at any moment and seize control from her, but she didn't want to give him up just yet. She had so very much to learn about him.

Her touch drifted over his erect penis, light as a

feather and then harder, a little rougher, testing her power. She felt the tracery of veins straining against the velvety skin and the strength of his desire. A tiny drop of pearly liquid formed at its tip, and she caught it on her palm.

"Caro, I don't think this is a good idea," he growled.

She smiled. "Do I need to tie you tighter?"

And she closed her lips around him, drawing him into her mouth. She had read of such things in racy French pamphlets hidden in the back rooms of bookshops, yet she'd never been able to imagine actually doing it. Here, now, with Grant, it felt like the most natural of acts.

He tasted salty and sweet at the same time, and she could smell the maleness of him. She slid her kiss along his steely length and back up again, her hand braced on his rigid thigh.

His body was taut under her touch, and he held his breath. He moaned, and a heady sense of power and pleasure grew within her.

"No more," he said, and she released him from her kiss.

She moved up his body, rubbing her skin against every inch of him in a delicious, damp, sweaty friction.

"Untie me," he said. His eyes were very dark as he watched her. "I want to touch you."

"Not yet," she panted. "I want to see something..."

She pressed her palms on the carved headboard and spread her legs wider over him. Slowly, carefully, she positioned herself over his erection and slid down onto him. She had never tried this before, either—poor Hartley had been strictly an under-the-blankets, man-on-top sort, and she had never dared suggest anything else. This felt strange and awkward, and wonderful.

Their connection felt deeper than before, and the pleasure of that knowledge washed over her like a hot, engulfing wave. He tilted his hips for a better fit, and she rose up and slid down, again and again. She found the rhythm she sought, and he found it with her. She rode him harder and harder until that now familiar burst of orgasm broke over her and made her cry out.

He shouted out incoherent words mingled with her name, his arms pulling the bonds taut Caroline collapsed on top of him as she struggled to breathe. The air was humid and heavy with their lovemaking and with the aftermath of the storm, both so elemental and unstoppable.

"You're right," Grant said hoarsely. "Belonging to you would not be so terrible, if this is what that means."

Caroline slowly raised herself up to stare down at him. His eyes were closed, his chest heaving as if he, too, couldn't catch his breath. He was vulnerable to her now, as she was always so vulnerable to him.

She leaned over him and held on to his bound wrists. "Grant," she whispered, "tell me why those Frenchmen are really here."

She felt his relaxed body grow tense. His eyes opened, and he looked up at her with a glittering stare.

"This hardly seems the moment to talk about them," he said. "Aren't we supposed to be murmuring endearments to each other?"

Caroline shook his hands in frustration. "There's

no time for that now! Morning will be here soon, and I'll have to see LaPlace and the others."

His lips tightened. "You could stay in here, like I told you in the first place."

"That won't work now, if it ever would have. They know I'm here, and LaPlace doesn't seem like a man to give up, no matter how jealous you are."

"Oh, and I am very jealous indeed, Caro my dear, as you've found out." He flexed his body against hers suggestively and laughed when she moved away.

She caught his shirt up off the floor and pulled it over her head before turning back to face him. The soft linen folds fell around her body, and she stuffed her feet into her slippers. "Are you in some kind of trouble?" she asked. "Do you owe these people something?"

"Not exactly." Grant sighed and added, "Can you possibly see your way clear to untying me? This is not the best position from which to converse."

Caroline nodded. "If you won't run away and lock me in again."

"I doubt I could ever run away from you, *gaolach*, no matter how hard I try," he said ruefully. "And obviously locking you in does no good."

She untied the bonds with difficulty, as their strenuous activity had pulled the knots tight. Once free, he found his breeches and put them on. Rubbing his wrists, he sat down beside her on the edge of the bed. "You won't like it," he said.

"I think I can safely anticipate that you're right about that. But I want to know anyway. I'm already involved, so surely I would be safer if I knew." If his goal was indeed to keep her safe, as he said. She could never tell what he was really about.

Grant gave a brusque nod. "Very well. The Vicomte is here to try and buy *The Chronicle of Kildare*."

"What!" Caroline did not expect that. LaPlace and his glowering kinsman Michel, not to mention the glamorous *mademoiselle*, hardly seemed the scholarly sorts. The Vicomte, while certainly interesting and charming, seemed too quiet and sickly to be the true reason for this visit. And he had not been in the library with Grant when she overheard the snatches of their conversation.

But when would she ever remember the hard lessons learned in the past? Appearances meant less than nothing. The truth was always hidden.

"Surely you have guessed in your conversation with him," Grant said. "His father was the French nobleman who once owned one of the three copies of *The Chronicle*, until his library was destroyed and he was sent to the guillotine."

"Yes," Caroline answered, remembering her talk with the Vicomte after dinner. "He did say he was trying to rebuild his family's Library."

"*The Chronicle* was a great treasure of the collection, or so the Vicomte says. He is willing to pay a very high price for it and claimed he could not wait any longer."

Caroline jumped off the bed and spun around to face him, her hands planted on her hips. "You cannot sell it!"

Grant shrugged. That blank, cold look that she hated was in his eyes again. "I have many responsibilities, Caroline."

"But *The Chronicle* is Ireland's treasure. It must stay here in Ireland." Appalled that he could even think of selling that book, which stood for so very much more than old vellum and ink, she took a step toward him. "It is your heritage."

He gave a humorless laugh. "Not mine, I fear. When my uncle turned my mother away from Adair Court, he said that in marrying a wastrel Englishman she had made her choice, and my choice, too. She turned her back on her Irish Catholic family and everything they stood for, fought for. And they turned their backs on her. So surely Kildare is not my heritage."

Caroline shook her head. In his old life, Grant had professed not to care about the McTeer family, indeed to hate them so much he tried to destroy them. He lived his life as an Ascendancy gentleman, more English than Irish.

But she had seen his library in Dublin. She had looked at his books on Ireland and had seen how they were well-read and lovingly cared for. Grant lived on this rugged island amid Irish fishermen. Surely that all meant something? Surely he could never completely abandon his identity with the land, just as she never could?

Her sisters had fought for Ireland, and she fought now to record and save its histories and precious stories. *The Chronicle* was such a part of that; it couldn't be lost. Grant couldn't be lost.

She carefully studied his face, but he gave away not a hint of his emotions.

"If you do need money," she said slowly, "perhaps you could sell the book to Conlan."

"I doubt my dear cousin could pay what the Vicomte offers," Grant said. "Plus that would entail him dealing with me, which I am sure he would never do."

"Then you could sell it to me!" she cried. "I have

LADY OF SEDUCTION

some money of my own from my marriage settlement, and I could raise more. You can't let *The Chronicle* leave Ireland, Grant!"

He caught her hands in his and pulled her against
his chest. She fought at first, too furious to accept the
touch she had craved so much before. But he held on,
gentle but implacable, and she went still. She had to
calm down if she was to make him see. Her emotions,
so distant from the rest of her life, always got the
better of her with him.

"How do you know the book wouldn't be safer
away from here?" he said. "The Vicomte would care
for it, and it couldn't hurt anyone there."

Caroline shook her head, baffled. "How can it
possibly hurt anyone?"

"Oh, Caro. If you only knew..."

A terrible scream echoed outside the chamber,
shrill and full of raw panic. Grant's arms tightened
around her, and his head went up. There was another
scream and another, coming closer.

"Fire!" a woman cried. "Fire!"

"*Mollaght*," Grant muttered.

Caroline looked up at him, remembering the
flames that destroyed his face and forced him out of
her life all those years ago. Was it happening all over
again?

He suddenly let her go. He caught up her dressing
gown from where she left it on a chair and tossed it to
her. As she wrapped it around her body, the noise
outside grew deafening. French words, full of confusion, were loud and insistent.

Grant quickly put on his boots and slid his coat
over his bare chest before grabbing her hand. "Stay

close to me," he said, and threw open the chamber door.

LaPlace and Mademoiselle Victorine were out on the landing, along with a few of the servants, but Monsieur Michel and the Vicomte were nowhere to be seen. Maeve had collapsed on the steps, sobbing into her apron. Her cap was gone, and her pale red hair was tangled on her shoulders, her dress damp and streaked with soot.

When she looked up and saw Grant, she let out a wail. "I saw smoke, sir! Clouds and clouds of it."

"Where?" Grant said tersely.

"At the bottom of the old tower. Monsieur Michel sent me to fetch more coal for the lady's fireplace, and I had to pass outside on the walkway. It was coming through the arrow slits."

"That's not possible," Grant said. "No one goes there."

"It was the ghost!" Maeve sobbed.

Grant turned to one of the footmen who hovered nearby and said quickly, "You get the others together and organize a bucket brigade as fast as you can. Make sure everyone stays far away from the tower."

"Oh, we will die here in this terrible place," Victorine moaned. "I knew we should not come! *Mon dieu.*"

Victorine fell into LaPlace's arms as she started to cry, and he absently patted her shoulder. His celestial blue eyes glittered with excitement at the prospect of destruction, or so it seemed to Caroline. Probably being sent on a voyage to fetch a book, however perilous, hadn't been interesting enough for him. A fire promised to liven things up.

But Caroline couldn't shake away the memories

of the warehouse, the sizzling heat of the flames licking at her heels, the acrid stink of smoke in her throat. The horrible crash as the roof caved in, with Grant beneath it. She never wanted to see such a thing again.

"Don't worry, *mademoiselle*," Grant said. "These old stones are thick, and the rains will quickly extinguish any flames. If there's really a fire at all." He turned to Maeve. "Maeve, go tell Mrs. McCann what is happening and have her ring the bell. She'll know what to do after. And take Mademoiselle Victorine with you. The kitchens are far from the tower; she'll be safer there."

Given a firm order, Maeve was able to collect herself, and she nodded as she rose to her feet. "Yes, sir. Follow me please, miss."

Mademoiselle Victorine, to Caroline's surprise, meekly went along with Maeve. Her thin white silk robe, trimmed with fur and swans down, trailed behind her like she was the ghost.

Grant glanced at Caroline and said, "I suppose it's no use asking you to go with them."

Caroline shook her head. "I won't be in the way. I'm useful in a fire, remember?"

"Unfortunately, I do."

CHAPTER

FIFTEEN

t was the ghost.

The maid's fearful wail echoed in Grant's mind, but he was quite sure she was wrong. Whatever havoc was afoot on Muirin Inish tonight was entirely man-made.

No one spoke as they made their way down the narrow, dark halls of the oldest part of the castle, and yet he was achingly aware of Caroline directly behind him. He heard every breath she drew, every swish of her dressing gown, the slosh of water in the buckets they carried. He had seen the flash of fear in her eyes as she remembered that terrible night in Dublin, but she had quickly collected herself and followed him.

His Irish warrioress. Fear never stopped her. And that was the thing about her he admired most, except for her gorgeous long legs, of course. She would stop at nothing to find out the rest of the half-truth he told her.

He couldn't think about that now, though. He had to stop the castle from burning down around their ears. The servants fetching buckets weren't enough.

As they approached the tower, the smell of smoke

grew sharper, and he could hear the crackle of flames mix with the clatter of rain on the ancient stones.

"Stay back," he ordered Caroline, and tested the thick planks of the door that led from the end of the corridor into the base of the tower. They weren't hot and neither was the heavy lock, but it was unlocked, which it was never supposed to be. He had the only key.

He opened the door, and a cloud of thick gray smoke billowed out. He could see no flames, but the smoke seemed to be coming from below in the dungeon.

"Help me!" he heard a weak voice cry out. "*Aidez-moi.*"

"Someone is in there, damn it," Grant said. His stomach clenched as he remembered how it felt for heat and flames to close in, and he knew he had to get the poor fool out of there. Even if that fool was intruding illegally in his home.

He held his handkerchief over his nose and dove inside. The cries, fading now, came from the dungeon, which could only be reached by a narrow, twisting old stone stairwell. High above, the ramparts opened up to the cloudy sky and fresh air, but below it looked like hell.

He ran down the steps, keeping close to the rough granite wall to keep from losing his way in the smoke and plunging to the flagstone floor below. Caroline and LaPlace were right behind him until they found the wide open door of the dungeon. Smoke poured out of it, and he could see the red-gold glow of fire.

They burst in, throwing the contents of their buckets on the fire, which seemed to be engulfing stacks of old crates and driftwood piled along the walls. Caroline stripped off her robe and beat at them with its smothering folds. The flames turned out to be more smoke than anything, and eventually died down, leaving the small, enclosed space filled with ashy, stinking, gray clouds.

Once they had cleared away, Grant saw the source of the cries. Monsieur Michel and the Vicomte were huddled in the comer, slumped on the floor.

"Arnaud!" LaPlace shouted, and ran over to kneel beside his cousin. "*Poutre*, what are you doing here?"

Caroline followed him and bent down to examine the Vicomte. "Monsieur," she murmured. "Monsieur, are you awake?" She dipped her handkerchief into a puddle of water and carefully wiped at his brow.

Grant knelt beside her. The surge of strength from fighting the fire subsided, leaving sadness and a cold anger. What were these men doing here? Had they set the fire for some unfathomable reason? For he was quite sure it had been set. That driftwood was not here before, and there were the remains of dry straw and paper along the edges of the walls.

The Vicomte came awake with a sputtering cough. He tried to sit up, his eyes full of terror, but Caroline gently pressed him back. "Careful, *monsieur*, you have had a shock," she said.

The Vicomte clutched at her hand. "Is it gone?" he whispered.

"We need to move them out of here," Grant said. He slid his arms around the Vicomte and lifted him up. The older man was thin and frail and racked by coughs as Grant carried him out of the smoke and up into the relatively fresh air of the corridor. LaPlace followed with Michel's bulky form over his shoulder.

The bell clanged in the distance, and he could

hear the clatter of the servants arriving with more water. As Grant directed them down to the dungeon, Caroline sat by the Vicomte on the drawing room sofa where Grant placed him, bathing his face and murmuring with him in quiet French. Once all was settled and quiet again, with the only remains of the fire the lingering smell of smoke in the air, Grant returned to kneel beside them again. The Vicomte's eyes were closed, and his breath labored, but at least he breathed.

"Is he well?" Grant asked Caroline quietly.

She nodded as she dabbed at the Vicomte's forehead with another damp cloth. "He will be, I think, if he rests quietly for a while. The fire was a great shock to his system. But I fear Monsieur Michel might not be all right."

"Michel?"

"LaPlace carried him up to his room a few minutes ago. It looked as if he wasn't moving."

The Vicomte stirred at her words. He opened his blood shot eyes to stare up at them. "I am sorry for it," he said. "Especially for my Victorine. She was in love with him, I fear, though I am not sure why."

"By Hades, what were you two doing in the dungeon of all places?" Grant said tightly, trying to rein in his anger. The force of his fury would only grind the man down even further, and he would never have his answers then.

"I was looking for the book, of course," the Vicomte said.

"In the dungeon?"

"You would not show it to me yet, *monsieur*, nor even tell me where it was kept. I fear my yearning overtook me, and one of your servants mentioned you

141

spend a lot of time in this tower. I asked Monsieur Michel to help me look around, to see if perhaps you stored some treasures there." The Vicomte paused. "I found that you do not."

Grant rubbed his hand over his face. He was weary of subterfuge, of always being on high guard, but this was an old battle that had no end in sight. He couldn't trust anyone or let down his armor for an instant.

Caroline watched him over the Vicomte's head. Her brow was furrowed in a suspicious frown.

"And the fire?" Grant said.

The Vicomte closed his eyes again. "I don't know, *monsieur*. We must have knocked over a lamp as we searched those crates, yet I have no memory of it."

"Those crates should not have been there," Grant said low under his breath. The old dungeon had long been empty, or so he thought. Once the smoke cleared down there, he would have a thorough look around. "Which servant told you I spent much time in the tower?"

"I cannot remember," the Vicomte said with a shrug. "A young, bearded man. I did wonder why you would employ such a person, but I am sure it is hard to find servants in such a place. He seemed most insistent I should look there."

Grant frowned. "Come," he said. "We need to get you to your bed, *monsieur le vicomte*. I fear there is no doctor on the island at the moment, so we will have to do what we can to see you well again."

"I am sure Mademoiselle Black is a most able nurse," the Vicomte said. "As well as a pretty one. You are a fortunate man, Sir Grant."

"Or a cursed one," Grant muttered. He slid his

arm around the Vicomte and helped him to his feet. The man coughed again, but he managed to hobble along. The foyer was empty again, all the servants having scurried back to their quarters belowstairs to speculate on all the strange events of the night. By morning his reputation on the island would be even blacker than it already was.

A wail suddenly floated down from the landing, high and thin like the mournful cry of a spirit. Mademoiselle Victorine appeared above them, her pale silk robe glowing in the shadows.

"He is dead!" she screamed. "And it is your fault!"

SIXTEEN

Caroline hurried up the hillside toward the ruins of the monastery. The bleak, gray sky threatened more rain but she didn't care. She had to be gone from the castle, with its terrible miasma of smoke and death and secrets, and be out in the fresh, cold air, alone. She needed to be in the world she understood, the world of history and legend.

She didn't understand *this* world at all.

The castle was in chaos this morning. Maeve had fled home to her mother, and most of the other servants were packing to leave as well. Even Mrs. McCann seemed flustered and unsure. The Vicomte was ill in his bed, still asking for the book, while his daughter sobbed in grief. Monsieur Michel was laid out in the old icehouse behind the castle's kitchen garden, LaPlace was in a fury, and Grant...

Caroline had not seen Grant all morning. The last anyone could tell, he had disappeared down to the dungeon at first light, and she couldn't quite bring herself to follow him down there yet.

The castle and all its weird occupants were on the

edge of some fatal precipice, she could feel it. One tiny breath of wind would send them right over and into disaster.

Caroline paused at the crest of the hill. From there she could see so much. The rugged green fields bisected by gray stone walls, whitewashed cottages, and the conical ruins of old beehive huts. A few shaggy sheep were the only living beings that she could glimpse. The cliffs stood out pale and jagged, beaten by the ceaseless stormy waves, and she could just glimpse the edge of the village down by the shore.

Were they harboring the "ghost," the mysterious figure who seemed to have started the fire? And what was the purpose of such an act? To drive away the French visitors? Or to drive out the castle's owner, once and for all?

She remembered Maeve's tear-streaked face as she hurried out the door with her hastily packed valise under her arm. "I've had enough of this place," she had said. "I just want me mum. And you should get away, too, my lady, quick as can be, before it's too late."

Caroline thought of her own mother Katherine, of her calm smile and cool touch, and her quiet, sensible air. She wanted her mother in that moment, just as Maeve did. She wanted to feel Katherine's arms around her and hear her sensible advice, even though Caroline rarely took it. But Katherine was far away in Switzerland with her new husband, visiting Caroline's eldest sister Eliza and her family. And Caroline couldn't run away. She couldn't leave Grant, not until she knew what danger he was in. It was as if some invisible but unbreakable tie bound their fates together, and they could not escape it. They were always borne back to each other, as if on the eternal ocean waves.

Even when she fought to swim away from him, even when she hated him, she was bound to him.

"I should have left him tied to the bed until he talked to me," she whispered. But even then, the infuriatingly stubborn, arrogant man would probably tell her nothing.

She kicked out at a rock with her boot. She wore her boy's clothes again, but they gave her no sense of freedom this time.

Caroline spun around and hurried down the other side of the hill. The monastery was deserted; there weren't even any birds crying in the old cloister. There was just the howl of the wind around the ruined spires. The ghosts of the monks were in hiding.

She sat down on the crumbling bench inside the church's nave, where she had sought shelter last time with Grant. The wind was cold on her face and tore at her hair, pulling it from its pins, but she liked the silence. She could think inside of it and feel more like herself again.

Obviously, *The Chronicle* was some kind of excuse for this French visit. No matter how eager the Vicomte seemed to have it, surely they would not have come now to fetch a mere book, unless it was a cover for something else. Who were they spies for, and was Grant their ally or their secret enemy?

Could he truly still hate his cousin so much that he would resort to treason to ruin all Conlan stood for —an independent Ireland?

She heard a sudden thud, like a stone falling to the ground. It was even louder and more startling in the sacred silence of the church. Caroline jumped to her feet in panic.

"Wh-who is there?" she called. "Show yourself!"

A man's face peered around a corner of the jagged wall, no ghost at all. Caroline studied him as she reached for the hilt of the dagger tucked into her boot.

He was young, but hard-faced, his green eyes blazing with anger. His long black hair and beard were tangled, and he wore rough clothes. He looked like a pirate or a brigand, yet he stared back at her with just as much caution as she held for him.

She suddenly remembered the Vicomte's description of the strange servant who lured him to the tower—rough and bearded. Could this be the "servant"? Why would he wish to create such a diversion?

"Who are you?" she demanded. "Are you following me?"

"Why would I do that?" he said. His Irish accent was very thick. "I came here to be alone."

"Do you live in the village?"

"I did once, afore my girl died, and I went to work on the mainland," he answered grudgingly.

"Your girl died?" Caroline remembered what Maeve's mother told her, about poor Bessie's heartbroken suitor. "You must be Mick, then."

"Aye, Mick O'Shea. And you must be the fine lady staying at the castle. I'd get away from there if I were you, milady."

"And why is that?" He was the second person to give her such a warning today, and he probably wouldn't be the last. She took a careful step toward him. He didn't back away or rush forward to attack her, but his face tightened.

"Because people die there, that's why. It's an evil place. First my Bessie, then what happened last night. No telling who might be next."

"Word travels fast, I see."

"It's a small island, is Muirin Inish. And we look after our own."

Caroline's glance fell on Mick's shirt sleeve. The pale linen was gray, as if streaked with soot. She took a cautious step closer and caught a whiff of sharp, stale smoke on the wind.

Her fingers tightened on the dagger hilt.

"And take revenge for your own, as well?" she said.

Mick scowled and tucked his arm behind his back. She saw that he wore pistols strapped to his waist. "You're just a stranger here, so you don't know what it's like," he said. "We live our own lives and don't bother no one, so we don't want them to meddle with us. The English, the French, they all just need to keep away. We won't let anyone else get hurt like Bessie."

"I'm not here to meddle with anyone. And I'm certainly not here to mess about with politics." She had quite enough of that in the Rebellion.

"I don't know why you're here, and I don't care," he answered. "Just consider this a warning. It won't be that old dungeon destroyed next."

"Consider me warned, then," she said.

He gave a brusque nod and spun away from her. Caroline watched cautiously as he disappeared over the crest of the hill. She let her breath out in a great rush, and her hand fell from the dagger. She had to get back to the castle.

The narrow road was just as empty as the

monastery, and the first cold raindrops were falling just as she ran up the stone steps into the foyer. All the tumult of earlier had vanished now, and all the servants were gone. Not even Mademoiselle Victorine's sobs could be heard. Caroline had to find Grant and demand some long overdue answers, and then persuade him to leave the island with her right now.

She went first to the Vicomte's chamber to look in on him. He seemed very pale and frail in the middle of the vast bed, propped up on the bolsters. An untouched breakfast tray sat on the bedside table. It was no time to ask him about the servant who sent him to the tower.

His eyes were closed and he seemed to be sleeping quietly, so Caroline started to leave. But as she eased the door shut, his eyes opened and he said, "Mademoiselle Black! Is that you? Do come in, please."

Caroline smiled at him. "I don't want to disturb you, *monsieur*. You need your rest. I only wanted to look in on you and see how you fared."

"I am well enough. Better than I deserve, I think, after all the trouble I caused last night." He held out his hand to Caroline, and she hurried over to take it in hers. "My daughter has made arrangements for us to leave this place. We will depart on the morning tide."

"Is that quite safe?" Caroline said, even though she had planned to do exactly the same thing. "It is still rough weather."

"I think we will be safer on the sea than here. And I must get Victorine away before her grief gets the better of her. I had no idea she was so very fond of that ruffian Michel, or I would not have agreed to him coming with us. I thought it was a mere trifle of an affair." He gave a deep sigh. "I was wrong about so many things, *mademoiselle*. And I was especially wrong to come here chasing a ridiculous dream."

"Grief and desire make people do such strange things," Caroline said. She thought of Mick O'Shea setting a fire to avenge his Bessie. And she thought of herself, chasing *The Chronicle* to Muirin Inish and getting trapped in the whirlwind of her feelings for Grant Dunmore. Where would it all end?

"You leave without *The Chronicle*," she said.

"It seems that particular dream was not to be, though I can hope for the future."

"And does Captain LaPlace go with you?"

The Vicomte frowned. "I really have nothing to do with LaPlace, *ma chere*. He was only a means for me to get here, just as I was his cover for his own errand. That was how it had to be for this voyage to happen."

"His own errand?" she said, feeling suddenly cold. "What is it?"

"I fear I do not know for sure. Only LaPlace and his friends in Paris know, including your Irish Monsieur Emmet. I have kept well away from all that." His hand suddenly tightened on hers, a strong grip that belied his frailty. "Mademoiselle Black, won't you come with us?"

Caroline tried to laugh even as her mind raced with the news that LaPlace surely was a spy. "Monsieur, I can't go to Paris."

"Then let us take you to some larger island at least. You should not stay here; it isn't safe."

So many warnings today. "Oh, *monsieur*. I do appreciate your concerns, truly I do. And I will leave as soon as my own work is done here." She gently kissed his brow. She had become quite fond of him in the short time she knew him, even if he did want to take *The Chronicle* away. "You should rest now. I wish you a very safe journey back to your library."

"And I you, *ma chere*." A faint smile whispered across his face. "I have enjoyed our talks. No one at home appreciates history as I do."

Caroline laughed. "I've enjoyed our talks as well. Maybe one day I will be able to come to Paris."

As she stood up to leave, the door flew open and Mademoiselle Victorine rushed in with an open valise in her arms. Her eyes widened when she saw Caroline there, and she threw the case onto the floor.

"What are you doing here, harassing my poor father?" she cried. Her eyes were red-rimmed with weeping, and her lovely auburn hair was falling from its combs. "He must rest if we are to leave this horrible place."

"I was just saying *au revoir, mademoiselle*," Caroline said softly. "I hope you and your father reach your home very soon."

"And we shall never leave it again! This is the most barbaric of lands, *mademoiselle*, and you would do well to leave it yourself." Victorine's stare raked over Caroline's tall figure in her boy's clothes and dirty boots. "If any sane Frenchman would have you."

Caroline hurried out of the room. She was vastly tired of all these French visitors, tired of their secrets, of all that had happened since they arrived. She just wanted the quiet of her own room, where she could think and sort everything out.

But she was not done with them just yet. Captain LaPlace waited for her in the shadows of the landing outside her chamber.

"You are very busy today, *mademoiselle*," he said

AMANDA MCCABE

with a smile. He seemed entirely unconcerned about his kinsman's death or anything else that might be happening around him. His hand rested casually on the balustrade, blocking her path. "Who would have thought there was so much to occupy a person on such a quiet island?"

Caroline watched him cautiously. She had the distinct sense their paths had not crossed accidentally. Why would he be waiting for her?

"I'm a scholar, *monsieur*," she answered. "I study the ancient history of Ireland, and there are a great many sites to be seen and examined."

"History! Such a dull subject for a lovely young lady."

"I do not find it so. Now if you will excuse me..." She tried to duck around him, to get into her room and lock the door against him, but he was too fast. His casual laziness was merely an act. He struck out, quick as a serpent, and grabbed her wrist in a hard clasp.

"Let me go!" Caroline cried. She tried to be firm and calm, and not give in to the fear that twisted her stomach. She attempted to wrench her wrist free, but he held her fast. LaPlace reeled her slowly toward him until he could spin her around and pin her against the wall. She felt closed in, surrounded, just as she had when he grabbed her the first time they met. He held her there with one hand, as easily as if she were a feather, and the other hand covered her mouth. But his first attack in the corridor had felt sexual, possessive. This time it felt only violent and controlling, keeping her in his power.

But that hateful, helpless feeling only fanned the flames of her anger. She kicked out at him, and he

152

laughed and lifted her higher. His eyes gleamed with a terrible enjoyment.

"Oh, *mademoiselle*, let us not lie to each other any longer. It becomes tiresome," he said. The more she fought, the more he seemed to enjoy it, so she went very still. She watched him carefully, waiting for a vulnerable moment.

"We should be friends," LaPlace continued. "We could be of much benefit to each other. But I fear that cannot be until we come to an understanding. I know that old, musty ruins are not the only thing that keeps you and Sir Grant here on this forlorn island."

Caroline shook her head.

"My master is not a fool, *mademoiselle*," LaPlace said. "He knows that not all of Monsieur Emmet's contacts can be trusted, and your lover is the most untrustworthy. After all, he has been known to change his loyalties before, *n'est-ce pas?* He is probably planning to do so again. But disloyalty is one thing my master will never tolerate. And I serve him in all things."

Caroline wrenched her mouth away from his hand, and he let her go. But he rested his fingers ever so lightly on her throat, ready to close in again in an instant.

She felt an icy numbness creep over her, as if she watched the whole scene from a distance. She needed that distance to get away from him. "I have no idea what you're talking about, *monsieur*," she said. "You and your master—whoever that may be—are no concern of mine. And Sir Grant does not confide in me."

"Of course he does not. No man of sense confides in his *putain*. But you are not merely a little whore, are you? I have watched you since we arrived, just as you have been watching us." His hand tightened, just enough to make it harder for her to breathe. "And if all goes as we hope, my master will soon be yours as well, and that of every person in your benighted Britain. It will be more than you deserve."

He leaned closer to her, so close she could feel the nauseating brush of his soft lips on her cheek. She feared she would be sick, and she closed her eyes against the clammy sensation.

"And then, *ma chere*," he whispered, "you will learn your place, as all good Frenchwomen have. The ancient regime was too permissive to you... how do you English say? Bluestockings. But that will be done now. A woman's true place is beneath a man..."

His mouth covered hers, and Caroline cried out. She had no time to struggle; he was suddenly flung away from her and she fell to the floor.

She opened her eyes to see that Grant had seized LaPlace and torn him away from her. He held the Frenchman in an iron grip by the neck, and the two of them grappled in one flashing, violent blur on the landing. Fists were flying, the air torn with shouts and grunts and the terrible thud of flesh on flesh.

Her legs trembled, but she managed to stand using the wall as support and slowly edged away from the furious combat She looked around frantically for some sort of weapon, anything she could use to drive them apart, but there was nothing. She was trapped there against the wall, able only to watch in horror as first one then the other seemed defeated.

At last Grant managed to catch LaPlace in a headlock and slam him down on the top step. There was a horrifying crack, and the Frenchman went still.

The sudden, vibrating silence was deafening. Caroline stared at Grant as he slowly stood up, his chest heaving as be fought for breath. His lip was cut, the blood bright on his skin.

"Grant..." she said, and he took a step toward her.

Suddenly, LaPlace's hand shot out and grabbed Grant's leg. Caught off balance, Grant tumbled backward toward the stairs. LaPlace leaped up into a crouch and shoved him down the old stones.

As Caroline watched in terror, Grant rolled down the steps, slowly at first, then faster and faster, with no sound but the awful thuds of his body.

"Grant!" she screamed. In that instant, her whole world seemed to change, and she was overcome by a wild desperation. All she knew was Grant was hurt, and she had to get to him. She lunged forward, but LaPlace caught her by the waist and threw her hard over his shoulder.

She had only a fleeting glimpse of Grant lying terribly motionless halfway down the stairs. She cried out, and LaPlace tossed her into the bedchamber. The door was slammed in her face as she threw herself at it, and she heard the metallic grate of the key in the lock.

"Grant," she sobbed, as she fell to the floor. "Oh, Grant. Damn you, don't you dare be dead!"

CHAPTER

SEVENTEEN

"Let me out!" Caroline screamed. She banged on the locked door with her fists until her hands turned bruised and bloody, shouting until her throat was raw. "Please, someone help me!"

But there was no one left in the castle to hear her, and even if there was, the old walls were too thick and secure. The place had been built to keep people out—and keep them trapped inside.

She pressed her forehead to the door and closed her eyes as she listened for any hint of noise. She could hear nothing at all. It seemed LaPlace had abandoned her there for the moment.

But where was Grant? Her last view of him haunted her, that image of him tumbling down the stairs and lying there so horribly still. He couldn't be dead. The ties between them were so tight, surely she would feel them snapping loose if he were dead. But her heart felt heavy with an icy weight of grief at the thought Her stomach cramped, and she thought she would be sick.

She fell to her knees, clutching at that hollow ache inside of her. He was not dead—she wouldn't

even think that. But he was here in this castle somewhere, hurt and in the power of that terrible LaPlace.

"He will find a way to get free," she whispered.
Grant was surely like the proverbial cat, he had many
lives, and he always seemed to escape from any trouble. Had he not survived his deprived childhood, the
warehouse fire, the stormy sea? He would escape
from this, too. He simply had to.

In the meantime, she had to find a way to help
herself. If she could get out of this room, she could
find Grant, and together they would find a way to
escape.

She forced away her fear and ran to the window.
In some of the Gothic romantic novels Anna liked, the
imperiled heroines sometimes escaped by tying
sheets together to make a rope and lowering it out a
window. But as Caroline peered outside, she immediately saw the foolishness of such an idea. Only cliffs
and ocean were below her window, and even the
narrow strip of dirt and rock was very far away. She
didn't have nearly enough sheets to reach safety.

She studied the room carefully. If only she could
scurry up the chimney, or simply vanish like one of
the fairy folk in an old story!

Suddenly there was a soft tap at the door. Caroline was sure she imagined it, but then it came again,
a little louder. Her heart seemed to skip a beat. Was it
one of the servants, crept back into the castle to help
her? Or was it LaPlace, corning to attack her again?

"Don't be silly," she told herself. He would never
knock.

"Mademoiselle Black? Are you there?" someone
called. To Caroline's shock it was Victorine.

"Yes, I'm here," she answered. She ran back to the

door and pressed her palms against it, as if she could will it open. "I'm locked in, by LaPlace."

"I thought as much. But I stole your dragon housekeeper's keys from the kitchen." Caroline heard Victorine rattling the keys. "*Sacre bleu*, such a lot of them! I will try this one."

After several tries, with Caroline's heart beating faster at every one, Victorine finally found one that worked. The door flew open to reveal Mademoiselle Muret standing there in her travel cloak, a victorious smile on her face.

"At last!" she said. "Such a nuisance. Come, *mademoiselle*, we must hurry."

Caroline knew the need for haste very well, yet she hung back cautiously for a moment. Victorine surely had no love for her or for Grant, after what happened here. She was French. This could very well be a trap, a game of LaPlace's. Victorine tapped her boot impatiently against the floor.

"What now? Do you wish to stay here?"

"Why have you come for me?" Caroline said tightly. "Did LaPlace send you?"

Victorine gave a most unladylike snort. "LaPlace! That *cochon*. If not for him, my Michel would be alive and my father would be safe at home. LaPlace decided to drag us all here to this hellish place. I would no more work for him than I would a snake. By helping you I thwart him in one small thing, yes?"

Caroline carefully studied the woman's face. There was anger there, and a hardness that transformed her fashionable prettiness into something fearsome, like the Celtic goddess of death Morrigan, after the demise of her lover. She certainly did bear a hatred for *something*.

And Caroline really had no alternative but to trust her. It was better than staying in this room waiting for something terrible to happen.

"Let's go," Caroline said.

"Very wise, *mademoiselle*. My father did say you were very clever. But grab your coat, it will be quite cold on the water. And you will have to be quick. I must take my father down to the boat, while you get Monsieur Grant and meet us there. We must make haste, or we will miss the tide."

Caroline snatched her coat up from the chair and slid it over her shoulders. As she checked to make sure she still wore the precious locket with her niece's picture, Victorine closed and relocked the door.

"Where is Grant?" Caroline demanded. "Is he hurt?"

"Is he alive, you mean? He was the last time I saw him, as LaPlace locked him in that dungeon. LaPlace won't want him dead, for then Grant wouldn't be able to answer his questions."

In the dungeon? Caroline thought of the stench of smoke down there, the damp, and the rats. Even if he was alive now, how long would he last—especially if LaPlace had "questions"?

"And where is LaPlace?" she asked.

Victorine smirked. "He is secure for the moment. I locked him in the icehouse with my poor Michel. But he won't be there for long." Victorine gave Caroline the heavy ring of keys. "Hopefully one of those will open that dungeon door. Now go, and meet us at the boat as soon as you can!"

Caroline had not a moment to lose. She ran as fast as she could toward the corridor leading to the old tower, her heart bursting. Grant wasn't dead! He lived, and she had to find him. But what shape would he be in when she did? She remembered his body on the stairs, lying so still.

"I'll just have to find a way to move him," she whispered. They had to get away from there. Together. Caroline slid around the comer to the narrow old corridor, lined with the archways of old windows that were now empty of glass and looked out on a narrow stone ledge and then the rocks below. The wind swept between the arches, cold and damp. It stung her skin, but she kept running. She was focused on only one thing—finding Grant.

Only to be brought up short when a figure stepped from the deep, purplish shadows near the door. It was LaPlace, escaped from the icehouse. His handsome face was bruised from the fight with Grant, and probably from Victorine, but his smile was as bright as ever, relishing yet another fight.

"I knew you would find a way to free yourself, my intrepid *mademoiselle*, just as I have," he said. "I've been waiting for you."

He had obviously learned nothing about her at all. She preferred her nice, quiet bookish ways, but she could fight when she had to, and her blood was definitely up. When she looked at LaPlace, she saw Grant's body falling down the stairs, Michel's body, even that crazed, blood-stained soldier who tried to rape her sister in the heat of the Rebellion. Anna had killed that man for what he did, and they were not sisters for nothing. A Blacknall never let anyone hurt her or the people she cared about.

Caroline remembered the way LaPlace threw her over his shoulder earlier. Perhaps she could push him down and thus crack his head on the stone floor. He watched her with that horrible smile, and he seemed to think she would try to flee. Instead, she ran forward as fast as she could with a loud shout.

She caught him by surprise. She had only a fleeting glimpse of his smile fading as she pushed him hard in the midsection with her shoulder. She pushed harder, with all her weight thrown against him. He lost his balance, just as she had hoped, and he fell backward. He couldn't regain his equilibrium, and his own weight carried him the rest of the way.

He fell through one of the archways with a shrill scream, and then there was only the sound of the wind. Caroline ran to peer down. He lay still on the stone ledge below, his limbs sprawled out.

"*Diolain*," she whispered. She had killed him. For the first time in her life, she had killed someone.

A sickening feeling seized her stomach, and she pressed her hands hard against that cold knot. There was no time to think of it now, no time to dwell on what she had done, what was necessary. She had to find Grant.

She backed away from the archway and dashed toward the old tower and down the stone stairs to the dungeon below. The farther down she went, the stronger the smell of stale smoke. It hung heavy in the humid air, choking and acrid, mixing terribly with the sickness she already felt. What if LaPlace was not really dead? The walls seemed to press in on her, but she kept going forward. Time was flying by, and she had so very little of it left.

The iron-bound door to the cell was locked fast. "Grant!" she shouted as she tried first one key then another in the thick latch. What if the housekeeper had no need of a dungeon key, and it wasn't here?

What if LaPlace had the only key, and now he lay dead out on the cliff? Her hands were shaking so much that she could hardly fit the keys into the lock, and worse, she could hear nothing beyond the door.

"Grant!" she called again. "Are you there? Can you hear me? Please say something!"

At last she heard a scraping noise, like something dragged against stone, and his voice answered, "Caroline? Is that you?"

Caroline sagged against the door in a rush of sheer, warm relief. "Yes, it's me! I have Mrs. McCann's keys. I'll get you out in a moment if I can just figure out which one..."

"There's a cross etched at the top," he said. His voice was muffled through the door, but it was definitely him, alive and conscious. Now if they could both stay that way in time to get off that cursed island! Grant could recover away from here, someplace safe and peaceful. And Caroline had to get home.

"How did you get away from him?"

"With the help of an unexpected friend," she answered.

She found the key with the cross. The lock was old and rusty, and it took all her strength to turn it, but at last, the barrier cracked open and Grant was there.

Caroline fell into his arms and held on to him as if she would never let him go. He was so warm, so alive, under her touch. She ran her hands over his arms and his ribcage to make sure nothing was broken. The sleeve of his shirt was torn away, and the linen was stained with blood, but he seemed whole.

She framed his face in her hands as she scanned every bruise and cut. She damned LaPlace for every one, and wished with all her might that she could push him off the ledge again.

"Thank God you are alive!" she said. "I was so afraid!"

He kissed her hard. "As was I. I've been going insane thinking of what might have happened."

"I was locked in my room until Victorine found a way to get me out."

"Victorine?" he said incredulously. "But where is LaPlace now?"

Caroline shook her head, trying to blot out the image of LaPlace's still body. "There's no time to talk now. They're waiting for us at the boat. I think it's time we were away from here for a while." She took Grant's hand and pulled him with her toward the stairs.

He went with her, but his hand was tense in hers. She glanced back to see that his face was set in that implacable expression she had come to know too well. It meant he had taken a position and would never be moved from it. "I must do something first."

"There is no time!" Caroline shouted. "We have to go. Please, Grant, come with me now."

He studied her carefully for a long moment. Whatever plea he saw in her eyes seemed to convince him. He nodded, and held her hand to lead her out of that frightening place. He went, not back to the stairs, but to a narrow door half-hidden in the rough stone wall. It led to a dank, narrow passage, much like the one Caroline once followed from the library.

The passage was dim, lit only by the door they left open behind them, but Grant seemed to know the way. The door at the other end opened into the vast, deserted kitchen, pots and dishes tossed around in the servants' haste to depart. From there he took her to the library, and headed straight for a small painting hung beside the fireplace. It was an unremarkable seascape, one Caroline hadn't noticed before.

"Grant!" she protested. "We have no time."

"One moment, then we will go, Caroline."

He took the painting off the wall to reveal a small, hidden safe. As he opened it, Caroline watched him in growing impatience. Every tick of the hands on the mantel clock seemed inordinately loud in her ears, counting off every moment that passed. She wanted so desperately to be away from this place!

"Take a deep breath, Caro," Grant said without looking at her. He swung open the safe, and seemed far too calm for all that had happened. "We'll make it to the boat. But I can't leave without these."

"What are they?" she asked. She peered over his shoulder into the safe, but all she could see were stacks of small boxes and bags.

"Money, for one thing." He handed her bundles of notes and a clinking bag of coins. "Put them in that valise over there. We can't get to Dublin without money, can we? Unless you want to walk every step of the way."

"Are we going to Dublin then?" She packed away the money as Grant took out a thick stack of papers wrapped tightly in oilskin.

He added them to the notes and said, "Of course. I now know that time is of the utmost essence. Events are progressing much faster than I expected." He took out a carved, shallow box and handed it to her. "We should take this as well."

Caroline peeked inside and gasped when she saw

the soft, worn green leather cover tooled in a pattern of Celtic knot-work that formed a dragon. "*The Chronicle*! You do still have it."

"Certainly I do." Grant shut the safe. "It seems I'll need your help to keep it secure." He took the box from her and packed it in the valise before he snapped it shut. He grabbed a coat that lay draped over the desk chair, tucked the valise under his arm, and took Caroline's hand in his.

Without another word, he led her into the hidden passageway, and they made their way in silence to the cave's entrance. The wind blew against her face, harsh and cold, but the rain had stopped. A faint, pinkish-gray light was spreading out from the horizon, a sign of a new day. And the boat waited for them down on the beach, the larger ship anchored offshore. A sailor was helping the Vicomte and his daughter into seats in front of the oars, and they waved up at Caroline.

She and Grant ran down the pathway to the beach. She was on her way home at last, though not in any way she could have imagined. Who knew what lay ahead?

As the boat pushed off into the surf, she dared to look back at the old tower. And LaPlace's body was nowhere to be seen.

CHAPTER
EIGHTEEN

Caroline closed her eyes as she lay very still on the narrow ship's berth. She felt the sway and heave of the sea under her, choppy and rough, but it seemed oddly soothing. It meant a change, an escape. They moved farther and farther from the island with every moment. Her whole body ached with a deep weariness, yet her mind was far too awake.

She listened to the murmuring voices of the Vicomte and Victorine as they talked together in French. He lay in the berth across from Caroline's in the small cabin, while Victorine knelt beside him. Grant stood by the open porthole, staring out in silence at the endless, empty sea.

Caroline opened her eyes and studied him as he stood there as the watchful sentinel. His fists were braced on the wooden wall, his alert gaze always searching. She had thrown in her fate with him, for fair or foul. She had spent the most intimate moments that two people could share with him. Yet at moments like this, she felt as if she knew him so very little. He kept so many dangerous, dark things hidden from her.

"What do you see out there, Grant?" she said.

He glanced at her over his shoulder and gave her a crooked half-smile. "Water and more water."

"And will for some time, I expect," she answered. "You should rest. Come and sit by me for a while."

For a moment, she thought he would refuse and insist on keeping guard. But he nodded and crossed the small cabin to sit at the edge of her berth. Caroline slid over to make room for him, and he finally lay down beside her. His arm came around her waist to draw her closer, and she rested her head on his shoulder with a sigh.

When she was with him like this, somehow those dark secrets seemed far away. She felt safe with him, as if all else were shut out by the mere nearness of him. All the fear and loneliness were gone for that one moment, along with fights, death, and disappearing bodies.

They would surely all be back soon enough. For now, she closed her eyes and let herself rest with him.

"We'll reach Mallorney Island by evening," Grant said. "The captain will put us ashore there, and then the Vicomte and Mademoiselle Muret can continue on their journey south."

"You are quite certain you won't go on with us?" the Vicomte asked.

"I have business in Dublin, which I fear won't wait," Grant said.

"And you are sure you will be welcome there?" the Vicomte persisted. "After associating with foreigners such as us?"

Caroline opened her eyes to look up into Grant's

face. His brow was creased in a frown, his eyes shadowed, but he shook his head. "I have to go, Besides, even if I did not have matters to see to there, I would have to make sure Caroline gets home."

"Do you have family waiting for you, Mademoiselle?" Victorine asked.

"Not really." Caroline thought of her mother and stepfather, and of Eliza, Will, and their son, all far away in Lausanne. Before they could even hear a hint of this adventure, she would be safely home. As for Anna, she would certainly not be happy if she knew Caroline was with Grant Dunmore. Luckily, she, too, was in blissful ignorance, occupied with looking after two estates and two wild little children. Caroline's stepdaughter and friend Mary was still on her honeymoon and wouldn't be home for some time.

"Most of my family is abroad," Caroline continued. "And my sister thinks I am on a research holiday in the north."

"Ah, *oui*, research for your project, *mademoiselle*!" said the Vicomte. He seemed tired, too, and weak. Surely the sooner he was back in his Parisian library the better. "It sounds so very intriguing. Can you tell us more about it now, and distract us from this tedious voyage?"

"Yes, please!" said Victorine. "Tell us a tale, Mademoiselle Black. Do you know any romantic ones? With happy endings?"

Caroline laughed ruefully. "I know many romantic stories of Ireland, but I fear few have happy endings. Tragedy so often seems the fate of the Celts. My work is to record as many old tales as I can and relate them to important historical moments in Ireland. Far too many are sad stories."

"What is one of your favorites?" asked the Vicomte.

Caroline thought of all the stories she loved. The tales of Etain the fairy, who was the most beautiful woman in the world, and the champion's prize at the feast of Bricriu, which made her so proud to be a part of Ireland, even a small one. There were far too many to choose from.

"When my sisters and I were children," she said, "we had an Irish nanny who loved to tell us the Three Sorrowful Tales of Erin. Not typical bedtimes stories for children, maybe, but we enjoyed them and always begged her to tell them again. My eldest sister liked Deirdre of the Sorrows and her poor, lost husband. My other sister liked the Children of Lir, who were turned into swans by an evil sorceress. I think she liked the idea of being able to fly away on grand adventures, while I liked to stay at home."

And yet it was Anna who was at home now with her family, and Caroline who was on a great adventure full of danger and peril. Caroline who pushed men over ledges and ran off to sea with her mysterious lover. Life was always surprising.

"What story did you prefer?" Grant said. She felt his touch against her hair, gently caressing.

She curled her fingers into his shirtfront and held on to him as if he could vanish from her at any moment. "I liked them all, especially the tale of the fate of the Children of Tuireann."

"Then will you tell us that one?" said the Vicomte.

"I'm afraid it's a rather bloodthirsty tale," Caroline said. "I was a terribly fearsome child."

"Victorine likes bloodthirsty stories as well as romantic ones, don't you, *chere*?" the Vicomte said. "Or she never would have come with me on this journey."

Caroline laughed, then proceeded to tell it as best she could. "Once upon a time, a man named Lugh of the Long Hand was with the high king of Ireland, when word came that their enemy, the Fomor, had landed at an ally's country, and had laid waste to that land. The king was not minded to avenge this act, but Lugh was. He gathered his three kinsmen, Cian, Cu, and Ceithen, and told them, 'Gather all the riders of the Sidhe to me.' They all set out, Cu and Ceithen to the south and Cian to the north, to the plain of Muirthemne. But there he met with his family's great enemy, the three sons of Tuireann."

Caroline closed her eyes so she could envision the old story unfolding before her. "Cian knew he could not fight them alone, so he prudently decided on retreat. Seeing a great herd of pigs nearby, he struck himself with a Druid rod and took on the shape of a pig himself. But the sons of Tuireann saw him and realized he was no friend to them. Two of them also used a Druid rod to make themselves into two fast hounds, and they ran on the trail of the pig that was not a pig. Once Cian was back to his own form, the eldest son, Brian, killed him, and they buried the body deep before going to the battle with the Fomor.

"But Lugh soon discovered what had happened to his kinsman. He declared, 'Ireland will never be free from trouble for this treachery, neither to east nor west.' He went to the high king, where he found the sons of Tuireann. He begged for vengeance, though the sons of Tuireann declared, 'We did not kill your kinsman, but we will pay the fine for him the same as if we did kill him.' They bound themselves to the king that they would pay the fine.

"But the fine was a heavy one, a great fearsome task indeed. He wanted the three apples from the Garden in the East of the World, which could take away wounds and sickness with one bite. The magic pigskin of the King of Greece, the spear of the King of Persia, the two horses and chariot of the King of Siogair, and the seven pigs of the King of the Golden Pillars. And that was not all! He also wanted the dog of the King of Iorurudh, which was the most beautiful of dogs and the most powerful in the hunt, and the cooking-spit of the warrior women of Inis Cennfhinne. Last but not least, they must find the hidden, sacred hill of Miochaoin, and give three shouts from its summit before being caught by its guards.

"And they traveled away on their task, leaving their father sorrowful and lamenting. They used their useful Druid rod to turn into hawks and steal the apples from the garden. Then they went in the guise of Irish poets, which were famous throughout the world, to the court of the King of Greece to steal the magic pigskin. They were discovered and there was a terrible fight, but in the end, they killed the king and moved on to find the spear of the King of Persia. Once again they went in disguise as poets, and once again they killed the king. The sons of Tuireann seemed indestructible, especially after they retrieved the chariot and horses and the herd of pigs, defeating all before them in battle.

"But they could not defeat magic. When Lugh heard they were close to completing the ransom, he put a spell of forgetfulness on them so they would not remember the rest of their tasks and would long for home. They turned back to Ireland and were reunited with their father, only to be sent again to complete their quest. They got the cooking-spit, thanks to their handsome faces, but when it came time to shout from the hill of Miochaoin, there was a great battle, for the hill was sacred and shouting was forbidden.

"The three sons of Tuireann were grievously wounded, but they made it to their boat. And once they saw their home again, they died. Their father cried and lamented over his sons, that had the making of a king of Ireland in each of them, and he, too, died, and they were all buried in one grave in Ireland's sacred earth."

Caroline opened her eyes at the end of the tale, still wrapped in vivid images of an ancient and brutal land, where men were set impossible tasks and died brave deaths. The Vicomte and his daughter were asleep, sunk deep in exhaustion, but Grant watched her with his unreadable dark eyes. She couldn't help but feel that they were also setting off on some unknown, unwinnable quest.

"Try to sleep for a while," he said. He took her hand and drew her back to lie cradled beside him on the berth. His arms wrapped around her waist.

"Will we find the magical spear?" she whispered. "And shout from the hill? I feel like our adventures are similar to theirs now."

He kissed the top of her head and said, "Time enough for our quest in the morning. Sleep now, *gaolach*."

Caroline closed her eyes again and drifted into an uneasy slumber, where there were dreams of danger and adventure—and a warrior with magical eyes who kept driving her onward into the endless night.

CHAPTER
NINETEEN

Caroline waved until the boat slid out of sight over the horizon. The Vicomte and his daughter were gone, on their way back to France, and Caroline was alone in the world with Grant.

"They can't see you any longer," he said. "They're too far away, and it grows dark."

She laughed and gave one more wave before she turned back to him. She surely should be frightened and ready to flee from him at a moment's notice. Yet instead, she felt free and strangely exhilarated. All the things that held her tethered to her old life, to her old self, were far away, and she could be or do anything she wanted. And she wanted to see what would happen next on this journey, with Grant.

"I hope they make it home safely," she said.

"You should be more worried about your own safe arrival home," he said. He took her hand, and they made their way to the path that wound from the small beach up to the light of Mallorney Island's village.

"You could probably find a boat here to take you back to the mainland," he continued. "And hire a companion for the journey."

"You promised *you* would see me safely back to Dublin," she said. "And I intend to keep an eye on *The Chronicle*. You can't hide it from me again."

"Stubborn woman," he growled.

"Not half so stubborn as you, Grant Dunmore." She swung around to face him. "What is your urgent business in Dublin?"

He was silent for a long moment, and she could feel the tension in his hand against hers. "It's growing cold. We need to find a place to stay for the night and hire a boat for tomorrow."

Caroline shook her head. "Very well. But you will not escape me for long. It's a long voyage to Dublin, Grant, and I am with you every step of the way. You will have to talk some time."

He gave a reluctant laugh. "Consider me warned then. But I caution you, Caro, you may not always like what you learn."

They walked on in silence and found the town's inn, a ramshackle building whose whitewash was flaking away from the walls, and windows were cracked. It seemed to be the only place to stay, though, and was quite popular, its public room crowded and noisy. It smelled of fish, spilled ale, smoke from the green wood in the grate, and damp wool. The eyes of the hardened fishermen and the harried barmaids followed them suspiciously as they made their way across the room. It seemed Mallomey Island never saw many strangers, as the landlady mentioned no boat had been seen approaching. She was full up with regulars.

But Grant's coins soon convinced her that she did have one empty room, and she would even send up one of the maids with a tray of food and some water for washing. The room was a small, cramped space under the eaves, but Caroline found there was a window to let in fresh sea air and a lock on the door.

The bed was a narrow one, piled with rough blankets, and the only other furniture was a rickety washstand, a table where the maid left their food, and two straight-backed chairs, which crowded the narrow space. Yet after the long night and day she had just passed, it looked like a luxurious refuge.

"It's not much," Grant said, "but we call it home."

Caroline wrapped her arms around his neck and went up on tiptoe to kiss him. His lips parted against hers, and he tasted of the salt air and that dark sweetness that was only Grant and that always drew her to him. The aching exhaustion of their hasty voyage faded away, and a sparkling excitement swept over her. She felt so very alive, and she wanted to grab on to it and never let it go.

His hands circled her waist and pulled her up against him. His kiss turned hot and hungry, as if he felt that same rush of new life between them. Through the blurry heat of passion, she felt him slide her coat from her shoulders and throw it aside, and felt his fingers on the lacings of her shirt as he tugged them free. The boy's clothes she still wore fell away.

The chilly air of the room made her tremble, but she wasn't cold for long. Grant's mouth traced a fiery ribbon of kisses along her throat to the vulnerable hollow at the base of her neck. He drew the linen of her shirt away as he went, kissing her, touching her, just where she most craved. He knew her body so well now.

Her eyes closed as he pressed a soft kiss just between her breasts. Surely he could feel the erratic pounding of her heart that said just how much she longed for him? She twined her fingers in his hair and tried to urge him even closer, but he evaded her. He spun her around to face away from him and drew her shirt off over her head.

"What are you..." she began, and gasped when she felt the slide of fabric over her eyes as he covered them with his cravat. The light was blotted away, leaving her in hot darkness where she could only feel. Every soft sound of his movement behind her was amplified.

His hands fell gently on her shoulders, caressing her as he held her still. She felt the rough strength of his long fingers slide down her arms to hold her hands still, keeping her from pulling off the blindfold.

He kissed the nape of her neck, his breath warm against her skin.

"You wouldn't let me touch you when you tied me to the bed," he whispered. "It only seems fair now that you can't see me. You can't see what I'll do to you..."

"Grant," she said weakly. His lips traced along her neck to her shoulder and bit at the soft curve where they met. Her legs trembled, and he caught her as she started to fall.

Her back was pressed against him, not even a breath of air between them, and she felt the hardness of his erection on her hips. His palms covered her naked breasts, caressing in rough circles until she cried out at the pleasure of it. The air felt so heavy around her that she couldn't breathe. He swept her up in his arms, the whole room whirling around her, and laid her across the bed on her stomach. The blankets chafed at her skin, so sensitive from his touch, but he drew them back until she lay on the softer sheets. She could hear his breath, his every movement, as he slowly removed her shoes and her breeches, leaving her naked. Her blindfold seemed to form an exquisitely sensitive connection between them, as if the whole world narrowed to just the two of them alone.

Caroline felt him leave her and heard the rustle of wool and linen as he shed his own clothes. The cold swept around her again, and she tried to roll over to face him, but his hands stopped her, gentle but firm. She was his prisoner.

"Not yet," he said. His body lowered over hers again, bare skin to bare skin, completely intoxicating. As he kissed her shoulder, she felt every caress, every movement, a hundred-fold. She wanted more, and more, and had to bite her lip to keep from begging.

She didn't need to say anything, though—he seemed to know exactly what she needed. He knew just where to kiss to make her cry out. She felt his open mouth, hot and wet, slide down the arch of her spine and bite at the soft curve of her backside. He kissed the top of her thigh as his hands slid beneath her and drew her up.

She pressed her hands flat to the bed in front of her to keep from falling again. Grant moved slowly down the curves of her body, exploring every inch. No soft spot went unkissed; he caressed the back of her knees, her feet. He licked at her ankle, touched each freckle and sensitive spot. Then he moved back up again, and she cried out as his finger slid deep inside of her damp womanhood.

"You are so beautiful, Caro," he whispered against her ear, as he pressed his touch even deeper. Another finger slid inside and another, and he knew just where to caress to make her want to scream. She lowered her head to the sheets, and buried her face in their softness so no one could hear her.

"So beautiful," he said again. kissing her shoulder as his fingers moved faster. "Like a fierce goddess of the hunt, Artemis or Babd. And when you find your pleasure your skin turns the loveliest shade of pink— just like that."

Caroline's climax exploded inside her, a burst of fiery pleasure. She screamed into the sheets as her hips arched back into his touch.

"God help me, Caro, I've never wanted anyone the way I want you," he groaned.

She had barely begun to float back to Earth from the heights of sensation when she felt him draw her hips back even higher and his manhood slid into her. There was nothing slow or careful about their lovemaking now; they surged together in hot need, rough and fast. His hands were hard on her hips as he slid back and thrust forward, deeper and deeper. His skin was hot and damp against hers, their bodies clinging together.

"Grant!" she cried, as the pressure carried her up again. "I can't bear it. I can't..."

"I'm here, Caro," he said. "You're safe. Just let go."

And she did. She let herself fall completely into his hands, let herself be only in that moment with him. And in losing herself, she found herself more fully than she ever had before. She was free.

As she shouted out her climax, she felt his body surge once more into hers and tighten above her.

"Caro," he groaned, as if in the deepest, darkest grip of pleasure and pain. His hands seized on her hips and then fell away. She felt him next to her on the bed, and she took off the blindfold to look at him. After the intensity of what she just experienced with him, it was almost as if she saw him for the first time.

Grant lay on his back beside her, his head turned away and his arm flung over his eyes. His lean, strong body glistened with the diamond-like sheen of sweat, his skin a glowing bronze in the dying lamplight. His hair was tangled against the sheets.

He had said she looked like a goddess, but surely he was the immortal spirit. He was so like her images of a Celtic warrior-god resting from battle, fierce and beautiful. Like those fighters, he protected what he cared for and what was his. But who protected him?

Caroline reached out and gently touched his hair. It was like a skein of damp, tangled silk that wrapped around her fingers and bound them together. He grew tense, but he didn't move away from her. He didn't uncover his eyes.

She smoothed the hair back from his brow and carefully traced her fingertips over the pattern of the scars on his cheek. She leaned over him and kissed them softly, every jagged line that spoke of his pain. If only doing that could erase all the hurt, and everything that was past! But it was the pain of the past that brought them together, so she could not change even a terrible moment of it.

She kissed his shoulder and pressed her forehead

against his chest. She wanted to curl up into him, to be part of him and know his secrets at last. Maybe then they would both be free.

But after the frightening intimacy of their love-making, she could feel him drawing away from her again. He was pulling back into himself even as his arm came around her and drew her against him. He held on to her as if she were a lifeline to the world.

"You should get some sleep," Grant said. "We'll have to leave early in the morning to make a run for the mainland."

"I'm not tired," Caroline said, even as she felt the tug of foggy sleep pulling her down. She wanted to savor this moment with Grant, just the two of them alone, without the demands and perceptions of the world pressing in on them.

She had a terrible feeling such moments grew fewer and fewer.

"Then tell me more about your life in Dublin," he said. She felt his hand smooth gently over her hair. He loosened the tangled curls from what few pins remained and spread them over his chest.

"My life in Dublin is quite dull," she said with a laugh. "For instance, while there, I've never been called upon to free anyone from a medieval dungeon or set out across the sea at a moment's notice."

"Then you're lucky you have me to fill your time now," Grant said. "But you must do something with your days there."

"Oh, yes. I visit the library of the Hibernian Society or one of the bookshops to see if they have any new arrivals. I take tea with my sister if she's in town. I drive in the park or go walking. Sometimes if I feel up to it, I sit with Anna in the visitor's gallery at Parliament to hear the debates, but it is dull since the Union moved all the interesting business to Westminster. In the evening, I go to a salon where there is talk of books and ideas, or to the theater, or if forced, I attend a ball or the assembly rooms. I play cards, though luckily for very low stakes since I am quite bad at it. Then I go home and write until it's time to retire."

"You say it is dull, but I think it sounds as if your life is quite busy."

"In the last few months it has been. My stepdaughter Mary, who is also my dear friend, got married, and I helped her plan the wedding. My own nuptials were a quiet affair, so I never realized what a lot of work invitations and bouquets could be! But since she left on her honeymoon, things have been dull again."

"So you came to chase danger on Muirin Inish?"

Caroline laughed. "I had not realized quite how dangerous it would all be. I only wanted a book, and..."

"And?"

She hesitated and traced a light pattern over his shoulder with her fingertip. "I suppose I wanted to see you again."

His arm tightened around her. "I would have thought you were overjoyed to be rid of me after all that happened."

"It seemed as if there was something left undone between us, something I could not quite let go," she said. "At first I thought you were dead, and we would never bring things to a close."

"What did you think when you heard I still lived?"

Caroline's hand stilled against his skin, and she

pressed her palm to his shoulder. She remembered when she learned Grant would recover from his wounds but would not come back to Dublin. It was in the midst of her wedding preparations with Hartley, when she was about to step into a new life. She had felt that tug toward Grant even then, a rush of longing that had to be buried deep. He was far away, and they had both chosen their own paths.

"I felt terribly relieved, of course," she said. "It was as if a grief had lifted, and I could move forward in my life with that chapter closed. You only seemed to be a strange aberration in my life, which had already been laid out on its path by others."

"And is that what happened? Did you move forward in your contented life as Lady Hartley?" he said. "That is how I always imagined you, happy and safe. Even though I could never see you again, I wanted that for you."

He had thought of her in their years apart? Caroline propped herself on her elbow to stare down at him. "I thought it had, until I saw you again. Then I knew all too well, but there were so many things my life as Lady Hartley could never give me."

"But you were safe in Dublin."

She smiled at him and traced the furrows on his brow in a caressing touch. They smoothed under her fingertip. "Perhaps safety is overrated after all."

He caught her hand in his and kissed it, each finger, one by one. "I promise I will get you back to Dublin, Caroline. I'll see that you get your life back, just as it was before I came into it again. I'll make sure you're safe, for good this time."

Caroline studied his face, all sharp, elegant angles in the dying light. How very dull her old life would seem without him in it! How dry and colorless.

"Dublin is a long way away," she said. "A lot can happen between here and there."

He stared at her intently, as if he wanted to argue with her. But he just tugged her down to lie beside him again, and wrapped his arm around her shoulders.

"It is a long journey," he said "And we'll have to make an early start in the morning. You really should sleep now."

Caroline nodded. "I think I can sleep."

He kissed her temple as her eyes drifted closed and sleep pulled her down deeper into misty forgetfulness.

"Oh, Caro," he said softly. "I think I couldn't leave you even if I wanted to."

"I NEED TO FIND PASSAGE ON A BOAT HEADED TO THE mainland tomorrow," Grant said. "Killorgin maybe, or another port, it doesn't really matter."

The hard-faced woman behind the bar eyed him suspiciously as she wiped at the dirty glasses. The loud merriment of earlier in the evening had faded, leaving a few people playing cards and muttering together as they watched Grant, a few drunks snoring under the tables. It seemed calm enough.

But Grant knew better than to ever let down his guard. He watched the woman steadily until her gaze fell away and she nodded. One good thing about his scars, they usually meant no one wanted to start any sort of trouble with him. They were a clear indication that he was no stranger to battle.

"Old Fergus over there, he's going out in the morning," she said, and gestured toward a grizzled man sleeping by the fire. "He can probably take you as far as Killorgin, if you have the coin."

"I can pay," Grant said in a hard voice. "But he doesn't look like he can even stumble out the door much less steer a boat."

"He's more spry than he looks. No one else wants to go too far out, not when they hear tell the French might be coming." She leaned closer over the bar. "You've been out on the waters, aye?"

"From one of the outer islands."

"See anything suspicious out there, did you?"

"There weren't any other vessels at all."

"Aye, not in this weather, I think. Not unless they have some special sort of errand." She gave the bar a swipe with her rag, as if she tried not to appear too curious. "One of the boys here came back from the mainland not long ago. He said that an Irishman had recently come back from Paris and was traveling through Kildare, trying to find some old allies and persuade them to raise their forces. Men have been gathering from all over Wicklow, Wexford, even Carlow. I don't condone such behavior myself. This is a peaceful tavern. But you should heed the warning if you're traveling that way."

"We'll be sure to avoid the southern route then," said Grant. He laid some coins on the bar. "If you would give Mr. Fergus my message when he wakes, I would be most obliged."

He went back up the rickety stairs and unlocked the door to their rented room to slip quietly inside.

Caroline still slept peacefully on the bed, the sheets wrapped around her like a cocoon.

Grant slowly sat down beside her, watching her as she slept. She smiled in her dreams, her face serene as if she had only good visions tonight. He didn't know how she could rest so deeply after all that had happened. The fire, LaPlace, fleeing the island—and yet she looked like she slumbered in her own luxurious feather bed without a care in the world.

He had promised that he would take care of her and keep her safe. But he was doing an extremely poor job of that so far. All he could do now was get her home again, back to that life of the library, tea parties, and balls.

Once he did that, he could go back to Muirin Inish or maybe to another, even more isolated island. He could emulate the ancient hermits and live in a cave. But even there, he feared he would never forget Caroline Blacknall. He would lie on his stone bed and dream of the softness of her skin, the springtime smell of her perfume, the way she called out his name as she found her pleasure. And the calm, steady way she looked at him with her large brown eyes, as if she could see everything he tried to hide from the world —and even hide from himself.

"You'll be my curse forever, Caroline Blacknall," be whispered to her. But he would not be her curse. Once in Dublin, he would leave her to regain her life and never see her again. No matter how hard that was.

She stirred in her sleep. A little frown creased her brow, but she didn't wake up. Grant tucked the bedclothes closer around her and lay down beside her on the narrow mattress. She nestled against him with a sigh, and he put his arm around her shoulders to hold her close. Her hair brushed against his neck, soft as silk and smelling of sea air and roses.

He feared it would be damnably hard to leave her in the end.

CHAPTER
TWENTY

Caroline came awake, startled. She had no idea where she was. The room around her was dark and unfamiliar, smelling faintly of fish, stale ale, and salt. Someone was stumbling down the corridor outside, bumping into the walls as they went and singing an off-key sea chantey. Her heart raced in her chest.

She sat up and felt someone's hard arm against her hip. Then she remembered. She was at an inn on Mallorney Island, with Grant.

She slowly lay back down and breathed in deeply. Grant still slept beside her, fully clothed. The sky outside the grimy window was dark, but turning a lighter gray at the edges. Soon it would be morning, and they would have to be on their way to—where? What was their next step, their plan?

Caroline carefully slid out of bed so as not to wake Grant, wrapped a sheet around her for a robe, and fumbled around until she found the candle stub and managed to light it. There was still bread and cheese on the tray on the room's one table, and an ewer of now-warm ale, and she found to her surprise that she was quite famished. Adventure seemed to create a hearty appetite.

As she ate a chunk of the bread, she noticed the valise at the edge of the table. Grant had packed his mysterious papers in there, along with *The Chronicle*. She knew very well she shouldn't open it—look what had happened to poor Pandora. And snooping had gotten her into enough trouble on this adventure. But surely he wouldn't mind if she just peeked at the book. It had been so long since she saw it last.

Caroline slowly lifted the lid and peered inside. Packed on top were the things Mademoiselle Victorine gave her before they parted, a dress and shawl, clean stockings, a pair of kid slippers, and a hairbrush. Beneath these were the oilskin-wrapped papers. Caroline ignored those and took out the book in its box.

It wasn't a large volume, but it was a precious one. She carefully unfolded the cloth tucked around it to reveal its worn-soft green leather cover, embossed with a twisting, writhing Celtic dragon with little emerald eyes. A tiny gold clasp set with more rough-cut emeralds held it closed.

She gently opened it to a chapter in the middle. It was a tale she had not seen before, a story of the Dragon of Adaislan, beautifully illustrated with illuminated images in reds and blues and yellows, so brilliant that they could have been painted yesterday.

It was a fascinating tale. In all the lands of Kildare, there was one that surpassed all others in beauty, that which lay between Killinan and Kilmoreland. Fertile green fields, orchards laden with fruit, streams rich with purple-silver salmon, restful shady woods filled with the song of the rare pure-white sparrow lay in this glorious kingdom. The inhabitants lived long lives of peace and plenty. This rare kingdom was called Adaislan, and it was unique in all the land, for it was ruled only by a queen and no king.

That was surely near her own family's home at Killinan!

Grant rolled over on the bed, and Caroline read the rest of the fascinating story in silence, studying the illustrations of the queen and her court of beautiful women in trailing medieval gowns, and the dragon that guarded her land.

It was Queen Keira who ruled Adaislan at the time of our tale. She received the lands from her mother, who received them from her mother before her, and onward into the mists of lost time. It was the goddess Cliodna who granted it to their ancestress, and decreed that it would be the realm of queens and a prosperous place.

Yet Queen Keira required a princess of her own to be her heir, and thus contracted to wed the prince of another kingdom, Sean of Kilmarrin. Prince Sean accepted the terms of this union, and agreed to never make a claim on the throne of Adaislan. At first, the marriage was a happy one, and Princess Ava was born, heiress to the two lands of her parents. The marriage was not blessed with more princesses, and one day Queen Keira died. She was to be succeeded by Princess Ava, then a beauteous and kind maiden of fifteen summers.

Yet her father dissolved this succession and sought to seize Adaislan from his daughter by the force of his armies. The goddess Cliodna saw what was becoming of her fair gift and was sore unhappy. She undertook to send one of her fiercest warriors, a dragon of massive size and fiery breath, to defend the lands of Adaislan and its true queen. For Adaislan could only ever be ruled through the female line or terrible destruction would follow.

Caroline looked up from the book with a puzzled frown. It was a lovely fairy tale, the story of the dragon who went on to defeat the king and turned into a handsome prince, to marry Queen Ava and rule by her side until the day their own daughter succeeded them. She had heard versions of it before, but never quite like this one.

Brother Brendan, who wrote *The Chronicle*, was very specific about the location of Adaislan, and that it was always ruled by queens and passed down through the female line. She knew there had actually been a Killinan back then, where her own family's lands lay, and a Kilmoreland, which lay on the other side of Adair Court. She had read about them in her studies, their history and folklore, though she hadn't found anything about dragons. But Brendan was fond of mixing legend and historical facts. It made his tales a fascinating puzzle for any scholar.

If Adaislan—Adair—was indeed ruled by women, what did that mean?

Before she could finish reading the story of the dragon, she heard Grant stir awake on the bed. He sat straight up, his whole body tense as if ready to leap into battle, until he saw her there at the table. He relaxed a bit, but his eyes were still wary.

"How long have you been awake?" he said.

"Not long. I thought I heard something in the corridor, and then I couldn't go back to sleep because I was hungry."

"Something in the corridor? Why didn't you wake

me?" He got out of bed, as graceful as an uncoiling jungle cat, and went to peer cautiously out the door.

"Because you need your sleep, and it was nothing. Just a drunk stumbling about."

Grant closed the door again and turned to look at her. His arms crossed over his chest. "It's a long way to Dublin, Caro, and who knows what we'll encounter on the way. I want you to wake me from now on if you hear anything at all."

That seemed a bit overly cautious to Caroline, but he looked so serious that she nodded. "Of course. Come and have something to eat. The bread isn't too bad, and there's some ale left."

He sat down across from her, and reached for the ewer and an empty pottery goblet. "I found someone who can take us to the mainland in the morning," he said. "We should be ready to go as soon as it's light, though God only knows if *he* will be."

Caroline nodded and carefully closed the book. "Where will we go next?"

"If we have good luck, we should make it to Killorgin by evening. Then we can try and find out what's happening and plan our safest route to Dublin."

"They have an ancient tomb near Killorgin," she said. "I hear that it's very well preserved and the carvings are extraordinary, though I have never seen it."

Grant laughed. "I doubt we'll have time for much sightseeing, Caro my dear. We'll have to make for Dublin as quickly as possible."

To Dublin, where they would part and never see each other again? Caroline felt the oddest sinking sensation. Dublin was far away, though. Surely much could happen before they got there.

"Perhaps there might be time for one tiny little peek at a ruin or two," she said.

"Or perhaps you've been reading *The Chronicle of Kildare* again, and it's giving you the urge to see the old sites," Grant said, gesturing with his goblet to the book in her hands.

"Yes, I was reading the story of the Dragon of Adaislan," she answered. "It must mean something, if I could just decipher it."

Grant's jaw tightened. "It's just an old tale concocted by a bored and fanciful monk."

"Well, I like it anyway," Caroline said. She wrapped *The Chronicle* up again and carefully replaced it in the box. "And I promise I did not look at the papers. I only took out the book."

"Caro." Grant put down his goblet and reached across the table to catch her hand in his. He gave it a gentle tug, making her look at him. "Perhaps it would have been best if you *had* looked at them."

She shook her head. "No, I want you to trust me, as much as you can. If you want to keep your secrets..."

"Trust has to go both ways, does it not?" he said. "I've certainly given you no reason to trust me. You must have suspicions."

"Oh, Grant," Caroline said sadly. She covered his hand with her other one, holding them together. "I often feel I know you not at all. I catch a glimpse, I think I know something, and then it all changes."

"I know, and I am sorry for it, Caroline. Truly I am. You are the last person in the world I would ever want to hurt. But I see now we will have to work together if we are to get safely home."

She felt a cautious leap of excitement. Was he

going to confide in her at last? "You know I will hold anything you tell me in confidence."

"I know that. But some of these secrets are not mine, they affect many others, and there are those who would stop at nothing to get them. I can't tell you all of it, but I can assure you of this, I am not a spy for the French."

"No?" she said softly.

His mouth tightened. "I can't tell you all of it as the tale is not mine alone. But I can tell you this. I heard that Robert Emmet and some of his friends were back from Paris, trying to find all the United Irish leaders who had gone into hiding or tried to lose themselves in the everyday world. They wanted them to gather their old forces and be ready to rise on a French landing. But they refused to divulge any detailed plans or show any proof of French intentions. The French are the most uncertain of allies, out for their own ends alone and apt to pull out at any moment. To be vulnerable to them could prove as bad as English rule in the end. My contacts know this, and they know Ireland is still wounded from ninety-eight. The English noose is still too tight. She's not ready for another rising."

"Your contacts?" Caroline asked. Some of her suspicions it seemed were correct, a rebellion was afoot. But Grant's part in it was nothing she could have guessed. She still did not know for sure what he was doing.

"I do still have some friends in Dublin," he said. "And they know that Muirin Inish is perfectly situated for French schemes. The Vicomte wanted *The Chronicle*, that was a good excuse for a covert visit, a chance for me to discover more about any plans

Napoleon might have. But we did not plan for such a villain as LaPlace. The man is a fanatic for Bonaparte."

"He is a villain indeed," she said, thinking of all the wounds LaPlace inflicted.

"He was obviously set on his own mission, and was prepared to do anything to achieve it," Grant said. "I doubt those include Irish independence. His papers tell us more, but I must get them to Dublin as soon as possible and see them into the right hands. Perhaps I can stop the disaster of another rising before it's too late. I fear I can say little else. I have to see you safe, and then go on with my work alone."

"So you work with Irishmen?" she said, her mind reeling with it all. She especially did not like that word alone. She feared it meant after they reached Dublin, she would not see him again.

"Yes. Do you see, Caro my dear? I just want to try and make up for all I did before, try to protect you," he finished.

Did she see? She had feared he worked for the French, even as her instincts told her he could not. It made more sense he worked for the British government, for that world of privilege he once lived at the center of. Did he still turn his back on his Irish heritage? Did he still hate it? If only she could be sure.

"Oh, Grant," she said. Her throat felt tight with the threat of tears. She leaped up and ran around the table to throw her arms about his neck. "I can help you with this. I know I can."

"No, Caroline," he said firmly. His arms were hard around her waist. "It's too dangerous. I told you what

194

to expect so you can be fully on your guard, but you can't be involved in this any more than you already are. Remember what happened to your sister Eliza in ninety-eight? She's living in exile now, and it could have been worse. I won't have that happen to you. My work is only mine; I can tell you no more about it."

"Maybe I can't shoot or fight like Eliza," she said. "But I know a great deal about Ireland. I can help in other ways."

"You help by writing your history. People are dispirited by the Union. They need to find their pride again, their sense of heritage. Books like yours have the power to do that. My job now is to get you safely to Dublin so you can finish your work."

"And so you can deliver those papers, whatever they are?"

Grant gave her a tight smile. "Yes, that, too. And it must be soon. We have very little time to get to Dublin."

"Then we must keep each other safe," she said. And she would have to persuade him that she really could help with his work. Ireland, their Ireland, was too precious to lose. Surely he saw that now, saw that they were a part of this country, just as it was a part of them. They had to fight for it, however they could.

Suddenly there was a pounding at the door. Startled, Caroline tumbled off Grant's lap and landed on the floor.

"If you still want passage with old Fergus, you'll have to hurry," the landlady shouted.

Grant helped Caroline to her feet and scooped her clothes off the floor to hand them to her. "You heard the lady," he said. "No time to talk now."

"Maybe not," Caroline said, as she tugged on her

breeches and pulled the wrinkled shirt over her head. "But surely you must know by now, Grant Dunmore, you can't escape me. I will find out the truth, one way or another."

He suddenly grabbed her wrist and spun her against him for a quick, hard kiss. "Then know you're the most damnably stubborn woman ever. But I can be stubborn as well, and I won't hurt you again."

"Oh, don't I know it? You *are* damnably stubborn," she whispered. She kissed the line of his jaw, the tiny pulse that beat there whenever he was being patient with her. "If nothing else, this should be a very interesting journey."

He chuckled and lifted her off her feet to twirl her around until she laughed giddily. "Oh, Caro. *Interesting* is going to be the least of it."

CHAPTER
TWENTY-ONE

C aroline leaned against the door of the livery stable as Grant negotiated to hire two horses. She studied the street beyond, her hat pulled low over her brow to conceal her hair and add to the illusion that she was a lad. With her tall, slender figure and her breasts bound with strips of linen, surely she could pull it off if no one looked too closely.

And no one paid her any mind as they hurried on their business. Killorgin was a busy port town, with brightly painted fishermen's houses lining the cobblestone streets, and the briny smell of fish and pickled vegetables on the fresh breeze. The shops had just opened for the day, and their owners swept the front steps and laid out their wares in the windows. Carts rattled past, laden with barrels and crates to be loaded on the waiting boats. It all seemed like a typical Irish coastal town.

But Caroline noticed that there were not as many boats in port as could be expected. Because of the unpredictable weather? Or because of something else that kept them away from the waters, like English patrols and French smugglers? Everyone seemed most intent on minding their own business, which was also odd for an Irish town. Usually curiosity and natural chattiness got the better of people when they met with a stranger who might have new tales to tell.

Back in '98, the town had been occupied by the army and the site of a raid and skirmish, one that was quickly put down. Since then, things were quiet in the area. Everyone just wanted to rebuild their lives and make a living as they always had from the sea and the ships. If the country rose up again against the English, or worse, if there was a French invasion, there would be those who went to battle again. And there would be those who kept their heads down, frightened of more war and upheaval.

She should follow their example now and try to stay as quiet and unobtrusive as possible on this journey. She had to listen and watch, especially where Grant was concerned. Could she trust him now? Everything was so precariously balanced, and it could all change in an instant.

"It felt as if I was negotiating the Treaty of Cateau Cambresis, but I have at last procured us two horses," Grant said as he came up beside her. "The proprietor's wife also sold us a basket of provisions, so we shouldn't have to stop for some time."

"The weather looks promising as well," Caroline said.

"I'm hoping we make it to Kilmallock by the evening, if we ride fast."

"Er, about that..." Caroline said slowly.

He looked down at her with his brow arched. "Is there a problem?"

"No, it's just—well, I am not what you would call an especially good rider."

"Really? I thought all Irish countrywomen learned to ride before they could walk. Your sister was a bruising rider, as I recall."

Caroline felt a twinge at the mention of Anna, who as well as being blonde, pretty, and stylish, was a veritable centauress. She was even one of the few women in the county to ride with the local hunt. Caroline was not like that.

"I do know how to ride," she said. "My father was a famous sportsman, and I think he bought us our first ponies the moment we were born. I just don't do it very often."

Caroline didn't think it necessary to mention her suspicion of horses. The way they looked at people from their soft brown eyes always seemed to her as if they were planning something secret and nefarious. As if they were just waiting to throw a person to the ground and then laugh at them.

As Grant laughed now. "Then we'll insist on the most placid mount in the stable."

"I don't want to slow you down," she cried, as he led her around the building to the stable yard in back. "Perhaps I should find passage on a post chaise."

Yet even as she suggested it, she knew parting with him was the last thing she wanted to do. Not when she was so close to finding out more of his secrets. And besides, what if there were an uprising again and the post coaches were stopped, as they were in '98?

He shook his head. "I shudder to think of the trouble you would get into on a post chaise. No, I said

I would get you to Dublin, and I will. Even if it's on a horse."

They quickly procured their mounts and transferred the contents of the valise into saddlebags before setting out on the road out of town. At first they traveled in silence. The traffic into Killorgin was thick for a couple of miles, carts packed with cargo for the ships, and families on foot with their market baskets. They had to maneuver their way through the crowds, and it took all Caroline's concentration to feel at ease in the saddle again and remember how to control the horse. Luckily, her gray mare seemed as placid as promised and not inclined to go running off into the woods.

After a while, the traffic thinned to a trickle, and they had the road almost to themselves. The sun climbed higher in the watery-blue sky, and beamed down on Caroline's hat-covered head. She actually began to feel almost warm for the first time in weeks. With Grant beside her and the open road stretched before them, she could almost forget the reality of their situation and imagine her elf on a pleasant country ride.

Almost.

She glanced at the bag strapped to Grant's saddle, where she knew the papers were concealed. Her gaze slid over the cloth of his breeches pulled taut over his hard thigh, and she thought of last night. The blindfold, the feeling of his body moving against hers...

Her face suddenly felt hot, and she looked sharply away. He grinned at her, as if he knew exactly what she was thinking, which made her cheeks flame even higher.

"I think the horse likes you," he said. "She hasn't

made even the tiniest move to throw you off and run away."

While Grant, damn him, looked born to ride a horse. He sat easily, almost lazily, in the saddle with the reins carelessly draped in his hand. "She's probably just biding her time, waiting for the perfect moment to dash my head against those boulders," Caroline said. "But perhaps we have come to an understanding."

"If you're tired, we can stop for a rest."

"No, I'm fine. It's actually rather pleasant, all things considered. The sun is out, we're not on a boat in the middle of a storm..."

"And you'll be back in a library in only a few days."

They turned onto another, narrower roadway lined with tall hedgerows. The sun smelled warm and soft on the thickets, and all she could hear was the silence of the countryside, broken only by birdsong and the faint bleating of sheep. She had forgotten what the country was like after her years in Dublin, the freshness and clean beauty of it, the green, earthy smell.

Her life was waiting up ahead. As Grant said, she would be back in a library. She loved her books, the feel of the soft, old paper under her fingers, the scent of leather covers and glue, the wonders of discovery to be found in the pages. She loved her writing, and thought it was important. But was that enough now? Was it really all she wanted?

"Yes," she said quietly. "It will be nice to be home and to see my friends again. My niece and nephew will be getting so big now! But I fear my little town house will be quiet and dull after all this."

"And quiet without Lord Hartley there?"

Grant had hardly mentioned her husband. Caroline turned to him in surprise, which her horse took as a sign it should also turn. She had to tug hard on the reins to keep them from plowing into the hedgerow.

Once they were on the path again, she said, "I do miss Hartley at times, though he never lived in this house with me. His son lives in the grand Hartley house now. I especially miss the evenings when we would sit by the fire and read together, or when we would go to the lectures at the Hibernian Society and then discuss them after. But he has been gone for some time now, and we were not married all that long anyway. Sometimes..."

Sometimes it was hard for her to remember his face or the pleasant, soft way he would kiss her. That life seemed to fade further and further away, the longer she was with Grant.

"Tell me about him," Grant said.

"You met him when you lived in Dublin. I think you even belonged to the same club."

"Of course I met him. Dublin is a small place; one always seems to run into the same people everywhere. But we didn't exactly have the same interests back then."

"No," Caroline said. It was hard to think of two more different men than Grant and Hartley. "Hartley wasn't much interested in politics or wars, unless they happened a thousand years ago. He had no ambitions except for his studies."

"He didn't go around smashing people's lives as I do?"

"No. He liked things quiet and calm so he could

concentrate on his work. I think he would have been happiest to stay in his library day and night, though I did occasionally coax him to the theater or a card party. It was a nice life. No fires or riots."

"And you were happy with him? He was the right husband for you?"

She looked at Grant. He seemed terribly serious, as if this was not merely conversation to pass the miles. He sounded as if the answer mattered to him.

"Yes," she said. "He was the right husband for me then. I needed rest and quiet, needed time to find myself. But I think perhaps what I needed at seventeen is not quite the same as what I need now."

"So when you return to Dublin, will you seek out another man like him? Someone steady and dependable, like that horse?"

Caroline laughed and patted the mare's neck gingerly. "I have no idea what I will seek out in Dublin. I've scarcely had a moment to think of late. But maybe I won't marry again at all. Just because my mother and my sister Eliza married again after being widowed doesn't mean I must. Maybe I will just be my family's old widowed aunt, who insists on telling Irish myths at the Christmas dinner table. I could teach Lina how to embroider—if I was any good at it. Or I could teach them how to ride their ponies. I seem to have the knack for it now, don't I?"

Unfortunately, the mare chose that moment to veer toward the hedgerows again, and Caroline had to jerk hard on the reins to get her to come back. Then the horse headed for a distant meadow.

Grant laughed and galloped after them. "I wouldn't become too ambitious an equestrian just yet, Caro."

"Well, maybe I won't teach them to ride," she said, as he led them back to the road. "But I can teach them about old Celtic ruins. What about you? What will *you* do when we reach Dublin?" Would she see him again once they were there? Or would he keep his word and stay out of her life?

"I doubt I would be able to teach children anything at all. I can't embroider worth a damn, either."

"You'll have to do something when we get there. Will you move back into your beautiful house? It's been all closed up since you left."

"I probably won't be in Dublin very long. I'm not planning to restore my house and renew my social life. Though it might be amusing to see people's reactions if I showed up at the Crow Street Theater one night, don't you think?"

Amusing wasn't exactly the word Caroline would use. All these years later, Dublin Society still gossiped about Grant and all that had happened before the fire. It would be like a galvanizing bolt of lightning if he suddenly appeared in their midst again. And what would Anna and her husband say? Would there be a duel?

Perhaps he was right, and their lives should not meet again after they reached Dublin.

"It wouldn't have to be the theater," she said. "There are always the Rutland Square assembly rooms. They're terribly crowded every week, since Parliament moved to London, and there's nothing useful for anyone to do but dance and drink. You could make your appearance there."

He gave her a wry smile. "And would you dance the first dance with me, Lady Hartley?"

Caroline imagined taking his arm and walking

with him onto the dance floor as everyone stared at them. He had been a fine dancer, though she had never had the chance to partner him. She used to watch him from her seat beside the wall, and envy the way he touched his partner, the way he smiled down at her, the smooth, powerful grace of his movements. She was only a passable dancer herself, but surely in his arms, being swept around and around, it would feel very different.

Even if everyone did whisper about them while they did that dancing.

"You know," she said, "I just might. My sisters always got to be the scandalous ones; now it should be my turn. But I must warn you, I am quite notorious for treading on my partners' toes."

"Then it's probably fortunate for us both that I will never go to the assembly rooms," he said.

"Yes," Caroline murmured. "Most fortunate."

"I will conclude my business in the city and then leave as quickly as possible. I don't want to cause more trouble."

"And where will you go? Back to Muirin Inish?"

"I doubt I would be welcomed there with open arms. I think I've stayed there long enough, anyway. It was a place of refuge when I left Dublin, someplace quiet where I could think about all that had happened, but maybe it's time to see a new place."

"What sort of new place?"

Grant shrugged. "I hear America is rather nice. Or India."

America? India? Caroline's heart sank. Those were so very, very far away. There would be no chance at all of meeting him again if he sailed off to some distant shore. No chance to...

To do what? She didn't even know. She had no claim on Grant, nor he on her. They were together for this short time only, this brief period when she got to leave her life and have an adventure. He would go on to more adventures, and she would go back to her work. She had always known that.

She shouldn't feel sad about it now, and yet she did. Very much.

She shook that pang of regret away and gave him a bright smile. "They both sound terribly intriguing. I was reading a book recently written by a man who lived in the forested wilds of America with the Indians. Shall you do that?"

"I may have to," Grant said with a laugh. "It's probably the only place in all the world where I could hide from you Blacknalls."

"Hide?" Caroline scowled at him in mock indignation. "I assure you, Grant Dunmore, there is no need for that. We can always find you, even in America."

"Hmm. Well, perhaps the South Sea islands then."

The afternoon passed in such engrossing speculation of what life would be like on a tropical island that Caroline almost forgot she was on horseback. She forgot they were on an urgent errand with those secret papers, that she was far from all she knew, and dependent on her own wits with a man she couldn't fully trust. They laughed together, shared a midday meal under a tree by the side of the road, and talked of their childhoods and all they had dreamed of doing then.

But as they neared the town of Kilmallock, where they planned to stop for the night, Caroline was painfully aware that she had been in the saddle all day. Her thighs and backside ached, and she clung to the reins to keep from sliding off. She forced herself to sit up straight and keep smiling, but as Grant lifted her down in the courtyard of an inn, a moan escaped from her.

Grant frowned and slid his arm around her waist to hold her up until the numbness faded. "Are you quite well, Caro? I knew we should have stopped at the last village and not pressed on."

Caroline shook her head and gave him her most determined smile. "We had to press on if we wanted to make good time. I'm perfectly fine. I just need to walk around a bit and stretch my legs."

He didn't look convinced. "I'll hire a phaeton to-morrow to take us to Ballylynan."

"Nonsense! I'll be able to ride tomorrow. Now go find us a room for the night. I'll just walk around a bit out here."

"You shouldn't be alone."

Caroline laughed. "I'm a lad, remember? And no one is here to see me except that boy coming to take the horses."

At last she managed to get him to go inside, and she immediately collapsed onto the nearest mounting block. She was sure her legs didn't want to hold her up for another minute.

Once she felt strong enough, she pushed herself up again and walked around the empty courtyard. The movement did help, and slowly the ache faded away to a faint twinge. A carriage clattered in, and more servants came scurrying out of the inn to tend to it. Caroline hurried past the gates to get away from the chaos and stood just outside on the walkway.

Kilmallock was a bigger place than Killorgin. full of shops and tall, old buildings built close together along the cobbled street. Carriages, people on horse-back, and pedestrians hurried by, and the shop-keepers were lowering their shutters and locking their doors for the night. The sky was a dark blue above the rooftops and chimneys, and a couple of faint stars blinked along the horizon.

The scents of roasting meats and stewed cabbage floated out of the inn, making her stomach rumble. It seemed a long time since their earlier meal.

A horse suddenly galloped around the corner at the end of the street and came careening up the lane. It was so fast, so out of control, that the other people scattered with shouted curses. The horse's hooves pounded like thunder on the cobbles, and the rider's black coat flapped behind him like a demon's wings.

A woman stumbled next to Caroline and dropped her market basket. Vegetables and a loaf of bread fell onto the walkway. Caroline stooped to help her gather them just as the out-of-control horse hurtled past them.

Caroline looked up to add her curses to the oth-ers, but the shout strangled in her throat. The rider wore no hat, and his angel-gold hair gleamed. The pure, etched profile looked just like Captain LaPlace.

LaPlace, whom she had pushed down the ledge and left for dead to rescue Grant from the dungeon. Whose body she hadn't seen as they left the island.

She pulled her cap lower to hide her face, but he was gone in an instant. There was only the street full of irate people left in his wake. Caroline handed the woman her basket and made sure she was unhurt, before running to the corner where the horse had turned and disappeared. She desperately scanned the street, but there was only more of the same, scattered pedestrians and vegetables spilled on the walkway.

Was it LaPlace? Could it possibly be that he had lived and found his way off Muirin Inish? He had seemed in a terrible hurry. If it was LaPlace, he was surely after the papers and probably after revenge, too.

Caroline turned and hurried back to the inn. She had forgotten her sore muscles in the excitement, but now they ached all over again. Her heart was pounding erratically.

"There you are!" she heard Grant shout. He ran out the gates to take her arm and help her into the inn yard. "I leave you alone for five minutes, and you vanish on me."

"Oh, Grant," she whispered, as she clutched at his hand. "I think I just saw LaPlace."

CHAPTER
TWENTY-TWO

"Are you certain it was him?" Grant asked. He and Caroline made their way along yet one more street of Kilmallock, scanning every face as they passed, looking in every barroom and doorway. The night was fully dark around them by then, the lamplighters tending to the street lanterns as girls in revealing, cheap satin gowns stumbled out to begin their rounds.

They had found nothing yet except people who remembered the wild horseman galloping down the road and were angry at being knocked aside. No one had seen him again, and the only other inn in town besides theirs had no such guest.

But Caroline's face had been pale with shock, as if she had indeed seen a ghost. If it was LaPlace, he was gone now. Grant had to protect the papers, and protect Caroline, too, above all. He knew men like LaPlace, men filled with anger and bitterness, determined to avenge themselves on the world.

Grant knew because he had been such a man himself once. Until a pair of solemn brown eyes looked into his soul and woke him up.

"No, I'm not entirely sure," Caroline said. "He went by so very quickly, but it looked like him."

She stumbled on a cobblestone, and he caught her arm. She still looked so pale, with dark circles like bruises under her eyes. Grant felt a sharp pang of guilt.

"If it was him, he is long gone," Grant said. "He won't find us tonight, and I have no desire to go chasing him across the countryside in the middle of the night. Let's go back to the inn. You need something to eat."

Caroline bit her lip. She looked as if she wanted to argue, to keep on looking, but she nodded. "You must be hungry, too."

"Mostly I just want to sleep in a real bed." With her beside him. "We can leave early tomorrow. With any luck, if that is LaPlace, we can avoid him by taking the country roads until we reach Dublin."

They made their way back to the inn, which was now blazing with light and filled with guests looking for a drink. Caroline seemed to relax as they came closer to the noise and bustle. The fear faded from her eyes.

But Grant felt his fury born anew that LaPlace could still frighten her, even after she had defeated him. He never wanted her to be afraid again. Her life should be only peaceful and happy, and once he had her safe with her family again, away from the darkness of his own life, she would be. He would make sure of it.

Once their chamber door closed behind them, he took her in his arms and kissed her gently. Her lips were soft beneath his, and her arms wound around his neck. He felt such a vast tenderness come over

211

him at her touch, and a fierce protectiveness. She was his, his beautiful, sweet Caroline. He belonged to her as he had never thought to belong to another living being, and it made him feel stronger—and weaker—than ever before.

"I have to go out for a while," he told her quietly.

"Go out?" she cried. "Now?"

"Not for long. I'll have them send up bathwater and something to eat, and I'll be back before you know it. Just keep the door locked and the pistol on the table."

Before she could question him some more, he kissed her again and slipped out the door. He waited until she heard the lock click into place and then hurried down the stairs. He had work to do.

CAROLINE SANK DEEPER INTO THE WARM WATER AND SIGHED with contentment. It had been too long since she had a proper bath. The water and the delicious, soapy suds seemed to melt away all the tension she held in her aching shoulders. LaPlace, the vast distance between her and Dublin—and her and Grant—it all seemed to dissolve. At least for the moment.

Grant had finally told her something of his work, but then he closed himself off all over again. He was so infuriating! She kicked at the water, splashing it against the side of the wooden tub. Infuriating, and yet still so maddeningly attractive.

"It's still a long way to Dublin," she whispered.

She sat up in the tub and reached for the bar of soap and sponge the maid left for her. The soap had a lemon smell that was wonderful after all the dust of the road. She lifted her leg and carefully rubbed the soap over her calf, singing, "And when will you return again, and when will we get married? When broken shells make Christmas bells..."

"Caro, I think we should..." Grant said, as he came into the room without knocking. His words faded abruptly at the sight of her in the bath, and she heard the door click shut.

She looked at him over her shoulder and smiled. She had never felt particularly beautiful or desirable, especially not next to her sisters and her lovely mother. She was The Studious One, and that suited her well. But the way Grant watched her now, all hungry and intent only on her, gave her such a thrill. It made her feel a power she had never experienced before.

And she feared she felt just as hungry when she looked at him. His shirt was unlaced, baring a deep vee of smoothly muscled olive skin. He had washed, too, and his long hair was damp and slicked back from his face. His scars were nearly invisible in the lamplight.

"We should... what?" she said. She slowly lowered her leg into the water and turned to face him. She rested her arms on the edge of the tub and watched him. The air in the room had suddenly gone hot and close; it seemed to crackle against her skin.

Grant leaned back against the door. His eyes narrowed as he watched her. "I was going to say we should leave as early as possible so we can make it to Ballylynan soon. But now I think we should stay here for a week or more, if it means more baths for you."

Caroline laughed. "It is nice here. I had quite forgotten how a bath can feel so wonderful."

She turned around and held out the sponge. "Can you wash my back for me?" she said. She held her breath. Just thinking about his touch on her skin made her shiver. She closed her eyes and listened as he moved slowly across the room.

For a moment, he just stood behind her. She could feel the warmth of his body mere inches from hers, could hear the sound of his breath. Would he touch her or would he not?

Just when she thought she might scream from the uncertainty of it, he took the sponge from her hand. He knelt beside the tub and reached out to softly sweep the damp tendrils of hair from the nape of her neck.

She kept her eyes tightly closed as he traced the sponge over her skin. He drew light patterns over her shoulders and down the line of her back, his fingers barely brushing over her. Then he leaned closer, his breath cool on her damp body. His lips brushed over the nape of her neck, and he tasted her with his tongue.

"Grant!" she cried. She spun around to face him, and his mouth claimed hers. She met his kiss with equal fervor, full of all the terrible, passionate longing she always felt with him. It was a primeval, overwhelming force she couldn't deny.

She wrapped her arms around his neck, holding him so close there could be nothing between them now. She wished she could be even closer, that she could make him entirely hers.

Not breaking their kiss, he lifted her from the tub and held her high in his arms as she twined her legs about his hips and rocked against him. He was hard beneath the flap of his breeches. He wanted her, too, as much as she wanted him, and that knowledge fanned the flames of her desire even higher. She feared she would be consumed by it, and yet at the same time, she longed to jump into that fire headfirst and be lost.

Her lips slid to his throat and to the bare skin of his chest where his shirt fell away. The linen was quickly soaked with her bathwater, and he tasted of salt-sweat, of clean sunshine, and of Grant. She wanted more and more of him, of everything. She became horribly greedy when it came to him.

He slowly lowered her to her feet and held her away from him. She whispered a wordless protest and reached for him.

"We have to be careful," he said. "You're sore after the ride today."

"I don't care about that," she said. She could feel no pain at all, not now.

"I do. I won't hurt you." He grabbed the towel draped over a chair and knelt at her feet.

As Caroline watched in fascination, he gently reached for her foot. He dried it slowly, moving the soft linen around each sensitive toe and up the curve of her leg. Then he kissed her ankle, traced his tongue over the arch of her foot. It tickled and tingled and made her want to laugh and cry out, all at the same time.

He did the same with her other foot, drying it then kissing the soft skin just behind her ankle. He lightly bit at it and traced his mouth up to her knee, the back of her thigh.

"Grant..." she whispered.

"Shh," he said. "Just be very still."

He rose up on his knees and gently urged her thighs farther apart. With the edge of the towel, he patted dry the dark curls between her legs, then eased the linen into a loop around her waist and pulled her closer. He softly blew on that extra-sensitive spot.

"Grant!" she cried out. The sensation of it all was almost too much. She tried to arch her hips away from him, but he wouldn't let her go. And she didn't really want to go. She wanted to stay with him, just like this, with a desperation she had never known before.

He leaned closer and kissed her just there. With one hand, he held her by the makeshift bond, and with the other he spread the damp, hot folds of her womanhood so he could kiss her even more deeply. His tongue plunged deep inside her, rough and delicate all at the same time, tasting her, pressing at that one sensational spot. She moaned, and her fingers twined in his hair to hold him against her. His actions were terribly intimate, somehow even more so than when they had sex, and she felt utterly open and vulnerable to him, joined to him. Yet she also felt immensely strong and powerful. She wanted to shout out with the wonderful joy of it all.

Grant's mouth eased away from her to kiss the inside of her thigh. He rose up along her body and caught her around the waist, walking her back to the bed as he kissed her mouth. He tasted of mint and ale, and scandalously of *her*, and it made her cry out against him.

The kiss tumbled into desperation as he lowered her to the mattress. Everything was hot and blurry around her, their movements full of artless need as they held on to each other. He came down on top of her as she slid her legs higher to cradle him in the curve of her body.

Caroline moaned again—it seemed all the sound she could make now. Her mind could hold no thoughts, only feelings, emotions that she had kept deep down inside for so long that they overwhelmed her now. Tears prickled at her eyes as she turned her head to the side, while his open lips traced the line of her cheekbone, her closed eyelids, and her temple, where her pulse beat frantically. He bit lightly at her earlobe, his breath hot in her ear, and she trembled.

Her hands reached under his shirt to trace the hollow of his back, the hard muscles of his shoulder. His skin was satin-smooth, taut and damp, hard under her caress. He felt warm and vital and alive, and he made her feel that way, too. So vividly alive.

Her hands moved down to unfasten his breeches and take his penis into her hand. His manhood was hard and ready, and she spread her legs wider in silent invitation. With a twist of his hips, he drove into her and buried himself to the hilt.

Caroline wrapped her legs around his waist, and they found their rhythm together, hard and fast. Her hands clutched at his shoulders, her nails digging in as if to make him entirely a part of her, as she was of him.

That rough pleasure built inside her, and she reached out for it with all her strength. It drove her higher and higher until she felt like she leaped off a cliff and went soaring free into the sky.

Grant let out a hoarse shout above her. A great tremor rocked through his body, and he fell down beside her.

"Caroline," he said hoarsely. "Caroline, I never thought I could feel like this."

"I know," she whispered. "I know."

And they held on to each other as they fell into a deep silence, and the night closed in around them.

CHAPTER
TWENTY-THREE

Caroline lay in the circle of Grant's arms, feeling lazy and languid. Despite the fact that they were in a strange room, far from home, she had never felt quite so relaxed. She wanted to laugh, to roll around on the rumpled sheets, and revel in this new feeling of freedom and release. It would be gone too soon, and she didn't want to lose it.

From beyond their door, she could hear the sound of laughter floating up from the public room, along with the sound of instruments tuning up. A party!

She peeked up at Grant. His eyes were closed, but his hand moved lazily up and down her back, a lightly caressing touch that made her tremble.

"Do you hear that?" she whispered.

"Hear what?" he said. He swept her hair back from her shoulder and kissed her on its soft curve.

"The music, of course. I think they're having a party downstairs."

"I hope they enjoy it, then. Just as long as they don't carry on all night and keep me awake."

Caroline laughed and slapped him on the arm. "You sound like my father once did! He couldn't understand why my mother liked to have balls at Killinan so often. He just wanted to sit by the fire with his dogs, cleaning his guns and dreaming of the next day's hunting."

"Sounds very sensible to me. Why *did* she want to have balls so often?"

"Because—well, I'm not exactly sure," Caroline admitted. "To find husbands for my sisters and me, I suppose. I usually sat by the fire with my father, reading my books."

"You were very sensible, too."

"Yes. Whatever happened to me since then?" She knew very well what happened to her—Grant happened. He made her see that always being sensible meant missing out on so much in life. She did miss her family and her books and writing, but she didn't want it to be everything she had.

She wanted to make memories, lots of them, to store up for the day when Grant was gone and things were quiet again. She wanted to be able to take those memories out when she was alone by the fire and remember when she had an adventure. And remember him.

"Grant," she whispered in his ear.

"Yes, Caro?"

"Do you think they will be dancing downstairs?"

He wound her hair around his wrist. "Very probably."

"I think I'd like to dance, too."

He opened his eyes and looked at her. Somehow he had stayed cool and calm in their escape from

Muirin Inish, all their travels, and even LaPlace's reappearance—but the fact that she might want to dance seemed to surprise him. "But you said you never danced at parties in Dublin."

"I was younger then. And just because I'm not especially graceful at it, like my sisters, I enjoy a quadrille now and again."

"I doubt they're doing anything so organized as a quadrille down there."

"Even better. No one will notice that I don't really know the steps."

"Aren't you tired? We have to make an..."

"Early start tomorrow. I know." She sat up and leaned over him to softly kiss his lips. He still held on to her hair, keeping her close to him. "Just one little dance?"

He gave an exaggerated sigh. "Very well. One."

Caroline clapped her hands. "It will be such fun, Grant, you'll see! Once we're back in Dublin, it will all be stuffy waltzes at the assembly rooms again, and you'll be glad we did this."

He tugged her down for another kiss, harder and longer. "Or we could just stay here," he said. "And be... sensible."

It was terribly tempting. His hands moved up her back and over her shoulders, and his body was so warm and strong against hers. She could feel herself falling into the kiss.

"Later," she said. "First we dance."

He groaned and let her go. She clambered down from the bed and hurried over to the tub. The water was cold now, but she quickly washed her face and dressed in the white muslin gown Victorine gave her.

Being back in a dress again felt odd, the short, tight sleeves confining her arm movements and the silky chemise soft against her legs. But it felt good, too. It felt like a slight return to normalcy.

Especially when Grant sat up on the bed and watched her intently. She shook her hair over one shoulder and slowly drew her brush through the dark waves.

"Here, let me," he said. "You're making the tangles worse."

"Sorry," she said, handing him the brush. "I've been without my lady's maid for some time now."

"Well, you're lucky you have me then." He gently smoothed her hair along her back, his hands taking their time as they skimmed over her bare neck and shoulders. She barely felt the first stroke of the brush.

She had him now. His words echoed in her mind. Did she have him? Truly? She feared he had *her*. She was captured by him, his maddening secrecy and all.

She closed her eyes and felt the slide of the brush, the touch of his hand through her thin sleeve. "You're quite good at this," she murmured. "My maid pulls too hard."

"Practice, I suppose."

"Ah, yes." All those mistresses in his past. Surely they all had lovely, silken hair that never tangled or snarled. Somehow the moment's fragile magic seemed to dim just a bit. Those mistresses were still there in Dublin, beautiful hair and everything. Maybe once he saw them, he would miss his old life after all.

"Since I've neglected to cut my hair for years," he said, "I've had to learn to take care of it. I confess I had never fully appreciated the trouble you ladies went to before. I'll be a much more considerate lover in the future."

Caroline laughed ruefully. It was silly, really. Surely it was nothing to her if he did go back to his old life and his old ways. They didn't belong to each other, not really. Once they reached Dublin, and he fulfilled what he saw as his duty to see her home, they could part again. Just as he said they would.

Yet she liked the new Grant. She even liked his hard solemnity, his new awareness, his solitude. She liked his hair, too. She didn't want to lose him to the old, glittering Grant. Both Grants were beyond her, but when they did part, she wanted to imagine him still finding his own path through the darkness. Just as she had to find hers.

"I'm glad you appreciate our efforts at last," she said.

"Oh, I've come to appreciate many things about you, Caro," he said as he tied off the end of the neat braid he'd made while she daydreamed. He leaned close to the bare curve of her neck. He didn't kiss her but instead seemed to just breathe her in, as if he could smell her perfume, the very essence of her, and he wanted to memorize her. To make her part of him.

"I appreciate the way you tremble when I kiss you just... here," he said. His lips brushed lightly, enticingly, over the curve where her neck met her shoulder. "I appreciate this little mark right here." His fingertip brushed over the bluish birthmark below her shoulder blade, just above the edge of her dress. "It looks like a butterfly."

"When I was a child, my nanny tried to bleach it away with buttermilk and lemon juice." Caroline said shakily.

"I'm glad she didn't succeed." Grant traced the outline of the mark with the tip of his tongue.

Her breath caught in her throat. "And Eliza would say, if I'd been born a hundred years ago, it would have marked me as a witch."

"Now that I think makes sense." He pressed an open-mouthed kiss to her back, and she leaped off the bed.

Grant laughed and lay back amid the blankets, his arms folded behind his head. His bronze-brown hair spilled over the white sheets. "Are you sure you wouldn't rather stay here after all?" he said.

She wasn't sure at all. She heard the music from downstairs, a pounding rhythm full of wild freedom and merriment. She did still want to dance, yet she wanted to stay, too. She wanted him, every confusing, baffling, maddening bit of him. If there was any witchcraft here, it was all his.

She knelt by him on the bed and reached out to bury her fingers in his hair. It was like rough, raw silk to her touch, smelling of the clean Irish wind.

"You won't cut your hair when we get to Dublin, will you?" she said.

Grant gave a half-smile, that inscrutable crooked grin that made her heart pound all over again. "Won't you be ashamed to be seen with a wild Irish barbarian?"

Caroline shook her head. She ran her fingers to the ends of his hair and pressed her palms against his shoulders. They tightened under her touch, and she felt the leashed power of his body. "I like your hair. I suppose I just like wild Irishmen."

"Then I won't cut it, for you. Maybe I'll get myself a pair of leather braies and wander the streets wearing only that so everyone can see my tattoos. I'll shout Gaelic curses at all the passers-by, and carry you off to my hut over my shoulder. Then everyone can see just how barbaric I've become."

Caroline laughed at the image of him striding up opulent Henrietta Street, shirtless and leather-clad, swinging a broadsword. But she liked it, too; maybe too much.

"Even barbaric Irishmen know how to dance," she said. "And I think they're playing my favorite song."

Grant threw his arms wide in surrender. "Very well, one dance, just for you."

"Thank you." Caroline leaned down and kissed him. She slid away quickly as he reached for her, before he could entice her to stay. "Perhaps later we could find you some leather breeches?"

Grant laughed. "You like that, do you?"

Caroline didn't answer. She scooped his clothes off the floor and tossed them at his head. "What I like is a man who dances. Now hurry up, Sir Grant—the night is half gone."

"*And who are you, me pretty fair maid, and who are you, me honey? She answered me quite modestly—I am me mother's darling!*"

The party was in full force as Caroline and Grant came down the stairs hand-in-hand to the crowded public room. Nearly every seat was filled, and the long trestle tables were pushed to the walls to make room for the dancers. A long line of revelers spun and twirled down the space, seeming to follow no particular pattern of steps except their own inclinations.

Everyone seemed dressed in their best, the women with ribbons in their hair and the men in wool coats and embroidered, bright-colored waistcoats. Even the children had clean, shining little faces and spotless smocks. The air was warm and heavy with the smell of smoke, ale, clean wool, and the women's lavender perfume. Barmaids hurried past with platters of fried fish and potatoes, and pitchers of ale. The musicians played in the corner, a fiddle, pipes, and bodhran, filled with more enthusiasm than talent.

Caroline stood on the bottom step to take it all in. She clapped her hands to the tune, and went up on her tiptoes to study the crowd. Everyone seemed to be having a marvelous time, and it put her in a party mood, too.

Tomorrow they would have to leave again. She would have to ride that cursed horse, and they would have to keep a careful watch out for LaPlace's doppelganger. Surely she could have fun tonight? Just for a little while?

On the step beside her, Grant was watchful and unsmiling. Caroline linked her arms with his and said, "Is it some sort of holiday we've missed? Everyone seems so full of merriment."

"I don't know what's going on," he answered. He sounded suspicious, as usual.

"Well, I need some ale. Let's try to get a seat over there." There was a small space open on one of the benches by the wall, and Caroline claimed it while Grant went for the ale. The dancers swirled so close she felt their skirts brush her as they swept by, and she laughed. It had been far too long since she went to a real party like this, and far too long since she heard such music.

In fact, it was last Christmas, when she went to see Anna at Adair Court, and they held a ceilidh for all the workers and tenants. It was a wonderful holiday, with spiced wine, mistletoe, and music, just like this. Her little nephew Daniel perched on her feet as she danced him around the room, and Anna and Conlan kissed under the mistletoe as their people cheered for them.

Caroline suddenly missed her family with a painful longing.

"You look solemn all of a sudden," Grant said, returning from the bar and sliding onto the bench beside her. He handed her an overflowing mug of ale, so dark it looked like molasses. "Sorry you wanted to come here?"

"Not at all." Caroline clicked her pottery mug to his in a silent toast and took a deep drink of the potent brew. "I was just thinking it's been much too long since I was at such a party."

Grant studied the gathering over the rim of his cup. He looked solemn, too, and pensive. "I don't think I've ever been to such a party. It's very... interesting."

Never been to such a party? In Ireland? Caroline wanted to ask him how that could possibly be. It was hard to avoid dancing and music in their country; it seemed to be everywhere. But he appeared to be in a thoughtful mood, so she turned to the old man who sat on her other side. His little granddaughter sat beside him. singing the words to the song as he tapped along on the table.

The crowd here seemed different from the last inn. Mallorney Island was mostly fishermen, whereas these people appeared to be farmers and town merchants. They seemed to be rather prosperous ones, as well. Their faces were not as hardened or watchful, and they weren't as suspicious of strangers.

"Is it a holiday here?" she asked the old man. "I fear we've been traveling and have lost track of the days."

"Aye, haven't you heard, miss?" he said jovially. "The Peace of Amiens is over! England's at war with France again."

Caroline shook her head. She was saddened by the news, but not surprised. The Vicomte and Grant had both said the peace wouldn't last. She just hoped the old gentleman and his granddaughter would get home safely. "And that's cause for a holiday?"

He laughed. "Aye! It means the English will have to pay attention to the Frenchies again and leave us alone."

She wasn't so sure about that. The Dublin harbor had been rife with press gangs for months before the peace, men kidnapped to reinforce England's navy. It had caused much violence. But perhaps it was different here in this distant country town. Maybe they were not so troubled by politics and war. But that sounded like an impossible dream, a place untouched by strife.

"You're not from near here, are you, miss?" he asked.

Caroline took another long drink of her ale. It rather grew on her now, and her toes tingled with a fuzzy warmth. Was it the ale, or Grant pressed so close to her side?

"No, we're from the south," she said. "We're returning there now."

"Are you?" He gave her a look of keen interest. "You wouldn't have word of what is happening there, would you? It takes a while for news to travel here."

Caroline shook her head. "I fear I know as little as you. But I did hear..."

Grant suddenly took her mug from her hand and plunked it down on the table. "I thought you wanted to dance," he said.

"Why yes, but... "

He took her hand and pulled her out into the very midst of the dancers. They were jostled and pushed by everyone swirling around them, but Grant held her tightly by the waist and spun her around and around until she laughed dizzily. The slippers from Victorine were too small and pinched her feet, but Caroline hardly felt it at all. She was too happy to be near Grant.

"I thought you didn't want to dance!" she cried.

"It's better than getting in trouble by talking politics," he said close to her ear. "We need to get out of here with as little trouble as possible."

Caroline suddenly felt foolish. He was right of course; discretion was vital in days like this. Trouble waited around every corner. She shouldn't forget that for even a moment.

"I thought he might have some news," she said. "And he seems harmless."

"It's the ones who seem harmless you most need to beware. Surely you remember that?"

The wild pattern of the dance separated them, and she found herself whirling away as the song grew faster and faster. *"I am me mother's darling!"* She

AMANDA MCCABE

swung from one pair of arms to the next, laughing and laughing until her cheeks ached and the room turned blurry around her.

It was so glorious. She glimpsed Grant over the dancers' heads as someone spun her around in the air. He was laughing, too, his face alight with joy as he danced with an old lady in a lace cap.

It seemed he needed fun as well. Had she ever seen him laugh? It made him look so young, so care-free. It made his scars seem to vanish, and he looked like the lighthearted man he might have become, if his life was less bitter in the beginning.

Caroline laughed in sheer joy as she spun to the next partner. She had to make sure Grant danced more before they parted. And she had to dance, too, dance and dance until she fell down from it.

She twirled back into his arms at last, and he lifted her high to spin her around. The room turned hazy like a whirling kaleidoscope, all shards of color and ever-shifting patterns.

Grant slid her down to her feet along his body, and she pressed close to him in the crowd. He dipped her low and kissed her lips as they came up. She could feel his laughter in the kiss, and it was achingly sweet.

Suddenly their perfect moment was shattered by the sound of breaking glass. Someone shouted, and one of the barmaids screamed.

Caroline was pushed against Grant as the crowd shifted and stumbled. More glass broke, and everyone was running, though no one knew where to go. People tripped and fell, and shoved each other as they tried to get out of the way of they knew not what. The merriment turned to chaos in an instant.

230

"What's happening?" Caroline cried. Grant lifted her in his arms and held on to her as he elbowed his way through the crowd. "Can you see anything?"

Grant grimly shook his head. They reached the edge of the room to find that one man held another pinned to the bar. His beefy hands were wrapped around the man's neck as he banged his head on the wood. Shattered glass lay in glistening shards on the floor, and the maid was still screaming as the landlord battered the attacker's head ineffectually with a towel.

"That's enough!" the landlord shouted. "Break it up now, lads! Who's going to pay for all this?"

The man strangling the other held on as his victim kicked at him. His bald head was bright red.

"You sent for them, you bastard!" he yelled. "I know 'twas you, you brought the redcoats down on us. We barely got away without them knowing it was us."

"Redcoats?" Caroline gasped. "The army is here?"

The man on the bar managed to push back his attacker and twist his head away. "It weren't me! No one sent for 'em. They're just marching this way on their way to someplace else."

"Then how did they know? It had to have been you!" He lunged for the man again, with the landlord and the maid struggling to drag them apart.

The rest of the crowd seemed to have been a powder keg just waiting for one spark to go off. The energy of the dance turned to a fight, a chance to settle some old scores. Furniture crashed to the floor and splintered amid the shattered pottery.

Crying children were ushered hastily out the door, and Caroline wished she could go with them.

But the door was far across the room, and her path was blocked by a tangle of shrieking, kicking, punching humanity. Someone pushed past her and sent her twirling to the floor. She fell into a puddle of spilled beer and felt something sharp slice painfully into her leg.

"Ow!" she cried. She drew her skirt away and saw a shard of glass lodged in her calf, her stocking torn. She pulled it out, and blood rushed forward in a thin red stream.

Grant grabbed the man who had pushed her and shoved him roughly away, with a punch to his face for good measure. He knelt by Caroline, and for once his cool, expressionless mask was gone. He looked furious and violent, and scared for her. He gently touched her leg and leaned down to examine it.

"Are you badly hurt?" he demanded.

"No, I..." Suddenly, over his shoulder Caroline saw the man rise up again—with a chair held over his head, about to bring it down on Grant.

"Grant, watch out!" she screamed. She rolled away, pulling Grant with her, and they escaped injury just in time. The chair crashed to the floor in a jagged, splintered heap. The man was much larger than Grant, but Grant was lean and fit. And, Caroline remembered from Dublin, surprisingly good at brawling. He let out a great roar and tackled the man, sending them both crashing to the floor. Grant landed blow after blow while managing to dodge away from the other man's flailing fists. Until one lucky punch to the head sent Grant reeling back.

Caroline scrambled to her feet. She scarcely noticed the throbbing pain in her leg in the wild whirl of excitement. She scooped up a broken chair leg and tried to bash the man over the head. But he kept lurching away from her, and she couldn't get a clear blow in without danger of braining Grant instead.

Someone pushed her hard from behind, and she whirled around to strike out with her new weapon. It was the attacker from the bar, with his victim nowhere to be seen. She landed a fortunate strike with her chair leg, and he fell to the floor.

Only for a moment though. He stumbled to his feet with rage on his beet-red face.

"For fuck's sake, Caro, run!" Grant shouted. He had his own opponent on the floor with his knee in the man's back and a lock on his head. "Get out of here now!"

She didn't need to be urged twice. Still clutching the chair leg, she dashed toward the door, dodging around the combatants. The battle seemed to be waning as everyone grew tired. People were slumped against the walls, but a few fought furiously on.

At the door, she glanced back. Grant's attacker lay on the floor alone, holding his head and groaning. She didn't see Grant anywhere. Surely he would follow her soon. She ducked out the door and into the night.

The street was surprisingly quiet. A few people reeled down the walkway, but most of the houses and shops were dark and silent. It was as if everyone was hiding out. Even the moon hid behind a bank of clouds. The fresh breeze felt good on her warm face, but the pain in her leg washed back over her once she was relatively safe.

She sat down on a wooden barrel outside one of the closed shops and drew up her hem to examine the wound. The cut didn't look particularly deep, but it still bled. She kicked off her slipper and removed the ruined stocking to tie it around the cut as a makeshift bandage.

There were still shouts and crashes echoing from the inn, though not as loud now. Caroline wondered where Grant was. Surely he should be here now? Had he gotten into another fight? She thought of how he grappled with that man, as fierce as any street brawler in The Liberties of Dublin. She nearly laughed to think what people would say about the elegant, sophisticated Sir Grant Dunmore in such a state. But he had seen him fight that way before, with Conlan on the steps of the Parliament building before the Union vote. He was fierce, and crafty, too. How else would he have survived in his strange world all these years? Yet she still worried about him now. Where could he be?

She stood up to go back in the inn to find him, but then she heard a low moan. It was so soft that at first she thought she imagined it, until she heard it again.

She made her way along the street, searching the darkened doorways until she found the noise's source. It was the man she had seen being strangled at the bar. He sat leaning against the door, holding his head in his hands. Even in the shadows, she could see his clothes were torn and stained with blood.

"Are you all right?" she said gently. "Can I help you?" The man jumped at the sound of her voice, as if she had shouted at him menacingly. His hands fell away, and she saw he was terribly young, probably only about sixteen. Too young to have been the cause of such a battle.

But she had seen so many people, just as young, whose lives were torn apart by the Rebellion, herself included. She was only fifteen when the family had to flee from Killinan. And there would be more of the same if there was another uprising, which seemed likely if the army was on the march again. Even this place, which she had thought so peaceful and cozy, wasn't immune to trouble.

"It's quite all right," she said, as he shrank back against the door. "I won't hurt you. Please, let me help if I can."

"I have to get home," he said. He tried to sound defiant, but his voice was shaking.

"So do I," she murmured. But home felt so far away. "But you should bind up that cut on your brow first."

He slowly nodded, and Caroline knelt beside him in the doorway. She turned her back to remove her other stocking, the only bandage she had, and used it to dab at the wound. The man sat very still and tense under her care.

"You caused quite a riot in there," she said.

"It weren't me, miss," he muttered. "Tom started it."

"Was Tom the man who had you pinned to the bar?"

"You saw that, miss?"

"Yes, I saw that. Right before someone knocked me down."

Guilt spasmed across his face. "I'm sorry."

"Not your fault. Not entirely, anyway." Caroline stopped the flow of blood and bound the stocking around his head as a bandage. Not very dignified, but it would have to do. "What was Tom angry about?"

"He's my brother."

235

"Your brother?" Caroline cried. She was suddenly very glad she had only sisters.

"He thought I told the English about... about what I found. That I sent them this way and that's why they were on the march toward Kilmarin. I never would!"

What exactly had he found? Caroline felt a little tremor of fear, all too familiar now. It seemed matters were progressing at a very rapid pace. They were even reaching this corner of the country. "I've seen no redcoats."

"Tom saw them at Kilmarin, which is only a few miles down the road. He said they were asking questions and are sure to come this way. But it weren't me that told them! You have to believe me, miss. Even if I'd known what Tom and his friends were up to all this time, I never would have told."

"I believe you," she said reassuringly. But she feared it was not her belief he needed. And what were Tom and his friends "up to"?

She heard a noise on the street, and she peeked beyond the doorway to see more people tumbling out of the inn. The landlord shouted after them. They ran off in the opposite direction of Caroline's hiding place, with a group of scantily clad women of the night laughing after them from their street corner. But she knew more people would come this way soon enough, including Tom.

"Can you walk now?" she said. "Do you think you can make it home? The sooner you can get there the better, I think." If he could just avoid his brother.

"I can walk, miss." With her help, he stood and slowly made his way back to the street. His bandage stood out stark white in the night. "Will you be all right, miss?" be asked.

"Oh, yes. I just need to find my-my husband. We were separated in the confusion."

"Thank you so much, miss. You've been an angel. Be careful on your journey." And then he stumbled away down the street.

Caroline leaned back against the wall, suddenly exhausted. An angel—that was what their tenants at Killinan used to call her mother, who would nurse them and help them whenever she could, never losing her cool, calm ways. Caroline wasn't like that. Dabbing at a little blood wasn't the work of an angel, and she feared the boy was in far more trouble than she could help. They all were.

Her leg ached, so she sat back down in the doorway.

That was where Grant found her a few minutes later. "Caro, there you are," he said as he knelt beside her. "I was so worried."

"So was I." She gently took his face between her hands and examined him closely. He looked battered but hardly broken. She kissed his brow. "Your hand-someness is quite ruined, I fear."

He laughed. "That happened a long time ago. Come along, let's get you back to our room so we can see to your leg properly."

"Is the fight over then?"

"All but the landlord's fury that his grand party was ruined." Grant scooped her up in his arms and carried her back toward the inn. She rested her head on his shoulder, deeply grateful for his strength. "He declares nothing like this has ever happened in such a respectable town before, and he doesn't know what's gotten into people."

"I think I might know," Caroline whispered.

Grant looked at her sharply. "What do you mean?"

"I happened to meet with that poor boy who was beaten on the bar," she said. "But I can't tell you what he said until we are quite alone..."

CHAPTER
TWENTY-FOUR

G rant paced the length of their small room and back again. "You are quite sure that's what he said? The redcoats are at Kilmarin and headed this way?"

Caroline nodded. She sat perched on the edge of the bed, her skirt drawn up to uncover the cut on her leg. The sight of it filled him with fury all over again —fury with the man who pushed her, and even greater fury at himself. He had dragged her into this.

"The boy had a head wound, but he seemed lucid enough," she said. "He didn't say what it was he had found, though, that would make such trouble."

Grant feared he knew what it was, or at least he suspected. It was a rebel arms cache. He knelt down beside Caroline and reached for the basin of water and a cloth. The cut had stopped bleeding but was crusted over and bruised. The wound stood out starkly against her pale skin.

"You won't be able to ride tomorrow," he said.

"Of course I will. I barely feel it now." She leaned toward him, her brown eyes solemn. "You know what it is, don't you?"

239

He didn't look up from his ministrations. "Know what what is?"

Caroline gave a frustrated sigh. "What that poor boy is so afraid of, of course."

Grant shook his head. He reached for a strip of linen and wound it around her leg. "We need to be away from here as soon as possible."

"And in the opposite direction of Kilmarin? I don't need to be protected, you know."

"Oh, yes. That's quite obvious." Grant gently kissed her leg just above the wound. He held on to her as if something terrible would happen if he let her go, just as she feared what might happen to him if he wasn't with her any longer. He could see that fear in her eyes whenever she looked at him.

"Oh, Caro," he said. "You were hurt because you tried to come to my aid, just like in that blasted dungeon."

Caroline shrugged. "I save you, you save me. It seems a good bargain. It's worked for us so far, hasn't it? We're still here."

"Our good fortune won't last forever." Grant wrapped his arms around her legs and rested his head on her lap. He had never felt such a longing before. No one had ever breached the walls built around his heart like this, and he hated it.

Startled, Caroline laid her hand on his hair. "We're each other's good luck, Grant. I know that together we'll reach Dublin. I've never had anyone as strong as you to protect me before."

"And I've never had anyone to protect me at all," he said.

"What do you mean?"

He sat beside her on the bed and held her hand in

his. He stared down at their entwined fingers. "I don't really know how to explain it. You've always had your family, and even in a clannish country like ours, the Blacknalls are famous for sticking together. But I've always relied only on myself. I know no one will help me in life, so I've always helped myself." He laughed. "No one ever waded into a brawl to help me before. My Babd."

He kissed her hand and pressed it to his cheek, and couldn't say anything else. All he could do was hold her.

GRANT TRIED TO LAUGH, TO SOUND CARELESS ABOUT IT ALL, about the deepest secrets of his heart. But Caroline felt a sharp tug that was surely her heart breaking. Her sisters often drove her mad, but she had spent her life knowing she could always rely on them. They were hers and she was theirs, no matter what distance was between them.

But Grant had lived his life alone. He had to take care of his shattered mother, whose family had turned their backs on them both, and fight alone for his place in the world. Her life was built on warmth and acceptance, his on cold solitude and a sadness that hardened into bitter anger.

Yet that was not who he was, not really. She had glimpsed his heart on this journey, she had seen how he had changed, and she knew he did care about people. He cared about Ireland and his place in it.

But still he was alone. If only he would let her in.

"Oh, Grant," she whispered. "I would wade into a

AMANDA MCCABE

hundred brawls to help you. You aren't alone on this journey." He raised her hand to his lips and kissed it lingeringly.

She pressed her palm to his cheek, cradling it in an achingly tender gesture. "And I will protect you with my dying breath. I swear it to you, Caroline."

Tears prickled at her eyes. Caroline blinked hard to try to dash them away, but a few fell anyway, splashing on their hands. "Please, Grant, don't talk about dying! I couldn't bear it."

"My course is set," he said. "But yours is not. Your life can be anything you choose to make it, beautiful Caroline, and you deserve to have all you desire. And I will do everything in my power to make it so for you."

What she wanted right now, what she wanted more than she had ever wanted anything before, was him. As she looked into his eyes, that cool, careful mask he always wore was finally gone, and she saw the torment he had held inside for so long.

She went up on her knees on the bed beside him and held his face between her hands. She carefully traced his features with her fingertips, the line of his nose, his brows, those elegant cheekbones, his sensual lips. He closed his eyes as if to shut her out from that precious glimpse of his heart. He tried to draw away from her, but she wouldn't let him go. She was desperate to hold on to him while she could.

She kissed his closed eyes and the furrow above his nose. He would protect her to the last moment of his life, but she could tell he was struggling to stay under her touch, to give her that small control.

"Caroline," he groaned. "I've never known anyone like you."

"Then we're quite the pair," she said. "I've never known anyone even remotely like you, either."

She softly kissed his lips, but when he reached for her to pull her closer, she slid away. She slowly unlaced his torn shirt and took it off him, leaving his chest bare and golden-smooth in the candlelight Then she climbed down from the bed to kneel at his feet, as he had done when he bandaged her leg. He watched her with caution in his dark eyes.

She pulled off his boots, encrusted with dried ale and dust, and tossed them aside. She unfastened his breeches, also dirty from the fight, and peeled them down over his strongly muscled thighs and calves, roughened with a dusting of bronze hair. At last he sat before her magnificently naked.

She traced the tense, corded strength of his legs with her palms. Slowly, ever so slowly, he relaxed under her touch, and her mouth followed her hands over his thigh, the sharp plane of his hip.

She found that tracery of scars on his torso and etched its texture with the tip of her tongue. How well she knew his taste now. How she craved it. She knew his body, how it felt and smelled, how it fit with hers. How wondrous it made her feel. But she wanted to know his mind and heart, too. All of him. Everything was different, she was different because of him.

Through that white-hot blaze of desire, she felt him take off her gown and chemise even as he continued their desperate kiss. The whole universe was only a humid blur of their mingled breath and lips, their sighs and incoherent whispers.

His mouth slid away from hers, and her cries of protest turned to a moan of pleasure as he took her aching nipple deep into his mouth. She threaded her fingers through his hair and held him against her.

But he moved away from her and kissed the curve of her waist, the flare of her hip. He gently urged her to lie back on the bed and spread her legs wider as he knelt between them.

As Caroline watched him, trying to breathe, he lifted her legs over his shoulders, parted her damp womanhood with his fingers, and kissed her just there.

A lightning bolt of pure, hot pleasure shot through her, and she cried out "Grant!"

"Shh, Caroline," he muttered. "Just let me. I have to taste you."

She closed her eyes tightly and let him do what he would, and it was delicious. She had never felt anything like it before, the wet heat of it, the pleasure that built and built until she would scream with it! Grant was—oh, he was so good at that.

She bit her lip to keep a scream from escaping as her climax exploded. Through the cloud of glittering sensation, she felt his body slide up hers, felt his open-mouthed kiss on her breast, her neck. And she needed him all over again. She spread her legs wider as he thrust into her, deep and hungry. She arched up to meet him, their movements as one now. He kissed her mouth, catching her cries and half-spoken words of need. He tasted of—of her, and of his own need that met hers and drove it higher and higher. She dug her nails into his shoulders and felt the heave and drive of his body as he thrust into hers faster and faster. Behind her eyes, she saw only a silvery, magical sun, hot and sparkling as her release built up again, deep inside her.

"Caroline!" Grant shouted, and his back arched as be found his own release. In that instant, they were as one.

He was hers, and she—oh, God help her—she was his.

She fell back to the mattress, her entire body feeling so heavy and weak. She wrapped her legs around his hips as he collapsed against her shoulder.

She feared she would cry with the overwhelming emotion of it all. She kissed his shoulder and held on to him to keep from falling.

GRANT WOUND CAROLINE'S LONG, TANGLED HAIR AROUND his wrist, watching how the fading candlelight brought out the gold, shining threads among the brown. It was so beautiful, just as every part of her was. Even that stubborn, kind, tenacious heart, that refused to let go of its hold on him.

She sighed in her sleep and burrowed closer to him. He would have to wake her soon so they could pack their meager belongings and be on their way. But he couldn't do it quite yet. She looked so young and free as she slept, free of all the trouble he had brought into her life.

When they had danced tonight, before the fight broke out, she had laughed with such glorious abandon. She made him laugh, too, and he could just be in that one sweet moment of happiness with her. Moments of happiness in his life were so few and far between, he hardly recognized it for what it was until it was nearly gone. Holding her in his arms, hearing her laughter—yes, it was happiness. As fleeting as a rainbow after a storm.

He wanted her to laugh again, because he sensed that her moments of pure, exhilarating joy in life were just as few as his. He wanted to give her a lifetime of only such moments, but that was one thing beyond his power.

He feared he could only give her happiness by letting her go.

He kissed her bare shoulder, and she sighed as she snuggled closer to him. He carefully slid away from her and retrieved his breeches from the floor. As he dressed, his gaze caught on their travel bags, and he remembered how she was reading *The Chronicle* earlier. He remembered the way her eyes glowed as she examined the pages. He took it from the bag and gently opened the soft, worn cover. The old vellum pages fell open to the story Caroline was reading—the tale of the dragon of Adaislan. It would be that one. That story had turned his life upside down, once he realized what it was really about. But he wouldn't let it hurt Caroline and her family, too.

"Grant," he heard her murmur. He turned to see her sitting up in bed, blinking sleepily.

"I'm here," he said. He went back to sit beside her on the bed.

"Is it morning? Do we need to depart?"

"Not quite yet. We have a little time."

She leaned against his shoulder and reached out to touch the book he held in his hand. "You were reading *The Chronicle*?"

"The tale of the dragon of Adaislan. I think you were reading it in Killorgin?"

"Yes," she said carefully, and he knew that she had grasped the meaning of the story as well.

"Then you can see why I let no one read this," he said. "Especially this tale."

"It's only a story," Caroline said. "A myth."

He gave her a wry smile. "Do you believe that, my dear? You, who have made a study of the myths and history of Ireland and how they tie together? Adaislan is Adair, and those are the lands ruled by queens. Passed from mother to daughter, even if it must be through a son—and my mother was the only female of her generation."

"If that old tradition had stood, then you would hold the lands for your own daughter," she said, and he knew that she understood why he hid that book. "In the old times, such things did happen. There were lands ruled by women by ancient traditions. But why..."

"Because I don't want Conlan to know about this tale, of course. Adair is his."

"Yes, and even if the old tradition is true, it wouldn't stand in a modern court."

"Since when does my cousin care about modern English courts? He cares about Irish law, whether it is legal now or not. He would search out more old records and tales, until he decided the land was not his by Irish rule."

"And that is why you wanted *The Chronicle* before?" she said. "To prove that Adair should be yours according to the old ways?"

"Maybe once I had just such a wild thought. But now I hold on to it just to keep the secret. And now it's your secret, too. My cousin must never know of this."

Caroline knelt beside him, and he could sense her astonishment. That he, who had once wanted nothing more than to snatch his cousin's lands and destroy him, held on to this secret astonished him as well. But he was surprised by her tears as she looked up at him.

"You *have* changed, Grant," she whispered. "You want to protect your family now, don't you?"

"Yes," he said simply. "And I must ask you to do the same."

"Of course I will say nothing of this story," she answered. "I would not want to hurt my sister."

He took her hand and raised it to his lips for a kiss that felt like a binding vow between them. It was one more secret they alone held. "Then I know it is safe in your hands, Caroline." And it always would be—even if he was gone.

CHAPTER
TWENTY-FIVE

"You should eat something," Grant said, nudging a plate of fish and bread across the table to Caroline. The inn's public room was deserted that morning, so quiet and well-swept that the previous night's melee might never have happened. "We'll have to ride far if we're to make the next town by evening."

Caroline nodded and nibbled at a crust, but she wasn't really hungry. She was still thinking over and over again about the dragon of Adaislan, and the secret Grant had been keeping for so long, all to protect Conlan and his family. She had known his time on Muirin Inish changed him, but this seemed to show just how very much. The question was—what was she to do with this knowledge?

The morning sun slanted from the windows across Grant's scarred, austere face. He seemed far too calm and quiet today. He said nothing about the dragon and Adaislan, and she knew he would not. They had to be onto the next stage of their journey, whatever that would be.

"Sir, your horses are ready," the stable lad said from the door.

Grant nodded and said to Caroline, "Shall we, then?"

"Yes, of course," she answered. She thought of the soreness from the saddle that awaited her and groaned. "I suppose we must."

Grant laughed and said, "We'll go slowly at first. If you want to hire a carriage..."

"No," she said "That will only slow us down. We need to get to Dublin soon, yes?"

"Yes, we do."

But she didn't find out just how fast they needed to get there until they made their way out to the stable yard. Three of the grooms were gathered in the corner, huddled over a news sheet and muttering together. At the sight of Grant and Caroline, they quickly dispersed to their tasks. So quickly, one of them dropped the sheet, and before he could retrieve it, Grant caught it up. The groom scurried away.

As Grant read it, Caroline could see a frown crease his brow. His eyes darkened, and she peered over his shoulder to read the broadsheet.

The words were smudged and blurry, as if hastily printed, but she could make out some of it. There was news from Dublin, a tale of an explosion at a house in Patrick Street that had the Castle government out in full force. A rebel explosion?

"What does this mean?" she whispered.

Grant crumpled the paper and stuffed it in his coat pocket. "We need to be on our way now," he said. "We can't talk here." He lifted her into her saddle, and they didn't speak again until they were well clear of anyone who could overhear.

"What's the meaning of this news?" Caroline asked, as they left the outskirts of the town behind. "What's really happening in Dublin?"

Were Anna and her family safe? Caroline felt a terrible fear for them, her sister and her darling niece and nephew. Conlan was the best protector they could have in the city, but if there was another rebellion...

"I know only what you do, Caroline," Grant said solemnly. "We should try to make it to Hakley Hall before evening. It's the nearest estate, and perhaps someone there has more news."

Caroline knew the Hakleys; they had once been friends of her parents. Sir Thomas Hakley was a Member of Parliament when it sat in Dublin before the Union. If they were at home, they might have news from Dublin.

And Caroline sensed Grant would tell her nothing more right now. His jaw was set in that hard line.

"I'll race you to that hill on the horizon," she said. "My equestrian skills seem to be growing by the hour."

"And your confidence, too," he answered. "Very well, last one there owes a shilling."

Caroline laughed and urged her horse into a run. This mount was faster than the first one, and eager to run. She felt surer in the saddle as well, and the wind against her face felt delicious and cool.

She felt the pounding of the horse's hooves on the ground as they galloped up the hill. She could hear Grant close behind her, gaining on her, and she urged the horse even faster. It was as if they could outrun their troubles and be free.

Yet that glorious freedom was over much too

quickly. They reached the top of the hill, and Caroline reined her horse in, with Grant barely inches behind her.

"A close-run race!" she cried. "But I think you owe me a shilling."

Grant laughed; his head thrown back. The sun gleamed on his hair, turning it to the bronze of an ancient metal. "Best coin I ever spent"

Caroline had to catch her breath, both from the fast run and from the glorious sight of Grant actually laughing. She shielded her eyes with her hand and studied the landscape around them. It was wondrously beautiful, with rolling hills of velvety dark-green, empty except for a few stray sheep and a crooked pattern of gray stone walls. The sky arching overhead was the palest of blues, dotted with puffs of white clouds so low they cast shadows on the ground.

The scene was everything she loved about Ireland, the vivid, rugged beauty of the land, so green and peaceful. It seemed to whisper to her of all it had seen, the brave people who lived their lives there, who loved and laughed and died—and who cherished the land as she did now.

There were violent battles here once, in the days of the Irish kings and their vassals, but all was quiet now. The land was healed over, silent. But for how long?

Caroline brushed her hand over her eyes to hide the sudden prickle of tears. On the crest of the next hill, she glimpsed the stony ruins of an old watch-tower above the tops of a thick forest in the valley. Its blank, empty windows seemed to stare back at her in silent, resigned observation.

"Where do we go from here, Grant?" she said.

"The next town is Ballylynan," he answered. "We could be there by nightfall, if you don't wish to top at Hakley Hall."

"No, I don't mean where on this journey. I mean..."

But what did she mean? She wasn't even sure herself. Where did they go once they were in Dublin and no longer had to stay together? Where did they go if there was a battle?

She smiled at him. Those were questions for another day, a day when they could no longer be avoided. "I'll race you to that tower. That will give you a chance to win back your shilling."

He grinned at her, and she suddenly wished every moment could be just like this. The two of them together, laughing under the endless Irish sky. "I'll take that wager," he said, and they were off again.

In the valley between the two hills was a thick stand of trees, silvery ash and stout oaks that seemed to tower over the horses as if they had been growing there for decades. Their thick branches blotted out the sky and cast wavering black shadows on the carpet of grass.

Caroline's horse leaped over a small stream and pounded along the path. The wind rustled in the leaves over her head, and it felt like she was caught in a fairy-tale wood. Maybe there were fairies and wood sylphs peering out at her as she dashed past.

Grant was right at her side as they burst from the trees and into the sunlight again. The tower cast its shadows above them, like the looming past. Caroline spurred her horse to get ahead of him.

Suddenly there was a sharp cracking noise, and she smelled the metallic tang of gunpowder in the air. Someone was shooting at them from the trees!

Her horse reared up in alarm, and she held tightly to the reins to keep from tumbling to the ground. All around her was a blur of confusion, the sky reeling over her head, the scream of horses. There was one more shot, then—nothing.

Caroline struggled to get her horse to stand steady on the ground. She urged it to a measure of cover behind a wall and patted gently at its neck, murmuring soft, incoherent words until it was still. But she could feel it shaking just as she was.

She sat up tense and alert in the saddle, listening for any hint of more shots or any movement at all. She couldn't hear anything. Even the birds had fallen silent.

She twisted around to find Grant. Her blood rushed so loudly in her ears that she could hear nothing else. "Grant, I think..." she said.

But his saddle was empty.

Icy fear crept over her skin, and the bright day suddenly took on the hazy tinge of a dream. Numb, she slid down from her horse and glanced around frantically. She didn't even think about the shooter or if he was still there. She could only think about Grant. He lay on the ground beside his trembling, neighing horse, face down in the grass.

"Grant," she said. She thought she screamed, a wail of anguish, but it came out a strangled whisper.

She ran to him and fell down on her knees beside him. She could not lose him. She had only just found him.

Shaking, she managed to strip off her gloves and reach out to touch him. His shoulders suddenly heaved on a breath, and she could have cried with utter relief.

"Grant," she said with a sob. "Grant, say something."

He rolled over onto his back and glared up at her. "You damn fool woman, run!"

Caroline choked with terrified laughter. He was alive and cursing. Surely that was a good sign. "I couldn't leave you," she said. "Besides, I think whoever it was is gone now."

Then she saw the blood on his shoulder. His coat was torn and stained crimson. "You're hurt!"

"It's nothing," he answered through gritted teeth.

"Of course it's not nothing, you stubborn man! You've been shot."

"It's just a graze, Caro. And I am not going to sit here and be shot at again. I'm certainly not letting you stay, no matter what your own foolish notions. Help me up."

"I'm not sure you should move," Caroline protested. He pushed himself to a sitting position, his face white and taut with the effort. She quickly slid her arm around his waist and helped him to his feet. He actually leaned on her, a sure sign it was more than a "graze."

She peered over his shoulder and could see no blood on his back. "Is the bullet still in you?" she asked. She remembered the night during the Rebellion when Eliza and their mother had to dig a bullet out of Will. The thought made her stomach lurch, but surely she could do the same if she had to.

"It never went in," he growled. "See. It's there on the ground."

Caroline looked down and caught a gleam among the flattened grass. Yet the shoulder still oozed blood. "It doesn't look good. It should be cleaned. Maybe if we went back to the stream..."

"And run right back into the shooter's arms? It's bad enough we're standing here."

Caroline bit her lip. "Of course not. Yet surely they're gone or they would have tried again?"

"Maybe they think they've accomplished their goal of getting us out of the way, or scaring us. We can go on to Hakley Hall. It's less than an hour's ride."

"You shouldn't be riding like this," she said. He started to struggle out of his coat, and she quickly helped him slide it down his arms. He grimaced as she concocted a sling and bound his arm up with it. Then he wasted not a moment in seizing the dragging reins of his horse and pulling himself up into the saddle.

He gave her a tight smile. "We don't have a choice, Caro my dear. Now, are you going to ride your own horse, or do I have to drag you off across my saddle? I personally would vote for the saddle."

"Stubborn man!" Caroline cried. He never would listen to her. But at least he was still there to infuriate her. For that one terrible moment, she had been so sure she had lost him.

And it frightened her how terrible that prospect had seemed, the bleak vista of years with no Grant in them.

She retrieved her own horse from behind the boulder and clambered into the saddle. He spurred his horse into a gallop, even though he cradled his arm tightly against him. Her wonderfully strong, delightfully stubborn, alive man. But could he stay alive to reach Dublin?

She would just have to make sure of it. No matter what she had to do.

CHAPTER
TWENTY-SIX

"I save you, you save me, has become a terrible habit of ours," Grant said. He watched Caroline as she leaned over a pot of water set to boil on the fire. She looked so achingly beautiful, her hair loose down her back in a river of dark waves and curls, her slender body in the thin shirt outlined by the flames.

Beautiful, strong—and yet so fragile.

She smiled at him over her shoulder. "It's better than the alternative, I think."

"Better than you safely at home and me with my just fate?"

"Better than me dead in a brawl and you dead in a field. Better for us to be here in this gamekeeper's cottage, together." She came to him and leaned over his chair with her hands braced on the wooden arms. "I was frightened there for a moment."

"Just deserts, *gaolach*," he said. "I've been frightened for many moments ever since you washed up half-dead on my beach."

"You see? I save you; you save me—it works well

for us." She took his face gently in her hands and stared down at him with wide eyes.

Grant could look into her eyes forever, could drown in them and be happy for such a demise. How had he come to this? He had lived his life only for himself for so long and had thought it the only way to exist.

Now he cared more for another person than he ever had for himself. No one but Caroline had ever slid behind his careful defenses like that. No bullet could be more frightening. He had to steel his heart again toward those soft eyes and concentrate only on his immediate goal—get her to Dublin, deliver her to her family, and see to his own business.

But that resolve was hard to keep when she kissed him gently on the lips. "Just don't scare me like that again," she whispered. "Please."

"I'll try not to."

"Not good enough."

Grant reached up to touch her cheek. Their days outdoors had tinged her skin pale gold with the sun, and the freckles across her nose stood out in amber relief. Loose, soft tendrils of her brown hair curled around her face.

She was the most beautiful thing he had ever seen, and her eyes were full of questions as she looked at him. But he could promise her nothing. Not yet, and maybe never.

He traced the curve of her lower lip, the tiny dimple in her chin, and felt her gasp. "I'm afraid it has to be good enough, Caro, my dear. It's all I have right now."

She studied his face carefully for a long, silent moment. "You do drive me mad, Grant Dunmore."

259

"Believe me, Caroline Blacknall, the feeling is entirely mutual."

She spun away from him to take the water off the fire. As it cooled, she set about tearing up a pile of old sheets she found in a cupboard.

"I'm sorry no one was home at Hakley Hall," she said.

"I'm not. This old cottage suits me well. I think I've become so accustomed to rougher accommodations that I wouldn't know how to behave in a fine house." Especially a fine house where they were bound to ask questions.

Caroline laughed. "I wager you would remember soon enough. But I was hoping they could give us news of what is happening in Dublin."

"I'm sure it's quiet enough. We're near enough now that we would have heard word if there was a rebellion in full force."

"I worry about my family," Caroline said. "Even before I left, there was unrest and strife. Press gangs roving the docks, riots, British ships trapped in ports because there aren't enough men to sail them. Even with the war with France, the troops in their barracks have been increased. If they're preparing for an uprising..."

"With luck, they know nothing of it yet."

"That's not likely, is it? They always have their informers." She turned back to him and stripped off his torn shirt to examine the makeshift bandage. "And the United Irish leaders are not always the most discreet, are they?"

"Perhaps they learned from their mistakes in ninety-eight."

"Do you think so?" She unwound the bandage

and carefully examined the scratch the bullet left behind. She squinted a bit, still somewhat nearsighted without her long-lost spectacles. "Someone knew enough to shoot at you."

"I thought we agreed it must be an errant poacher," Grant said. He gritted his teeth as she prodded at the reddened wound. "I doubt it was some English Orangeman hiding in the woods, just waiting for an Irishman to happen by."

"But we don't really know who it was, or what they were waiting for. It could have been anyone. It could have been..."

"Captain LaPlace?"

Caroline grimly shook her head. She rubbed a cake of harsh lye soap she also found in the cupboard over the wet cloth and pressed it to his shoulder.

"Damn it, Caroline!" he shouted. It stung like the devil. "Are you trying to kill me yourself?"

"With lye soap and hot water? I may be only a quiet scholar, but I'm sure I could come up with a more efficient way to kill you than this." She washed the wound gently, with her other hand pressed to his shoulder to hold him still. "And I don't know that the man I saw in town was LaPlace. I was tired. I probably imagined it."

"Whoever it was, we need to get to Dublin quickly. And then you should go stay with your sister until things are quiet again."

She glanced at him from under her lashes. Her gentle ministrations didn't falter, but he thought she pressed a bit harder than necessary with the cloth.

"Why is that? Kildare was a dangerous place in ninety-eight, and there are still plenty of people there with secret Green tendencies," she said.

"And many of the rebels who escaped there have taken refuge in Dublin's crowded streets. The two factions have been living cheek by jowl all these years. It's a powder keg just waiting for a stray spark."

"So Dublin is their planned center?" Caroline asked.

"I don't know yet. That's why I have to get there fast."

"To meet with—who?"

"That's not important," Grant said. Caroline knew a lot now, more than she should. But she didn't yet know whom he was really working with, and she didn't need to know. She probably wouldn't believe it anyway. "What's important is that you not stay in the city any longer than necessary. You need to be well away before anything happens. I would tell you to take a ship to England, but I know you wouldn't do that. The next best thing is your family's protection."

"If Dublin does rise, the surrounding counties are sure to follow. Kildare, Wicklow, Wexford, Queen's—there's more than enough discontent there still." She probed at his wound. "I don't think it needs stitches."

"You should stay with your sister. If there's a fight, you'd be safe with her."

She looked at him, her eyes sharp. "With Anna? Is she mixed up in all this?"

"How should I know? Your sister is hardly likely to confide in me, of all people. But she and her husband have influence with their people. Adair Court is its own little kingdom. No one would dare attack it, not the rebels or the army."

Caroline nodded. She dabbed a sticky concoction of honey on his shoulder and wound a clean bandage around it before she answered. "You are eager to see me away."

He reached out and caught her around the waist. He drew her between his legs and held on to her. "I only want you to be safe. I've put you through enough already."

She laid her hands gently on his shoulders and smiled down at him. "I've brought it all on myself, Grant. You didn't ask me to come to Muirin Inish, I went of my own free will. And I wouldn't have wanted to miss this journey."

He gave a humorless laugh. "You enjoy being caught in brawls and shot at, do you?"

She laughed, too. "Maybe *enjoy* is not the right word. But it's been terribly exciting, and I would have missed out on it all if I'd stayed at home. Maybe I'll write a novel about it one day."

"I would definitely read it if you did."

She gently smoothed his hair back from his face, twining her fingers in the wind-tangled strands. "And I've learned so much. About Ireland, the real Ireland, not just the one in my history books. And about myself, and about..."

"About what?"

"You, of course. You are entirely unexpected, Grant. Every time I think I know more about you, you change."

"That is my goal, Caroline. To keep you baffled."

"You're doing an astounding job with that."

He leaned toward her and kissed a long lock of hair that lay over her shoulder. "Could you bring *The Chronicle* to me from my bag, my dear?"

She gave a puzzled frown, but she nodded. "Of

course." She fetched the volume from its place at the bottom of the bag and placed it carefully in his hands.

Grant drew back the wrappings and stared down at its soft, green cover. The dragon's emerald eye glittered in the firelight as if it were alive. How obsessed he had been with this book for so long. How it had driven him, first to possess it and control its secrets, to use it to prove his place in the world. Then he had tried to hide those secrets away. It had almost destroyed him. But it had never really been his.

He handed it to Caroline, pressing it into her hand and closing her fingers around it.

"It's yours now," he said. "You must keep it safe."

Her brow furrowed as she stared down at the book. "I don't understand. You want me to look after it until things are quiet? Of course I will, but..."

"No. I mean it is yours entirely now. Study it, write about it, lock it away, whatever you like," he said. "But I know you'll keep the secret of the dragon, for your sister and her children."

"Grant, no." Her gaze lifted from the book to meet his. Her brown eyes glittered with unshed tears, like dark stars. "I can't keep it. It belongs to you."

He shook his head. "It never belonged to me. You are its true guardian. Will you look after it now?"

She nodded silently. "I will always keep it safe. One day I will give it to Lina, and I will teach her to do the same. I promise."

"Then it's done." Grant slumped back in his chair. His shoulder throbbed under the clean bandages, and he felt very tired. *The Chronicle* had been his treasure, his curse for so long, and now it was gone. Caroline was really its true guardian, and she would be a far better one than he ever was.

Now he just bad to persuade her to take the book —and stay far away from the trouble that was coming to their land.

CAROLINE CAREFULLY TUCKED THE BLANKETS AROUND Grant where he lay on the straw mattress up on the cottage's sleeping platform. His eyes were closed, his face grayish with pain, but he didn't seem to be asleep. His shoulders were tense under the bedclothes, his hands curled into fists. She wished she had some feverfew, which her mother used to mix into wine to help her patients sleep. But even though the deserted cottage was comfortable enough, it lacked such provisions.

She lay down beside him and stared up at the darkened ceiling beams. She also ached with tiredness, but her mind raced too fast to let sleep in.

Grant had given her *The Chronicle*. The book he had coveted and hidden and protected for so long— he had placed it into her hands forever.

She had told him he was a puzzle, that whenever she thought she knew him, he changed on her. He had revealed one more facet of his soul. Who was the real Grant? What did he truly desire and really work for?

Giving her the book seemed to show the old, selfish Grant was truly no more. He had learned from the hard lessons of his youth, and sought a new path. But what was that path, and how could she be a part of it?

How could they set the past aside once and for

all? She felt his hand touch hers, the soft brush of his fingers over hers. "You need to sleep," he said.

She turned her head on the pillow to look at him. His eyes were still shut, the skin taut over his cheekbones as if be held back all the pain. "So do you. I was not the one who got shot today."

"I'll sleep later, once we reach Dublin."

Caroline doubted that, considering the terrible possibilities of what might wait in the city. If only she could keep him right here, in this little cottage, for days and weeks. He could rest, drink healing possets, put up his feet by the fire, and tell her everything she longed to know. He could recover fully then.

But she knew he would never stay here, not for a moment longer than they had to. He was set on his course. They only had tonight, alone together in this quiet place, the wind singing down the chimney and the fire dying down in the grate. One night to learn all she could before he slipped away from her again.

She remembered his words, telling her she should go away with her sister to the countryside, that Anna could keep her safe. Such concern for her sister, the woman he once planned to marry. Did he still think of her and see her as a part of that glittering life he lost? Such a thought had dwelled in the back of her mind for years.

"There is one thing I have wondered," she said.

He didn't open his eyes, but a half-smile touched his lips. "Only one, Caro? I'm quite astonished."

She whispered into his ear. "Were you in love with Anna when you were paying court to her?"

That question did make him open his eyes and look at her. "My dear, I didn't even know your sister.

Not really. So how could I have been in love with her?"

"You wanted to marry her. There must have been a reason," Caroline persisted. She had wondered this for a long time, ever since she once sat on the edges of ballrooms and watched him dance with Anna, saw the flowers he had sent, and saw the fury that exploded when she refused him for Conlan.

There had also been a part of her that didn't want to know, not really. That part of their lives seemed so very distant now, and that Grant was a man who no longer existed.

But that Grant would always be a part of him, no matter how buried. She had to know now, before there was any chance at all of moving forward.

"Of course there was a reason," he said. "Your sister was beautiful, and your family an old and respected one in Anglo-Irish society. She was so much sought-after then, and seen as a great prize, so of course I had to be the one to win her." He gave a rueful laugh. "And the fact that my hated cousin seemed to want her so much just made the pursuit all the better.".

"So she was your prize," Caroline said. She felt so sad for her sister, and for Grant. too. A prize to be won. What prize did be seek now?

."Caro, she was everything a man in my position needed in a wife, at least outwardly. No one could anticipate how deep that Blacknall stubborn spirit ran, in all of you." He gently twisted his fingers with hers, as if he thought she would pull away from him. "I want to tell you something, if you will let me."

She gave a reluctant nod. Had she not decided

this was the time to learn about him, no matter what she found out? "Yes."

"As you know, when my mother and I were turned out of Adair Court, she was heartbroken and terribly bitter. I promised her I would become very rich and powerful one day, enough that I could give her the fine life she deserved—and to have revenge on them for hurting her. I did that. I went to Trinity College, which never would have admitted me if I was a Catholic McTeer, and there I made very useful connections that I could exploit in business and in Society. I did anything I had to do to make a strong place for myself in the world."

"Anything?" she whispered.

"Yes. I lied and cheated, and I schemed to bring my cousin down. And you know very well, I resorted to kidnapping. Even when my mother died, I held to my promise. Your sister was only a part of all that. But I went further than I ever wanted when I hurt you, and I'll always be sorry for that."

"But you are trying to make amends now! You hid *The Chronicle* away when you saw it had the potential to hurt your family. You took care of me."

"Not as well as I should." He slid down on the bed to gently touch the bandage on her bare leg.

"I would have been dead a dozen times over if not for you, starting with drowning on your beach."

He kissed the soft curve of her knee, his teeth lightly nipping at her skin and making her gasp. His hand slid slowly up the back of her leg.

"Grant," she whispered hoarsely. "You're hurt. We can't do—this."

"Shh," he said against her skin. "It's just a kiss."

"It's never 'just a kiss' with you and me," she said.

But as his mouth slid up the angle of her thigh, she fell back weakly to the pillows. It was always like this when he touched her, kissed her, like a drop of alcohol meeting a flame and burning out of control. With him alone did she ever feel such pure emotion and need. With him alone could she just let go and feel.

She wore only her loose shirt, and as he moved up her body, he grasped it by the hem and pulled it over her head. He sat back on his heels and simply looked at her, studying her bare, pale skin, every curve, every freckle. Caroline felt suddenly shy, unaccountably so, since he had already seen and kissed every inch of her. She was tempted to pull her long hair down to cover herself, but she couldn't move. She held her breath and stared down at him in the crackling, hot silence.

His gaze met hers, and in that instant, Caroline felt something deep and profound shift between them. They saw each other, they understood, and every breath and every heartbeat was like one. She loved him, as she could never love anyone else.

And that realization shook her deeply. She reached out and gently touched his face. Those old scars were slightly rough under her hand, his skin warm. She wanted to catch him in her arms and cling to him, to never let him go. She wanted this moment to be forever.

But the wind rattled the shutters outside, and she remembered the hard, cold world that waited for them. But they did have tonight. That was hers, and it could never be taken away.

He turned his face to kiss the hollow of her palm. Caroline felt a great rush of bittersweet tenderness, and she laid her other hand on the tangled fall of his hair. She longed to say those life-changing words aloud—*love you*—but her throat was too tight with unshed tears. She couldn't bear it to know for certain he didn't feel the same, couldn't stand to see pity in his eyes. This was her secret alone.

"Lie down beside me," she whispered. She curled her fingers around his band and urged him up onto the bed. He lay back on the pillows, and she leaned over him to kiss his lips. Their mouths met softly at first but then desperately, full of the hot rush of need for each other. He caught her around her hips and tried to roll her to the bed beneath him. but she slid under his arm and eased away from him.

She rose above him on her knees and smoothed her touch over his bare chest, his flat nipples, the sharp line of his collarbone, his strong shoulders. She had to memorize every inch of him, the feel and taste of him. She had to remember all of this.

He watched her with narrowed eyes, and she could feel how he held his breath. Trust was so foreign to him, but he let her explore, let her do what she would. She unfastened his breeches and peeled them away from his hips, freeing his erect penis to her soft touch. It was hard and soft at the same time, hot velvet stretched taut over iron, and she stroked it down to its swollen tip.

She heard Grant's breath catch in his throat. His hips twitched under her touch, and his hands tightened convulsively on her waist as be dragged her closer. He sat up and captured her nipple deep in his mouth, hard and hot and wet. Caroline cried out and wrapped her arms around his shoulders as he rolled her nipple over his tongue and nipped at it with his teeth. His hand covered her other breast, roughly caressing.

He shifted her so she sat on his lap, her legs around his waist as they rocked together.

She felt the roughness of his bandage as her hand slid down his chest, and she tried to pull away, afraid she would hurt him. His mouth slid from her breast, but he wouldn't let her go.

"We shouldn't do this," she whispered. "Your shoulder will bleed again."

"It won't," he insisted. "And if it does, I don't care. I only want you."

"And I want you."

"Then forget everything, Caro," he said against her neck. He nuzzled at the soft curve just above her shoulder. His breath and lips were warm on her skin, and she shivered. Her eyes fluttered closed.

In the darkness behind her eyes, bright sparks of white and red exploded in the darkness as she reveled in the feel of his body against hers, the friction of their damp, hot skin, the frantic need that built up inside her. He could always make her feel that way.

In the sizzling darkness, she felt the press of his fingers against the wet seam of her womanhood, parting her for the heavy thrust of his penis as he entered her. She arched her back to lift upward, sliding him even deeper into her, so deep it seemed be touched her very soul.

She held him there until she had to move, had to reach for that hot, wondrous pleasure now, and their movements coordinated like a dance.

He moved faster and faster against her, calling out her name. She dug her heels into his back, reaching, reaching, until at last she touched that brilliant, burning sun and shattered into a hundred sparkling pieces.

"Grant!" she sobbed. And he held her in his arms as they fell to the bed, entwined and gasping for breath. "Grant, Grant."

Inexplicably, she burst into tears. Such beauty was too fragile, too fleeting, and her heart ached with it all.

Grant cradled her against his chest as she sobbed, his caress a soothing, soft motion on her hair. He said nothing, which was a good thing, for she had no explanations for her tears. She had no words for anything at all.

At last the storm was spent, and her body grew heavy with exhaustion. She held on to Grant as she slid deeper and deeper into dark sleep.

"My beautiful Caroline," she heard him whisper as she slipped into darkness. "I will make everything right for you again, I promise. I won't let anything hurt you."

But maybe those words were all in her dreams.

TWENTY-SEVEN

"**A**re you sure you can ride today?" Caroline asked worriedly. She watched as Grant saddled their horses outside the cottage. He seemed to be moving well enough, but she feared he was also moving too carefully. She felt a bit guilty for their night of lovemaking.

Grant merely laughed. "That wasn't a concern last night, was it? I rode well enough then."

Caroline felt her cheeks grow hot as she remembered just how very agile he had been the previous night. "We should at least wait until this afternoon, so you can rest for a while longer. If it starts to bleed again..."

"It won't. You bandaged it too tightly this morning."

He left the horses and came to her, laying his hands on her shoulders. He gently kissed the tip of her nose. "I've had the very best of nurses."

"The best nurse would have made you sleep last night without, you know."

"Seducing me?" He grinned down at her. "Believe

me, that was the best medicine possible. I feel entirely well today."

Caroline carefully peeled back the edge of his shirt to check the new bandages she had applied just before they packed up their belongings. The white linen was blessedly free from any spot of blood. There were no red streaks of infection on his skin.

"Very well," she said. "But I insist we stop early for the night. No pressing on to Dublin until tomorrow."

"We'll see," he answered. "Are you ready?"

"Yes, I suppose so." Caroline glanced once more at the little cottage. So very much bad happened there that she hated to leave it so soon to jump back into the real world. But that world would not wait.

Grant helped her into her saddle before finding his own mount, and they galloped away from the little clearing. She didn't look back again.

The road from Hakley Hall that led to Dublin was usually a busy one. Caroline's family often took a stretch of it when they traveled from Killinan to the city, and it always seemed crowded with farm carts, lumbering travel berlins, and young rakes roaring along in their high-perch phaetons, especially in the summer like now. But they met only a few vehicles, which passed them hastily and left them alone again.

It seemed everyone hid out in their houses, waiting for something. Even the pale blue sky overhead seemed empty and silent.

Grant's good mood faded into tense watchfulness, and they spoke very little as they rode onward. They glimpsed Hakley Hall from a distance as they passed on a ridge, and the stolid gray stone house was still shuttered and quiet, as it was when they stopped yesterday. There were no cows or sheep in the meadows, and very few workers in the ripe summer fields.

The other houses they passed, Ballyornen and Pierce Court, where Caroline had often gone visiting with her mother when she was a girl, were just as quiet. Had they gone to Dublin, or sought passage to England as so many had done in '98? That sense of fearful waiting was the same as she remembered from those days.

At last, as morning slid into afternoon and the sun grew warmer, Grant broke their silence. "There's a stream up ahead where we can stop and drink if you're thirsty."

"Yes, I am," Caroline said, surprised to realize she was quite thirsty, and her backside was getting sore again. She had been distracted by her thoughts and worries.

But they never reached the stream. As they turned off the main road to a narrower path lined with hedgerows, they found their way blocked by another man on horseback. He wore a caped greatcoat and a brimmed hat tugged low on his brow, but those angelic blue eyes were much too familiar.

It *was* LaPlace, alive after all. She *had* actually seen him on the street in Kilmallock. And he held a pistol leveled at them as if he had been expecting them.

Caroline's mouth went dry, and her heart leaped with sudden panic. She tugged her horse around hard, but another man stepped out from the hedges with a gun in his hand. To her shock she saw it was Mick O'Shea, poor dead Bessie's suitor. His face was

275

pale, his eyes wild as if with a panic even greater than hers, but still he held on to his gun.

"Ah, Sir Grant, *mon ami*! And the lovely *mademoiselle*," LaPlace said affably. "I knew if I just waited in the right place you would come to me. It is meant to be."

Caroline slid her hand toward her waist where a dagger was strapped just beneath her coat. She tried to move carefully, but LaPlace *tsked* and shook his head at her, as if she were a schoolgirl sneaking a cake.

"I would not do that, *mademoiselle*," he said. "Not with my friend's gun aimed right at your pretty breast. Nor you, Sir Grant. I'm sure you want nothing to happen to the fair lady."

"What is your game, LaPlace?" Grant said tightly.

"My game? Oh, no, *monsieur*. I did not begin this little play of ours. I merely came here to do Bonaparte's bidding. He doesn't want to entrust his troops and arms to helping your country if such assistance is not desired, and if your countrymen aren't prepared to act on their own behalf. Your messengers indicated your little island could be of benefit to us, so I was sent to discover the level of dedication to a rebellion."

LaPlace's cold blue eyes swept over Caroline, and his smile faded. "It seems my master was quite right to have doubts. You double-crossed me, *monsieur*, you and your little whore. And that means you have double-crossed my master."

Caroline glanced between LaPlace and Mick O'Shea. Mick certainly didn't seem to share LaPlace's chilly confidence. The hand holding the gun trembled, which made the firearm wobble about in a terrifying way. What if it went off?

"And you, Mr. O'Shea?" she said as calmly as she could. "What is your part in this? Do you serve First Consul Napoleon as well?"

"Of course he does," LaPlace said. "He has for many months, sending us messages of much interest. How else could we have known so much about Sir Grant and his Dublin friends? And in return, Monsieur O'Shea was handsomely rewarded."

"You were a spy?" Grant said in that low, soft, tight voice Caroline had learned to fear. It was worse than any shouting. Grant twisted around in his saddle to look steadily at O'Shea. "On your own island, against your own people?"

The gun shook even harder. "I needed the money! Bessie and I couldn't marry without it. I only passed on what I overheard, what Bessie told me she found. I never meant harm by it. I never meant..."

"And then she died," Caroline said. She thought of Maeve's tale of poor Bessie the housemaid, falling from the walkway of the old tower. Her ghost wandering the halls, moaning for someone to avenge her death. Yet it seemed "poor Bessie" was not so very helpless after all. She and her lover were spies, all for a few French coins.

O'Shea's face went even whiter, and his brow shone with sweat. Caroline had a sudden terrible suspicion.

Moving very slowly, her hands extended in a non-threatening way, she slid off her saddle and moved carefully toward Mick. She tried to ignore his gun and look only in his eyes.

"Caroline!" Grant shouted.

"It's all right, Grant," she answered. "I only want to ask Mr. O'Shea a question."

"I don't want to talk to you!" Mick cried.

"I am bored with all this," LaPlace said. "Give us the papers you stole, Sir Grant; that is all we want."

Caroline ignored him. "What really happened the night Bessie died, Mick?"

He licked his cracked lips. "I wasn't there! How should I know? I heard that he killed her."

She gazed steadily into Mick's wild eyes. All her reading did have one advantage now, she had learned a great deal about the unpredictability of people. They had motives and desires no one else could understand, and they were often driven by them to do awful things. But unless a person was unnaturally cold like LaPlace, the guilt of it haunted them. She had seldom seen anyone quite so wretchedly guilty as Mick O'Shea.

"And you let them think that, didn't you?" she said. "But I think you know what really happened."

"It were an accident," he cried. "I wanted to stop sending them any information, but Bessie said we needed the money. She said the French couldn't be no worse than the English, but I knew she was wrong. We met in the tower to talk about it, where no one else could hear. But we argued, and then she..." He broke off with a sob.

"And she fell?" Caroline said softly.

"I told you, it were an accident!" The gun suddenly swung up and pointed at Caroline's face. "I only wanted it to stop!"

"Caroline!" she heard Grant shout. He leaped down from his horse and strode over to grab her arm. "Get away from him now."

He dragged her down just as an explosion went

off, deafeningly loud. The birds scattered from the hedges in a wild flurry, and Grant threw her to the ground, his own body over hers. The clear country air smelled of metallic gunpowder and new blood.

"*Diolain*, Grant, are you shot?" She ran her hands desperately over his back and shoulders, searching for any wounds. He still breathed and seemed blessedly whole and unhurt-this time.

He raised himself as his gaze scanned over her, searching for wounds in turn. "It's not me. For fuck's sake, woman, what were you thinking, going to him like that?"

Caroline peered over his shoulder to find that it was Mick O'Shea who had been shot. A puddle of bright red blood spread over his chest, and he tilted precariously to one side but didn't fall down. His eyes were wide with disbelief, just before they went glassy and empty. The gun in his hand, still unfired, fell to the ground, and he toppled after it.

LaPlace still sat on his horse, the smoking pistol leveled in his grip. He shook his head and said, "So regretful. He was useful for a time, but he had obviously lost his nerve. That botched shooting in the woods, where he missed you by mere inches, Sir Grant, showed his use was quite at an end. The Irish fool."

Grant leaped to his feet and pulled Caroline up with him. He gave her a hard shove and told her, "Run now!"

LaPlace tossed away his emptied pistol and drew a long dagger from his belt. He climbed down from his horse and stepped toward Grant. "This has all become quite dull, *monsieur*. Let's be at an end now."

Caroline drew her own dagger and tossed it to Grant before she did as he suggested—she ran. But she didn't go far. She couldn't leave Grant, not now. She caught up Mick's gun and dashed to the end of the lane. She took what shelter she could behind the hedge and tried to get a clear shot at LaPlace.

He and Grant circled each other warily, never taking their eyes off each other. The sunlight glinted off the daggers they held in their hands. They were like two primitive warriors, each poised to make the killing strike. Only one of them could prevail, and both had the fury of revenge behind them.

Caroline couldn't breathe. Suddenly, LaPlace lunged forward with his knife raised to strike. He let out a shout, but Grant just slid to the side, lithe as a dancer. Grant parried with his own blade and drove LaPlace back.

Grant kept driving him back with a furious series of thrusts and defensive strikes, until he landed a hard blow on LaPlace's arm. A line of blood appeared on LaPlace's sleeve, and finally his cold mask cracked in anger. He lashed out with his foot to kick Grant hard on the leg and tripped him, sending him falling hard to the ground.

But Grant seized LaPlace's wounded arm as he went down and dragged him along. They fell heavily to the dirt and grappled. The dust flew in a blinding cloud, but Caroline saw Grant go down, LaPlace's arm raised to land a killing blow. Seeing the knife only an inch from Grant's face, she screamed—only to have the sound strangle in her throat as Grant twisted the Frenchman's arm sharply and pushed him off in one great heave. Blood and sweat flew with the dust in a nightmare whirlwind. Every time Grant shouted, she wanted to cry.

Caroline watched them in terror as first one then the other seemed to get the upper hand. It was a horribly confusing scene, a tangle of limbs and blows and shouted curses. She couldn't see who was where, and her arm ached with holding the heavy gun. She knelt on the ground with a frustrated sob.

Suddenly, Grant's dagger thrust upward and landed deep in LaPlace's chest. The Frenchman fell face-first and lay in the dirt, very, very still as blood slowly pooled beneath him.

Grant lurched to his feet to stare down at his fallen foe. He carefully turned LaPlace over with his boot, and Caroline could see LaPlace was truly dead this time. There would be no more miraculous risings for him. His eyes stared sightlessly up at the sky, and a thin line of blood trickled from his mouth. Grant's face was completely blank, his eyes very dark.

Caroline dropped the gun and ran to him, throwing her arms around his neck. She buried her face in his shoulder and held him as hard as she could. He was alive! They were alive. It hardly seemed possible after this terror.

But then she saw that the shirt over his shoulder was stained with fresh blood.

"Grant," she sobbed. "You're hurt again."

She felt him kiss the top of her head. "It's just the old wound. I think it reopened in the fight, nothing to worry about." His voice was cold and calm.

"Nothing to worry about?"

"Come, we have to get out of here." Grant lifted Caroline back up into her saddle, his face still blank.

As she gathered up the reins, all the fear of the

last few minutes faded into numbness. She watched as Grant quickly and efficiently dragged the two bodies into the hedges and searched LaPlace's saddlebags. After he retrieved a packet of papers, he sent the horses galloping off alone down the lane. Then he swung up into his own saddle and led Caroline in the opposite direction—toward Dublin.

CHAPTER
TWENTY-EIGHT

T he walls of Dublin looked as if they were
preparing for a siege.

Caroline and Grant were halted just beyond the gates, held up at the end of a long line of
people waiting to enter the city. Carts filled with vegetables, eggs, milk, and squealing pigs, destined for
tomorrow morning's markets, jostled with fine carriages and sedan chairs. No one was getting inside
any faster than anyone else, and nerves and tempers
were fraying. It didn't help that the evening sun beat
down on them and the air was still, with no cooling
breeze.

Caroline shifted the reins to one hand and patted
her tired horse's neck. The animal was nervous with
the press of the crowds and the tangle of loud voices,
and so was she. She had forgotten what it felt like to
be among so many people, bombarded with the
sounds and smells of the city, after Muirin Inish and
the quiet country roads and towns.

And Dublin hadn't been quite like this when she
left. Things had been tense but quiet, the social
season still going, but winding to a close. Usually by

this time, most people had returned to their estates, and the city was silent.

Now it was busier than ever. Caroline shaded her eyes from the sun's hard glare and studied the dark gray stone walls. More cannons lined the parapets than usual, their ominous black mouths pointed on the throngs below, and more soldiers patrolled those heights and guarded the gates. They were checking papers and examining the carts before they let anyone pass, which slowed the lines down. Other soldiers worked on repairing the weak spots in the old walls, which had been crumbling since long before the last rebellion. Now the men slapped on mortar and shoved new stones haphazardly into place.

Caroline felt sure if there was an invasion, the walls wouldn't hold back the forces for even a minute.

She shifted in her saddle and adjusted her skirt over her knees. She had changed into her washed and mended dress and wore her boy's coat over it, not exactly a proper riding habit. But hopefully it would shock anyone they met less than her breeches would have.

Her companion—well, Grant was sure to shock everyone immensely as soon as they saw that he was back in Dublin. He sat beside her, watching the activity around them in silence. His hat was pulled low, casting a shadow over his expressionless face. He had said hardly a word since they left LaPlace behind, only what was necessary as they rode hard across the countryside. It was as if he already withdrew from her into a place where she could not follow. Where he would not let her follow.

At last, it was their turn at the gate. The farm cart

ahead of them rolled on with its load of squawking, malodorous chickens, and the barouche behind them pressed at their heels with squawking human passengers. The soldier who seemed to be in charge examined her closely, his beady eyes narrowed.

Caroline sat up straighter in the saddle. She might be tired and windblown, tanned from the days under the sky, but she was a lady. She would not be intimidated by anyone, not after all she had seen and done. She stared back at him steadily.

"And who might you be, miss?" he said. "You wouldn't be coming from Kildare, would you?"

Before Caroline could answer, Grant edged his horse between her and the soldier. "This is Lady Hartley," he said, in that cultured, contemptuous accent she remembered so well from the "old" Grant. "And I am Sir Grant Dunmore. I'm charged with seeing her safely to her sister, the Duchess of Adair. Your commander wouldn't like it if you were to impede the sister-in-law of a duke, would he?"

The soldier swallowed hard as Grant stared at him steadily with glittering, golden-brown eyes. "I have no wish to impede her ladyship, sir. If you have some identification..."

Caroline had no identification of any sort. All her papers were long lost at the bottom of the sea. But Grant drew out a document from inside his coat and handed it over. The light flashed on a gold signet ring on Grant's smallest finger, a piece she had not seen him wear for a long time. The soldier gave it a cursory glance and waved them through.

Once they were through the bottleneck of the gates and into the city streets, the crowds fanned out and the noise was not as loud. Everyone seemed to be hurrying on the everyday errands of a warm summer evening—maidservants walking by with market baskets on their arms, fine ladies in feathered bonnets flying past in their carriages on their way home to change for the night's parties. But there were more soldiers there, too, marching in formation down the street or loitering in doorways with their firearms on prominent display.

The smells of the city—the sweet ladies' perfumes, roasted meats, and sugary spiced almonds from vendors' carts, mixed with the tang of human waste in the gutters and the fishiness of the river, all blended with something acrid and odd. Something very like fear. She remembered that smell too well from '98.

Grant looked at her from under that shadowy brim, and she saw a flashing glimpse of his intense tenderness as a lover in their private bedroom. "Are you all right? It's been a long journey."

Caroline nodded. "I'm just a bit tired. I'll be glad for a hot bath and a real bed."

"Henrietta Street isn't far now."

"Henrietta Street? My town house is near Rutland Square."

"The Duke and Duchess are at Henrietta Street. I'm sure you must be anxious to see your sister."

She was eager to see Anna, desperate to see her in fact. But how did he know they were there? And what would happen when they saw her with Grant?

But he was already far ahead of her on the street, and he didn't look to see if she followed. Infuriating man! She tugged at the reins and hurried to catch up with him.

"You shouldn't be alone right now, Caro," he said. "You'll be safer with your sister, at least for now."

"How do you know that?" she asked. "What's going to happen?"

"I don't think anyone knows what's going to happen. But you have to stay out of it, whatever it may be."

Yet he knew more than he would say, she could sense it. They made their way past the streets of shops, the rows of narrow, respectable town houses, and onto the wider lanes of the Ascendancy's grand mansions. He was quiet as they went past the large, silent edifices of pale, austere stone ,with glossy black doors and shuttered windows.

Everything seemed so quiet in these aristocratic streets. Once in a while, a maid would scurry along the walkway, or a curtain would twitch. Even Henrietta Street, one of the grandest, oldest addresses of all, was quieter than usual. One carriage clattered past, so fast that the painted crest on the door was blurred, and a maid scrubbed at a set of marble front steps. Near the end of the street was her family's house, all soaring columns and classical carved pediments.

It had once been her sister Eliza's house, part of her widow's settlement from her first marriage, and she had used its vast rooms and hidden corridors for her work with the United Irishmen. After Eliza left for the Continent, Caroline and Anna and their mother used it when they were in the city. It was certainly grand, but Caroline preferred her own cozy house, and now left Henrietta Street to Anna and her children.

"Are you sure they're here?" she asked as Grant

helped her from the horse. "It's very quiet. Perhaps they—and everyone else—have gone to the country?"

"No, they are here, and so are their neighbors, I'm sure. Matters in the country are even more uncertain, at least for some people." Grant took her arm, and she felt strangely reassured by his strong, warm touch. He wasn't gone yet; he was still with her.

Caroline pounded the brass lion's-head knocker on the door and listened to the solid thud of it echo inside. It suddenly swung open, and to Caroline's surprise, it wasn't the butler who stood there, but Anna herself.

"Caro!" she cried, and grabbed Caroline in her arms. "Oh, Caro, you're here at last. I've been so horribly worried!"

Caroline held on to her sister and tried not to break into sobs. Anna smelled of her own perfume, white roses and lilacs, and her golden hair was soft on Caroline's cheek. How she had missed her sister!

And Caroline realized that there had actually been moments on this long journey when she feared never to see her family again. She had pushed it away until then, concentrating only on the next moment, the next town. But now that fear was transformed into a fierce wave of love and relief.

"Let me look at you," Anna said. She held Caroline at arm's length and took in every inch of her. "You're not hurt?"

Caroline laughed and tucked a long lock of tangled hair behind her ear. "Just saddle sore and not very presentable."

"And such an interesting fashion statement." Anna herself wore a fine day dress of blue-embroidered white muslin, as soft as a cloud, and a blue cashmere shawl. Pearl-tipped combs held her blond curls in their elaborate coiffure, and pearl drops hung from her ears.

Of course, Anna would be a fashion plate even in the face of a rebellion. It was part of her bravery.

"It's been a long journey," Caroline said. "I didn't have time to find a modiste."

"You never do. And I want to hear about every minute of this journey of yours. Don't think I'm not furious that you lied to us about where you were going! I have been off my head with worry." Anna glanced past Caroline—and her expression froze.

Caroline had half-forgotten Grant in the rush of reunion, but now she sensed him close behind her. He stood very still, almost like one of the Roman statues lining the marble foyer—stoic, watchful, and wary.

Caroline held on to Anna's arm and half-turned to Grant. He had removed his hat, and the light from the frosted window above the door cast strange, fractured shadows over his scarred face. His hair fell over one shoulder as he bowed.

"Your Grace," he said quietly.

Anna's arm was stiff under Caroline's touch, but she didn't run at Grant and claw his eyes out, as Caroline almost expected. She didn't move at all.

"So it's true," Anna said. Her stare never left Grant, but she reached out with her free arm and drew Caroline even closer to her. "I almost didn't believe Conlan when he told me you were coming."

"Conlan knew Grant was coming here?" Caroline cried out. Suddenly she was more confused than ever. Nothing had been as she expected or planned ever since she set foot on the boat to Muirin Inish. It was all more complicated, more terrible, and more wonderful. But this...

Anna's arm tightened. "Thank you for bringing my sister here. Conlan is at McMaster's Tavern with the others. He's expecting you."

Grant bowed again, and with not another word, he turned to leave. As he opened the door, the bright light of day spilled into the dim foyer, dazzling and blinding.

"Grant, wait!" Caroline called. She broke away from Anna and ran after him. On the front steps, she caught his arm and kissed him, hard and desperate. He was slipping away from her, and she didn't understand what was happening. She didn't know how to hold on to him.

He kissed her back, and he felt so wonderfully familiar to her now, yet so full of dark depths she had yet to explore. She'd thought she could let him go when the time came, and go back to her old life. But she didn't want to do that now. She wanted more of him, more of what they'd found together so miraculously.

He gently set her back from him with one brief kiss on her temple. He touched her hair, his gaze following that caress as if he wanted to memorize what it looked like, felt like.

"I have to go," he said.

"Will I see you again?" she asked.

"Yes." That was all he said, but Caroline knew that a "yes" from Grant was a promise.

He kissed her on the cheek once more, softly, and then he turned and went back to the horses tied upon the street. Caroline watched as he swung up into the saddle and left the house. She lingered until he turned the corner and was lost from her view. The street was quiet again.

She felt Anna's touch on her hand and glanced back to find her sister watching her with sadness in her blue eyes. Sadness, yes, but not anger. Not even any surprise.

"Come inside now, Caro," she said. "You must be hungry and tired."

She *was* tired, bone-deep tired, but not only from the journey. It had been exhilarating and strange, teaching her things about herself and the world—and about Grant—that she could never have imagined. She had learned she could be strong and brave, and that Grant could be kind. They had both found themselves. That wild ride surely wasn't over yet.

Anna led her into the drawing room, stopping only to instruct the butler to arrange for food and for "Lady Hartley's" room to be prepared at once. Caroline almost didn't know who Lady Hartley was anymore; she had become a stranger to herself. She sat down gratefully on a blue satin chair by the open window and studied the room. It hadn't changed since she left. The fine blue and yellow damask draperies, the gilded French furniture and paintings, the fanciful plaster roses wreathing the ceiling—they were all just the same.

Somehow, she had been sure the whole world transformed while she was gone, but it seemed to have remained perfectly still.

Anna moved her workbasket from a chair next to Caroline's and sat down, watching Caroline the whole time. "The children are having their naps, but they'll be overjoyed to see their Aunt Caroline when they wake."

Caroline smiled. "I'll be overjoyed to see them, too. I've missed them terribly, and you too, Anna."

"Why didn't you tell me you were going to find Grant Dunmore?"

"Tell you I was going to find Grant?" Caroline said with a laugh. "So you could stop me?"

"Of course, I would have stopped you. That island he hides away on sounds like an absolute wilderness, and he's—well, he's..."

"I know. He is Grant Dunmore. But he has changed so much, Anna. He's not the same man he was back then."

"So I have heard."

Caroline looked at her in surprise. "You've heard?"

"Yes, I've learned quite a great deal about Grant in the last few days, from Conlan."

Caroline slumped back in her chair and crossed her arms over her waist. She wasn't sure she could take many more surprises. "I think you had best tell me what you mean, Anna dear."

Anna pressed her lips together as if she didn't want to say any more.

"Anna! Surely I have a right to know. Whatever is happening here, I'm a part of it now, whether you like it or not"

"Yes, I suppose you are," Anna said sadly. "And I know the terrible feeling of being left out, not knowing what's happening to the ones I love. Conlan didn't tell me everything, either, until I threatened to go out and search for you myself. You are our baby sister; we always wanted to protect you, to let you have the life of study you loved so much. We didn't want you involved with anything unpleasant."

"Oh, Anna. I am not a baby now."

"No indeed. You are a grown-up, widowed lady." Anna nodded and said, "You see, Caro dear, Grant has been working with Conlan for many months now..."

MCMASTER'S TAVERN NEAR THE DOCKS WAS DESERTED. Only one man sat drinking in the corner, his greasy hair falling forward to hide his face. The bright sunset was dimmed by the narrow windows, and the smell of spilled ale and old cigar smoke was stale in the air. It was as if the place stood still in time, waiting for whatever was going to happen next.

McMaster stood behind the bar and wiped at a stack of dusty glasses. He didn't even glance up as Grant walked past and let himself into the back room.

It was also dark, the air warm and close, but it wasn't empty. A group of men were huddled around a table in the corner with their heads bent over a map. Their voices were low, angry mutters.

And at their center sat Grant's cousin and erstwhile enemy, Conlan McTeer, Duke of Adair. Conlan said nothing, merely listened to the others with an impassive look on his dark face. He smoked a thin cheroot, and the silvery smoke curled around him.

Conlan had always looked like an Irish devil, dark and glowering, to Grant's former bright charm. Now he looked even more so, harder and leaner than ever, as if having a family to protect made him even fiercer.

Grant knew something of that feeling now. He thought of Caroline's soft smile as she drifted into sleep beside him, and the gentle touch of her hand on his face. He would fight any foe to protect her, go into any battle.

Conlan saw him there, and his bland expression flashed to surprise. He stubbed out the cheroot and rose to his feet. He slowly crossed the room, and Grant wasn't sure if he should brace himself for a strike from his cousin. Though they had corresponded for many months, forming this uneasy alliance and working together, they hadn't seen each other since the long-ago day of the fire. Grant could see the anger still simmering deep in Conlan's eyes.

But his cousin held out his hand for Grant to shake. "I see you've decided to join us at last, Grant."

Grant glanced at the men still huddled around the table. They went on with their arguments and plans, but Grant could see them shooting secret, wary looks his way. "I couldn't let you and your friends have all the fun," he answered.

One of Conlan's dark brows arched. "Friends?" he said. He drew Grant to a shadowed corner and asked quietly, "Did all go as planned?"

"In some ways." Grant took out the packet of papers that he had purloined from LaPlace and handed them to Conlan. "The French emissary showed upon Muirin Inish as arranged, and he was most informative—even if he did not choose to be. He had his own ends to accomplish."

"I would expect nothing else," Conlan said as he sorted through the documents. His frown grew fiercer the more he read. "Napoleon has his own ambitions; he cares nothing at all for Ireland. To rely on such an uncertain ally can only do us harm."

"And so you've told the others."

"Much good it does. Emmet has been in Paris all

these years. He can't see anything else. Yet I read here that Bonaparte says he fears the Irish people have grown complacent under the English yoke, and no longer care to fight for their independence. He needs proof of Irish intentions before he commits to aid."

"LaPlace declared that if Dublin should rise, the north would follow, and Napoleon would see the seriousness of Irish purpose," Grant said. "Then he would send troops to land at Galway and supply more arms."

"By then, it would be far too late," Conlan said grimly. "Ireland has no stomach for a large scale rising on its own now. We have barely begun to recover from ninety-eight, and the Castle is tightening control even as we speak. General Fox has taken over command from Meadows, and he's already increased garrison strength here in Dublin and at Dunboyne and Kildare. He's added even more patrols in the city, sent ammunitions supplements to the barracks, and he's threatening to resume martial law. He's no fool. He and his troops will be ready if there's a fight."

"And will there be a fight?" Grant asked quietly.

"Right now, in these conditions, it would be utterly foolhardy. Emmet can't win, and another rising, brutally put down, would only make the English tighten their control even more," Conlan said. "It would put us in an even worse position, and I won't risk my family or my people at Adair for such an abortive scheme."

"You've grown cool-headed, Cousin," Grant said.

Conlan laughed ruefully. "I've had to be. If we want our freedom, rash actions and senseless bloodshed will never gain it. We have to wait, watch, and carefully plan until our time comes."

"And that time is not now. I saw it myself on this journey. The people in the counties aren't going to rise."

"I suspected as much." Conlan refolded the papers and slapped them down on a nearby table. They sat there in a rumpled heap, a silent reminder of all the violence and blood that got them here.

"I heard about the explosion," Grant said. "Even in the countryside, it's talked about, and it has people scared."

Conlan nodded grimly. "The armory at Patrick Street. They were making signal rockets, the fools, and sparks caught on some spilled gunpowder. It blew a hole in the roof and started a fire. They managed to move the wounded and clean up a bit before the watchmen arrived, but it attracted a great deal of unwanted attention. General Fox has sent soldiers to look for other depots. Emmet's officers say that argues for an early rising, before the stashes of arms around the city are found."

"How early?" Grant asked.

Conlan shrugged. "I haven't yet heard word. Within days, I would think." He glanced at the other men. "Some of them would go charging into the streets right now, the damnable fools."

Grant thought of Caroline in the house at Henrietta Street, the last pleading glance she gave him as he left her. That house was vast and strong, with thick walls and deep cellars. But would it hold fast in a war?

He rubbed his hand hard over his face. Damn it, he should have left her in Ballylynan, or at least insisted on taking her to Killinan.

Conlan gave him a shrewd look. "You said matters

went as planned in 'some ways.' What did you mean, Grant?"

Grant sat down heavily in the nearest chair. "You won't like it."

"If it has to do with you, Cousin, I'm sure I won't," Conlan said. He sat down on the edge of the table. "Tell me."

"I did not return to Dublin alone. I brought Caroline with me."

"So your note to Anna said. You found her on this research journey of hers? I'm surprised she agreed to come with you."

"I didn't tell Anna the whole truth. I didn't want her to worry about her sister, and I thought she should know Caroline was on her way to Dublin."

Conlan crossed his arms over his chest. He leaned back with deceptive laziness, but Grant could see the taut tension of his shoulders. Family was everything to Conlan, and Caroline was his sister now. "Then what is the truth, Grant?"

"We've been together for weeks. She came to Muirin Inish looking for *The Chronicle of Kildare* for her research, just as LaPlace arrived. She left the island with me, and I brought her here. With me."

Conlan suddenly slammed his palms down on the table with a crash loud enough to make the other men cease their arguments and turn toward their corner.

"What do you mean together?" Conlan shouted. "I thought your work with us meant you had changed, but if you seduced her, I swear..."

"I care about her," he said simply.

Conlan stared at him with a stony, burning glare, a perfect stillness, and somehow Grant had to admit it all to his cousin. "I love her," he said. "Once I thought you were a fool in your passion for Anna Blacknall, but now—now I understand."

Conlan eyed Grant warily for a long moment before he nodded. "You do love her."

"Yes," was all Grant could say.

Conlan laughed. "I knew no man could resist a Blacknall woman, not even a bastard like you."

TWENTY-NINE

"Caro? Are you asleep? May I come in?"

Caroline heard her sister's soft knock on the chamber door, but she didn't stir from the bed. She had been lying there for hours, on her side, facing the window as she watched the daylight fade and the city slip into the dark blue-black of a summer twilight. The servants had taken away the used bathwater and left a pile of clean clothes, and a maid lit the lamps, but still Caroline stayed there, thinking about all Anna had told her.

Grant worked with Conlan, and had for many months. He was certainly no French or English spy, nor even a newly minted fiery revolutionary. He worked with his cousin, a man he had once hated so bitterly, to protect the land and the people they both loved. He had come back to his family at last.

And now her love for him, so fierce before, only grew and grew. It seemed her heart would burst with love, it was so vast and wondrous. But he had left her here and gone off into some unknown danger, and she wasn't sure if she could bear it.

4 4 4 4

4 4 4 4 4

Anna's knock grew more insistent. "Caro, what are you doing in there?"

Caroline rolled over to face the door. "Come in, Anna. I'm not doing anything nefarious, just resting."

As Caroline sat up against the lace-trimmed pillows, Anna opened the door and stepped into the chamber. She was dressed for a party in a fashionable high-waisted gown of pale lavender silk, embroidered with a gold Grecian pattern at the hem. A necklace of amethysts and diamonds sparkled at her throat, and her golden hair was piled up in curls and twined with pearls.

"You look beautiful, Anna," Caroline said. "Going somewhere special, or is this just how a duchess chooses to dine at home? Setting standards and all."

Anna tossed a cushion at Caroline's head and sat down on the dressing table stool. "I'm going to a waltzing party at Signora Rastrelli's, and you should come, too. You remember the signora, she was my friend Jane, Lady Cannondale, before she married again."

Caroline certainly did remember Lady Cannondale. She had once seen her kissing Grant at a party. "A party tonight, of all nights?"

"Yes, it's been long planned, and no one refuses an invitation from Jane. Conlan sent a message saying he won't return home until very late, but that I must go. It will show everyone we have nothing to hide and that there is nothing to fear." Anna suddenly gave a dazzling smile. "And I do love to waltz. Don't you, Caro?"

Caroline had to laugh. "I have never tried it at all. They say it's a terribly scandalous dance."

"Oh, it is! Deliciously so." Anna leaped up from

her seat and caught Caroline's hands to tug her to her feet. She twirled her around the room, faster and faster until they were both giggling madly. "You see, it's very easy."

"I'm sure there's more to it than this," Caroline said. "Proper steps and all that. I never could remember those."

"No, it is just like this. One, two, three, and one, two, three. Spin, leap, turn!"

They fell into a dizzy heap on the floor, Anna's silk skirts and Caroline's nightdress billowing around them. "You see," Anna said. "It will be great fun."

"Until someone breaks a leg," Caroline answered. "I'm not sure I feel like dancing." Not when she was so worried about Grant. Not when she was trying to figure everything out in a world suddenly gone topsy-turvy.

"Then you don't have to dance. Just sip some wine and listen to some gossip." Anna suddenly looked very serious. "It really would be best if we went out tonight. Staying here and fretting won't do any good."

Caroline pleated her sleeve between her fingers, not looking at her sister. "I'm not fretting."

"No? I certainly am." Anna gently touched her shoulder. "Conlan's message said that Grant is with him. They're trying to stop this futile madness before it gets out of control. They'll be safe together, and we need to stay together as well."

"I couldn't bear it if he was hurt," Caroline whispered. Anna's arm slid around her shoulders and drew her close.

"I know," she said, and Caroline knew she really did. Anna loved Conlan with all her heart, had faced danger many times with him, and she was always brave in the face of it. Caroline just had to do the same.

"You really do care about him, don't you?" said Anna.

Caroline nodded. "I love him."

Anna's lips tightened. "You love Grant Dunmore?"

"I told you, Anna, he's not the same now. Surely his work with Conlan shows that? He wants to make amends for what he once did. He wants to be a good man. He *is* a good man! If you only knew all he's done —for all of us." But she couldn't tell Anna about everything Grant had done. She couldn't tell her about the secrets in the pages of *The Chronicle*. Grant had entrusted those to her.

"What has he done, Caro?"

"Lots of things," Caroline said. "He's different now, that's all. I know it."

"Yes. He must be, if you love him." Anna gave a deep sigh. "I confess I did not trust him when he first wrote to Conlan and said he wanted to help us. But family is everything to Conlan, and he wanted to give his cousin a chance, though cautiously until Grant had proved himself. You have always been the most sensible and practical of us, Caro. If you trust Grant..."

"I do."

"Then I do, too." Anna kissed her cheek. "We are a sad lot, we Blacknall sisters. We never want men with calm, safe lives."

"No, we don't. Not even our mother wanted that in the end. Do you think she is happy with Monsieur Courtois?"

"I know she is. We had a letter from her and Eliza just a few days ago, and they are disgustingly happy in Lausanne. The *monsieur* paints, Eliza writes her memoirs, and Mama nurses all the villagers. She wants us all to come and visit next year, if we can travel on the Continent, thanks to these horrid wars."

Caroline's heart ached suddenly with missing her mother and sister. If only they could all be together again, whether at Killinan or in the cool shadows of a Swiss mountain. She and Anna, Conlan, and Grant, all the children—they would all go there one day soon. "And so we will. In the meantime, I think I feel like a dance after all."

SIGNORA RASTRELLI, THE FORMER LADY CANNONDALE, lived in one of the largest, newest houses just off St Stephen's Green. The gleaming white-stone edifice, faced with soaring Palladian columns and tall windows sparkling with candlelight, seemed to positively vibrate with merriment. A long line of carriages inched toward the front steps, where a stylishly dressed throng waited to enter the packed foyer.

Caroline leaned her elbow on the ledge of their carriage window and peered out at the laughing gathering. It all seemed so strange and disconnected from everything else that was happening in Dublin. Here there was no strife, no threatened violence, no furious rebels lurking in the shadows. Only music and gossipy chatter.

She smoothed the pale blue silk skirt of her gown. It was her own dress, fetched from her town house in a hastily packed trunk, but it felt alien against her skin with its long skirt and tight, short sleeves. Even the pearls around her neck, a wedding gift from Hartley, seemed strange. Had she really been away from her life so very long?

I shouldn't be here, she thought. She should be with Grant, fighting with him in whatever he was doing. Their journey bad shown they could be a good team. It had shown her she could be strong, stronger than she had ever imagined. And that she loved Grant more than she ever thought she could love anyone.

But she also didn't want to distract him at such a delicately balanced moment, and she had to reenter the world at some time. Perhaps she could even discover something useful here, among all these powerful people. They would be dancing and drinking, trying to forget their troubles and not minding their words. Especially around quiet Lady Hartley.

She did wish the party wasn't at Signora Rastrelli's, of all places. She remembered well the former Lady Cannondale, Anna's old bosom bow and her partner in mischief before she became the Duchess of Adair and settled down, and before Lady Cannondale married her young Italian lover and went to live abroad for a time. Caroline especially remembered seeing Lady Cannondale passionately embracing Grant in a darkened corridor at a long-ago party.

"You are very quiet, Caro," Anna said. "Perhaps you are too tired for a party. I should not have dragged you here."

Caroline smiled at her sister across the carriage. "I'm quite well, Anna. I was just thinking how odd this seems after—well, after everything I've seen in the last few weeks."

"Dancing while Rome burns, you mean?" Anna said with a strange little smile. "It is odd indeed, but that's always the way of Dublin, isn't it? Danger seems to give a desperate edge to our party-loving ways. I would rather stay home with the children, but it's important to know exactly what's going on with the people who will be at this dance."

Anna peered outside, her eyes narrowed as she examined the people pouring through the doors. Caroline suddenly felt rather foolish. Her sister was not just here to dance, after all. She was here to do just what Caroline herself was thinking, to see what useful information she could gather.

"People aren't as cautious when they've had a few glasses of fine French wine," Caroline said.

Anna smiled. "Exactly, Sister. They're also quite free with their words when they're in familiar surroundings among their own kind. They're wary with my husband, but not so much with me, even after my years of marriage to Conlan. They still think I'm just Lady Killinan's feather-headed daughter, sadly seduced by a ducal title and concerned only with the latest style of bonnets. I hear so many things at parties, and so will you."

Caroline leaned toward her sister and said quietly, "Anna, where exactly are Grant and Conlan tonight?"

Anna's brow wrinkled, and Caroline saw a shadow pass over her eyes. "I'm not sure. But I know where to send a message if it's needed, and so can you." She reached for Caroline's gloved hand and squeezed it hard. "Oh, Caro, I am so happy you're here now. I have a true friend and ally."

Caroline squeezed her hand back. "Are you happy, Anna? I was afraid you wouldn't approve of my being with Grant for all these weeks."

Anna shook her head. "I do wish you could have found someone else to care for—anyone else. Except maybe someone like General Fox or Lord Hardwicke. I would definitely *not* have approved of that."

Caroline laughed. "No chance of that. I hear they're both terribly old and bad-tempered."

"All that and they're Tories, too," Anna said with a laugh. "But I could see even back before the fire that there was something between you two. We don't choose whom we fall in love with, and sometimes it's with someone terribly inconvenient."

"Like with you and Conlan?"

"Yes. He was a wildly imprudent choice. Yet look at us now."

"You're a family," Caroline said. "True partners, just like Eliza and Will, and Mama and her *monsieur*."

"Bad choices all. You say Grant has changed, and Conlan thinks that as well."

"He *has* changed, Anna. I've seen it in so very many ways."

"We'll see soon enough," Anna said. "I want you to be happy, Caro. No one deserves it more than you. Just be very careful."

The carriage finally jolted to a halt at the foot of the marble steps, and a liveried footman opened the door for them.

"And the curtain rises," Anna said. She stepped down in a flurry of lavender skirts, a bright smile on her face. She flicked open her lace fan, and no one watching her would suspect she had anything on her mind but an evening of frivolity.

Caroline would just have to follow her example. She pasted on her own sociable smile and alighted from the carriage to follow Anna up the front steps.

The foyer was crowded to the silk-papered walls with people. They tumbled up the winding staircase and into the open doors of the library and a small sitting room. Their laughter blended with the strains of music floating down from the ballroom above.

The air grew heavy and thick with the scents of hothouse roses and perfumes and of close-packed bodies. Caroline's head swam with it all, but she kept on smiling. She looked around to see who was there and listened carefully to hear what they might be talking about.

"My dearest duchess!" she heard Signora Rastrelli cry. Caroline turned to see Anna embrace the signora, who wore an amber-yellow muslin gown, cut perilously low in the very latest fashion. Her auburn hair was piled high and dressed with golden feathers. She was as glamorous as ever. "I'm so glad you could come tonight," the signora said. "It would not be the same without you."

"Well, we must distract ourselves the best we can these days, Jane," Anna said. "And what better way than with dancing? I have long wanted to try the waltz."

"It's just as scandalous as reported, I assure you," Signora Rastrelli said. "And I do hope you'll partner with Lord Childress tonight, Duchess. He has just arrived from a privy council meeting at the Castle. Such a stuffy nuisance on such a lovely day."

A fleeting glance passed between the two women. Caroline only saw because she was watching very closely. Signora Rastrelli worked with Anna and Conlan as well. Who else was part of this web?

Caroline shook her head. How very much she missed while buried in her books.

"I am sure you remember my sister, Lady Hartley," Anna said. She reached for Caroline's hand and drew her forward. "I hope you don't mind that I brought her along. She's just back from a research holiday in the north."

"Not at all! The more guests the better, I always think." Signora Rastrelli glanced down at Caroline's gown and up again to her face as they curtsied to each other. "I haven't seen you since before I left for Italy, Lady Hartley. I declare, you are quite grown-up now."

"I hope so, Signora Rastrelli, since I am a widow now," Caroline said with a laugh. "Much has changed in Dublin since you left."

"And yet so much has stayed just the same," said the signora. "I hope you have come prepared to dance, Lady Hartley, as your sister has. There are so many interesting partners to be had, if you are inclined as the Duchess is."

"I daresay I might be," Caroline said.

"That is excellent to hear." Signora Rastrelli held out her hand, and an impossibly handsome raven-haired man hurried over to kiss it. "This is my husband, Signor Gianni Rastrelli. He will escort you into the ballroom. The dance master will give a waltzing lesson before we begin."

The signor offered his arms to Anna and Caroline with a soft, "Ah, *bella duchessina*! Such an honor to assist two such beautiful ladies."

He saw them up the stairs and into the rose-lined ballroom, where a small man atop a tall dais was demonstrating the turns and swoops of the new Viennese dance. Anna quickly found Lord Childress and took his arm with a sweet smile and a murmured,

"Poor Lord Childress! I heard you had such a dull and trying day."

Signor Rastrelli himself partnered Caroline in the lesson. He was most charming, even though he didn't seem to speak much English, and Caroline soon found herself laughing and enjoying the swirling, skipping steps of the dance. It was much more fun than a staid minuet or intricate reel. Perhaps she could even like this sort of dancing—especially if Grant would one day partner her. Surely she could waltz forever with his hand on her waist and his eyes gazing into hers.

But she was not at the party to daydream and have fun. She was there to help Anna if she could. Once the lesson was over and the dancing began in earnest, she sought out partners who worked at the Castle or in the barracks. They were full of warnings that "young ladies" should mind where they traveled in the city, but not much of real use.

Until she found herself dancing with a young officer who had clearly been dipping deeply into the signora's excellent punch. His steps were stumbling in the dance, his hand clammy on hers, even through their gloves. Caroline steadied him and guided them both until the end of the dance.

"You are at the Cork Street barracks, are you not, Captain Williams?" Caroline said, as he stumbled against her shoulder again.

"Yes, Lady Hartley, and a blasted nuisance it is now," he answered, his words slightly slurred.

"How so, Captain?"

"All the new reinforcements they've brought in these last few weeks, of course. Rustic troops, most of

309

them, with no idea how we do things in the city. And there's no time to train them."

"How will they ever learn the proper procedures, then?"

"On patrol, mostly. They send them out with us to look for arms depots that the blasted rebels have put around the city. More trouble than they're worth, Lady Hartley. Their bumbling scares off the Irish, and the caches have been cleared by the time we get there. And then we're the ones reprimanded."

"How dreadful!"

"They're demmed sly, these rebels. There'll be trouble any day now. You should leave Dublin, Lady Hartley, or at least don't venture into unsafe sections of town. Can't be too careful these days."

"You're quite right, Captain Williams. It's most fearsome. What sections of town would you advise me to avoid? Where has your regiment been ordered next?"

The evening swirled onward, dance after dance, punch bowls and wineglasses emptied and refilled. The ballroom grew even more crowded and warm, the music louder. Caroline's feet ached from dancing, and her cheeks hurt from smiling, but she had gathered some quite useful tidbits along the way.

Until everything was shattered by a loud explosion. Bright, sparkling lights glittered outside the windows like fireworks on the king's birthday. But this was surely no harmless spectacle.

Confusion broke out on the dance floor. Ladies screamed and gentlemen swore, and there was a stampede to the windows as another explosion lit up the night.

Caroline ran to the windows with everyone else.

She managed to squeeze in front of the crowd just as yet another explosion went off overhead. It was no cannon.

"Signal rockets from Coal Quay," Captain Williams said. He sounded shocked into soberness.

"Oh, dear Lord, it's starting!" a woman shrieked. "We'll all be piked to death."

Caroline pressed her ear closer to the window. She could hear crackling sounds in the distance, like gunfire and the echo of shouts made louder through the glass. Was that woman right? Was it all starting right now? It was so much faster than anyone expected.

She suddenly felt a touch on her hand and turned to see Anna. Her sister's face was very pale, but she looked calm. "Caro, we need to go now," she said. "I've had a message."

Caroline nodded and followed Anna from the room. The staircase and foyer were deserted now, as everyone had run to look out the windows. Their passage was quick, and they were soon safe in the quiet of their own carriage. Only once they were rushing through the streets did Caroline say, "What sort of message?"

Anna drew in a deep breath, and her lip trembled. Caroline suddenly saw that her sister was not quite as calm as she pretended. She was holding herself under iron control. She took a tiny, folded paper from her beaded reticule and handed it to Caroline. "Conlan has been brought to Henrietta Street. It seems he is wounded."

CHAPTER
THIRTY

Caroline hurried behind Anna as she dashed up the stairs of the Henrietta Street house. There were four men in the foyer, hard-faced men in dusty coats and muddy boots, with daggers in their hands, but Anna didn't even look at them. The house's vast halls and rooms were silent and dim. Most of the servants had gone home to their families for the evening. But from above, Caroline could hear the echoes of a hoarse shout and a child's thin cry quickly hushed by the nanny. Anna lifted her skirts above her ankles and ran even faster.

She threw open the door to Conlan's chamber, and over her shoulder, Caroline saw her brother-in-law sitting in a chair by the fireplace. Despite the warm summer night, a fire blazed there. A young, be-spectacled man leaned over a case filled with bottles and ominous looking metal instruments.

"It's just a scratch, man—don't fuss like an old woman," Conlan shouted. Just like his cousin when wounded.

"Well, I'm glad to see you're not at death's door after all, Husband," Anna said. "I was terrified when I got your message. I was sure I would be a widow before I even arrived home." She ran over to kiss her husband. "You must cease doing this to me, Conlan."

Conlan slid his arm around her waist and drew her against him to kiss her back. "I told this fool not to alarm you, *cailleach*."

"Well, I'm very glad he did. I need to know what's happening. Now, let me see this scratch of yours."

As she knelt beside the chair to examine the bleeding cut along her husband's ribs, Conlan's gaze met Caroline's over Anna's head. "I see you arrived home safely, Caroline."

"No thanks to that cousin of yours," Anna muttered. She reached for a nearby basin of water and a sponge and carefully dabbed at the wound. "Your family is terribly reckless. I ought to lock all of you in the cellar."

"And the Blacknalls aren't reckless at all, I suppose," Conlan scoffed. "By the way, Caro, this young man is Dr. Linden. He's useful sometimes, and a dashed nuisance at others. But he's usually discreet, if you should ever need him."

"I really ought to bleed you, Your Grace," the doctor said.

"The last thing I need is to lose more blood, man," Conlan said. "Bandage it up; that's all it needs. I need to get back out there."

"You certainly will not," Anna said sternly. "What happened to you?"

Conlan gave a fierce frown, but Anna merely scowled back. "They rose too soon, of course, even after we warned them. They had some grandiose plan to block the artery roads and overwhelm all the power centers of the city—the Castle, the army barracks, Kilmainham Gaol. It's been obvious all along that they don't have the support needed to succeed. Not enough men, not enough arms, and no way to distribute the ones they have, and the government ready for them. But their blood is up. Old anger over the flogging and killing of their comrades won't be contained any longer. Emmet is losing control."

"How did you get hurt?" Caroline asked. She sat down on the edge of the nearest chair and balled her fists in her lap. It was hard to sit still and listen, to not fly into a panic and dash around like a bedlamite.

"One of my men heard a rumor that Lord Kilwarden, chief justice of the King's Bench, was dragged from his carriage and piked on his way to the Castle. The troops are pouring out from the Royal Barracks, loyalists hammering on the Castle gates to be let in for shelter. Panic is overtaking this whole place." Conlan let out a shout as Anna prodded at the wound.

"It needs stitches," she said. "You're going to have another scar, I fear. And you're fortunate that is all it is, if you went running into a fight, Conlan McTeer. You've been telling them for weeks to hold off. It shouldn't be your battle now. You have to think of your people at Adair, of the children."

"I think of them all the time, and of you," Conlan said. "If those bloody fools want to fight, they'll fight, no matter what. But we heard there were troops headed for the south quay, where a large rebel armory is hidden. We had to warn them."

"He ran into a skirmish on Thomas Street," Dr. Linden said, as he rummaged in his case for a needle and thread. "One of his men brought him back here after a dagger caught him in the ribs and then sent for me."

"I'm glad someone showed some sense tonight," Anna said. "Where are the men now?"

"On the south side of the city with Grant."

"Grant!" Caroline cried. "He is out there in the battle?"

"He said someone had to continue on and warn them to move the arms out," Conlan said. "He was to make his way back here after."

"How long ago was that?" Caroline demanded. Grant was out there in all that violence and chaos. Maybe he was hurt—maybe even worse. She was overcome with a frantic fear, and she couldn't sit still. She jumped up to pace the room, stopping only to peer out the window. Henrietta Street was quiet enough, all the large houses dark and silent. But in the distance she saw the glare of bonfires and heard the crackle of gunpowder and shouts, like holiday fireworks.

But this was no holiday. This was all too real. Captain Williams had said the regiments were being called out from the outlying barracks to make their way to the south edges of the city. They would be there at any moment, and Grant was right in their path.

"He's been gone for a few hours," Conlan said. "He should be back by now, unless he got caught in another skirmish."

Caroline pounded her fist on the windowsill. "I have to go find him now."

"Caro, no!" Anna cried.

Caroline looked over her shoulder at her sister and tried to smile. "Oh, Anna. If Conlan needed saving, wouldn't you go after him? Despite the danger?"

"Certainly I would," Anna said immediately. "Oh, Caro. I see. He is your Conlan."

"I don't know what nonsense you two are talking," Conlan shouted. "But no one is going anywhere."

Anna laid her hand gently on his arm. "I just don't think we can stop her, darling, no matter how much we try."

He looked into his wife's eyes for a long, silent moment, as if wordless thoughts passed between them. Then he nodded, and held out a tightly folded note to Caroline. "I need someone to trust to deliver this message. I know I can trust you."

"Those men in the foyer are yours, aren't they, Conlan?" Caroline said, taking the note and tucking it in her sleeve. "One of them can come with me to show me the way. We can follow the back streets and alleys and try to avoid the fighting. I'll need some breeches to change into, and any weapons you might have handy."

She hurried out of the room, Conlan's shouts ringing after her. Caroline had one thought, one focus alone—to find Grant and bring him back safely. That was the only thing that mattered.

THE WIDE STREETS AND SQUARES OF THE SOUTH SIDE WERE eerily silent as Caroline and her guard hurried through them. The summer night was warm and lit by bright stars, which made it even stranger. Dublin was a sociable, raucous place, and usually on such a fine evening open carriages would be dashing past, their inhabitants calling greetings to each other as they made their way from party to party.

But the silence didn't last. As they crossed over into the Thomas Street area, Caroline heard shouts and gunshots. The noise grew louder and louder as they headed southward. People ran by them. not slowing down in their great haste to be away.

Caroline swam against the panicked stream, toward danger rather than away. Grant was out there somewhere, and she would never turn back until she found him.

The streets grew narrower and darker, crisscrossed by alleys and lined with old brick warehouses and ramshackle offices. They were moving closer to the river, and the smells of rotting fish and burning wood grew thicker and more pungent, as did the crowd.

A large man in a rough wool coat ran past and knocked Caroline against the wall. She stumbled and nearly fell, and Conlan's guard caught her arm. He pulled her into a doorway just as another group surged past with torches and blunderbusses.

"They must have opened up the arms store on Thomas Street," he said. "You should go back now, my lady."

Caroline peeked around the edge of the doorway to see that the sky near the river was tinged red-orange, and the smell of smoke was even thicker. She shivered as she thought of the warehouse that once burned around them, the heat and the fear of it all. She had never wanted to experience such a terrible thing again. But she had to move ahead. There was no choice. Her need to find Grant was stronger than any fear. She shook her head. "Just a little farther."

They ducked out of the doorway's meager shelter and hurried on their way. The streets were littered with pikes, their tall wooden handles splintered, some of the steel tips stained with crusted blood. Caroline leaped over them and kept running.

They crossed over one of the bridges spanning the Liffey River. On this side of the river, the chaos was even greater. Mobs of people hurried one way then the other, as if no one knew where to go or what to do. Barricades were being built across roadways out of heaps of old crates, broken furniture, stones, and bricks. One alley was blocked by a toppled cart, its horse dead in its traces. Bonfires burned close beyond the barricades, their flames dancing higher and higher toward the sky. Windows broke with a metallic tinkle that somehow seemed even more frightening than the gunfire.

From the city walls came the hollow boom of cannons. Caroline kept her head down and kept going. Conlan had said Grant would be found at Thomas Street, which was not far away now. Yet the few short streets might as well be miles.

"We can go around this way and find a back road that might be quieter," the guard said.

He led her behind a large, empty building, its boarded windows staring out blankly at the war-torn night. A thick roof beam lay across one narrow alley entrance. Caroline started to step onto it, but the guard grabbed her arm.

"No, my lady!" be cried. "It's filled with explosives to hold off the soldiers if they come this way." He carefully lifted Caroline over the beam, and they made their way to the end of the alley.

It opened onto Thomas Street, usually a place of

lively taverns and cheap shops, a favorite of the dock
workers. There was one small, obscure book dealer
there that Caroline liked to visit from time to time. It
had been quieter of late, thanks to the roving press
gangs, but tonight the street was utterly desolate. The
lanterns were broken out, leaving complete darkness
in their wake. More pikes were tossed haphazardly
into the gutter.

A paper blew against Caroline's foot, and she bent
to pick it up. It was torn and stained, the printing
hasty and smudged, but she could see it was a procla-
mation calling for "a free and independent republic in
Ireland." It was signed by Robert Emmet.

She stuffed the paper in her pocket and went on
to the end of the dark street. There they turned in the
direction where Conlan said Grant would be. If he
had not been caught in the battle.

The old warehouse serving as an armory had its
doors thrown wide open. A small group of men ran
out with guns in their hands, so Caroline knew
someone was still inside. Waiting for the army that
was on its way.

"Stay behind me," the guard said.

Caroline crept with him through the ground floor,
which was littered with crates and heaps of rough-
chopped firewood. At the back was a rickety staircase,
and faint lamplight spilled from the door at the top.
She could hear the rise and fall of voices.

She tiptoed up the steps and listened carefully for
an accent that sounded like Grant's. The guard drew
his pistol, and she did the same.

"Who's there?" a man's frantic voice shouted. A
silhouette appeared in the doorway, blunderbuss
aimed at them.

"I came from Conlan McTeer," her guard answered. "I'm looking for Grant Dunmore."

"How do we know that's true?" the man with the gun demanded.

Caroline stepped out into a beam of light. "I'm also looking for him. Tell him Caroline is here."

The door was shoved back, and Grant appeared there. "Caro! *Mac an donais*, woman, what are you doing here?"

"I came to find you, of course," she said, echoing the words she used on Muirin Inish. She rushed up the stairs to catch him in her arms. He seemed unhurt, with no bleeding wounds. He was not dead in some filthy gutter. If only he would stay that way. "And to deliver a message from Conlan. He said he needed someone trustworthy to deliver it."

She held out the note, and he hugged her so fiercely he lifted her off her feet. "My cousin must be insane to let you go wandering the streets," he growled.

"I had Conlan's guard to show me the way," she said. She pulled back to study his face. His hair was hastily tied back, and his cheek was smudged with gunpowder. His eyes were dark-rimmed, but he was the most beautiful thing she had ever seen. "And Conlan and Anna couldn't stop me. I had to find you."

"It seems the battle has moved northward." Caroline glanced around the room. Gun boxes were broken open and empty, with only the sawdust they were packed in left to spill onto the floor. The men who had been standing around the walls disappeared out the door.

"As you can see, I think our work here is done,"

Grant said. "There's nothing left here for the soldiers to find."

"What were you doing exactly?"

"Handing out the guns and pikes that were stored here to anyone that would take them. We had to clear out the stash quickly. What else did Conlan say?"

"That Lord Kilwarden was dragged from his carriage and piked earlier tonight. And that reinforcements are being sent from the outlying barracks."

"Damn it all." Grant rubbed his hand over his face. "Troops will be pouring through these streets and alleys at any minute."

"What can we do? Can we spread the warning?"

Grant grimly shook his head. "As I'm sure you saw, it's utter chaos out there. Any modicum of control Emmet and his officers had is long gone. They'd all do well to take shelter in The Liberties. Come with me."

"Where are we going?"

"Back to your sister's house, where you never should have left, Caroline."

She grasped his hand tightly in hers. "After all we've been through, it would feel far worse to sit and wait, not knowing."

He lifted her hand to his lips for a quick kiss. "Then together we'll stay."

He led her out onto the stairs, where a few of the men still waited. "Reinforcements are coming from outside the city," Grant said quietly. "If there are any other arms stores, they need to be cleaned out right away."

"I'll go to McMaster's and let them know there," Caroline's guard said.

The others all hurried out into the night, and

Grant led Caroline after them. They turned back the way she had just traversed, away from the fires and explosions along the river.

Grant held on to her arm as they hurried down narrow back lanes, taking a circuitous route that changed in an instant whenever they glimpsed trouble. Troops marched by, their boots ringing on the cobblestones, just behind bands of rebels fleeing for their lives from the barricade. Ragged bands of beggars slipped by, loaded with looted goods, and once Caroline saw a most horrible sight—a cart filled with bloodied bodies.

Grant pulled her even closer to his side. "We'll be home soon," he said.

She nodded, but in a very strange way she felt as if she was home. She would never choose to be in such a frightening, nightmarish place, seeing the worst of what humans could do, but she was with Grant. When they were together, they were stronger.

Suddenly, there was a loud bang, much too close, and something swift and sizzling flew over Caroline's head. Grant dragged her to the ground at the base of a brick wall and threw himself on top of her. There was another crack, and a stone pediment high above them broke apart.

"What is it?" she whispered. She felt frozen with alarm, every sense vibrating as she waited for another explosion.

"Bloody sunman," Grant said tightly. He wrapped his arms hard around her and held her close in the shelter of his body.

"Army or Irish?"

"Could be either. They're surely all over the place

tonight and not asking questions before they shoot. Lie very still."

Caroline carefully turned her head just a bit to peer past Grant's arm at the building across the lane. She thought she glimpsed a moving shadow in one of the upper windows, a glint of metal in the moonlight, but she wasn't sure.

"That top window on the right, I think," she murmured. Grant's hand slid very, very slowly toward the gun at his waist. But he didn't have to try to get off a shot. A large wagon careened around the corner and came clattering noisily down the street toward them. It was loaded with enormous barrels that made a tall barrier, and Grant and Caroline jumped to their feet as it passed. They ran alongside it, keeping it between them and the figure in the window, until they spilled out onto a much wider street.

The lamps here were not broken out, and as they collapsed onto a doorstep to catch their breath, Caroline bad a glimpse of Grant's face. He looked utterly furious.

He caught her by her arms and roughly dragged her close. "You crazy woman!" he growled. "What if you had been killed?"

"What if *you* had been killed?" she cried. Her own anger bubbled up in her, all the fear and danger of the night boiling together with her fierce love for Grant.

"I couldn't bear it if something happened to you," he said, and gave her a little shake. "I could never live with myself if you were hurt, if I lost you."

As Caroline stared up into his burning eyes, she couldn't breathe. "Because you would feel guilty again? Because I would weigh on your conscience?"

"No, you fool woman. Because I love you, and I can't ever lose you again."

"Oh, Grant," she sobbed. "I love you, too. I know I shouldn't, I know we shouldn't, but I can't escape it."

"I save you, you save me," he said. "I think it's our fate, even if we fight it."

"Then don't fight it anymore."

Grant kissed her fiercely, his mouth hard on hers and full of the desperate, wonderful, all-consuming passion they bad found against all the odds, in the most terrible of circumstances.

Even with the chaos of explosions in the distance, panic and pandemonium all around them, she had to laugh.

"Oh, Grant," she whispered. "I feel so ridiculously happy at this moment, despite where we are. Does that make me entirely mad?"

"We're both entirely mad. I'm completely convinced of that." He kissed her once more, quickly, and tugged her to her feet. "Come on, Caro. We're almost home."

CHAPTER

THIRTY-ONE

Caroline propped her elbow on the piles of pillows on the bed and watched Grant as he slept. The daylight was bright yellow-white as it streamed through the window and over his face. His brow was deeply furrowed, and his fists curled atop the sheets as if he went on fighting even in slumber.

It had taken many hours for her to persuade him to rest, even after their mad flight across the city to land back at Henrietta Street. Grant and Conlan insisted on staying up as the news of the night came to them in frustrating spurts, messages that contradicted and canceled previous news. Finally with the light of day, it became clear the rising had been decisively put down, just as Conlan had feared.

Despite the way it had felt to Caroline while in the very midst of it, the way it seemed the whole city was a battle zone, the fighting had been rather localized. Some districts had seen no violence at all, though where there had been skirmishes it was fierce and deadly. The dead were still being gathered up and piled in the courtyard of the Castle. Soldiers explored every street and alley, and the rebels who had not fled were soon found and thrown into Kilmainham Gaol. Bridge crossings and roads out of the city were guarded, and houses were searched.

But not the houses of Henrietta Street. Not the houses of dukes, even Irish ones. All those houses rested uneasily in the bright day, waiting for the next chapter to begin. Caroline gently took Grant's hand in hers and studied his long, elegant fingers. The palm was scraped, and there were still gunpowder smudges beneath the nails, a reminder of last night's turmoil. She had the feeling that life with Grant would mean there was always a "next chapter," always excitement and trouble. Yet she wouldn't have it any other way.

She pressed a soft kiss to his fingertips, and his eyes opened. He started to sit up, but she gently pressed him back down on the bed. "What time is it?" he said.

"Oh, terribly late, I should think," she answered. "But you need to rest."

"So do you." Grant kissed her fingers, one by one, slowly, as if to savor her. He held her palm against his chest, and she could feel the steady, reassuring beat of his heart.

He was alive. They were both alive, and together. Caroline wanted only that, forever and ever. She slid down beside him on the bed and rested her head on his shoulder. "I'm not tired," she said. "I know I should be, but when I close my eyes, I keep seeing everything that happened last night. It seems like a nightmare now, so hazy and unreal. After 'ninety-eight, I thought I would never see such a thing again."

The corners of his mouth turned down, and his

hand tightened over hers. "You must try and forget it now, Caro. It is done."

"Is it? I think it will never be done, not here. Not until Ireland is its own country. Conlan won't give up the cause, will he? And neither will you. I can't hide in my books forever. I have to fight, too."

"*Gaolach*," Grant said. "There are many ways to fight and to help those who need us. You have to hide in your books—that is your work."

Caroline laughed. "When you put it that way, how can I say no? I suppose we all must use the talents we are given."

"I wouldn't say that. You fought fiercely on our journey and last night. I doubt I would be here without you, my Badb. But I would much prefer that you were safe in the library."

"I think we've learned libraries can sometimes be the most dangerous places of all. What will you do now?"

"I think it would be best if I left the city for a time and stayed quiet until things have settled down. Conlan and Anna say they will go to Adair as soon as the roads are open. I may go back to Muirin Inish."

"Muirin Inish?" Caroline said in surprise. "I thought you said the people there probably wouldn't welcome you back."

Grant laughed wryly. "I'm sure they won't be overjoyed to see me. But it's my home now. If I work hard enough, I'm sure they'll learn to accept me. In a decade or two."

"It is a beautiful place, despite everything." Caroline thought of the rocky, wave-tossed shore, of the old monastery and all the sites yet to be discovered, the rolling gray-green fields. "But can you bear to live in the castle again?"

Grant shrugged. "The castle does seem cursed, I'm afraid, or at least the islanders will always say that. Perhaps I'll knock it down and build something else. Something entirely new with no ghosts."

"A fine Palladian villa?"

"If that's what you would want, Caroline."

"Me?" She sat up and stared down at him in surprise.

He looked up at her. His face was set in that cool, wary expression that he so often wore, but his eyes held a bright gleam in their dark depths. "I have no right to say this, I know. I've led you into danger time and again ever since we met, and if you had any sense at all, you would run as far from me as you can."

"I think we have quite established that I do not possess any sense," Caroline said. Her stomach fluttered with tiny, nervous butterflies. Was he going to ask her what she thought—hoped—he was? She had the feeling that in the next moment the course of her life would truly change, and she would have to decide once and for all—safety or passion?

"I must have none, either, for I know I can't be without you, Caroline," Grant said. "I've lived my whole life alone, serving only my own selfish ends, until I looked into your eyes and saw the goodness of your soul. You showed me a better way to be, and I never want to go back to the way my life was before. So I must do one more selfish thing."

"What is that?" she whispered.

"I have to ask you to be my wife, to come back to Muirin Inish with me and help me build a life for us there. I love you, Caroline, and I will spend the rest of my days trying to be worthy of you. Please, give me a chance to do that." He took her hand and raised it to his lips for a tender kiss. "Please."

Caroline let out a ragged sob and gently cradled his scarred cheek in her palm. He had asked her, and now she knew her decision was clear before her—she chose passion. She chose a life with him, always and forever.

"Yes, Grant, I will marry you," she said. "I could do nothing else. We belong together, don't we? I think we always have. And I love you, too. So very much."

Grant threw back his head and let out an exultant, triumphant shout. He caught her in his arms and kissed her, their mouths meeting in a joyful burst of passion and hope. And Caroline knew that even in the midst of difficult days, they would always have that. They would always have each other, true partners and a port in any storm. It was all she could ever want.

They tumbled down onto the bed, laughing, their arms and legs entangled as the morning sun washed over them. "We'll always take care of each other now, won't we?" she said.

"Always," Grant answered. And she knew it was the most solemn, most precious promise she had ever been given.

EPILOGUE

MUIRIN INISH, ONE YEAR LATER

Caroline, Lady Dunmore, sat atop the rise of a green hill with her sketchbook propped on an easel before her and a pile of books beside her. It was a warm day, the dawning of summer after a long winter. The skies had cleared, the sun peeking from behind the pale gray clouds, and she had come out to sketch the ruins in order to illustrate the newest chapter of her book.

She smiled as she studied the shadow-dappled monastery in the valley below her perch. She wasn't the only one who had come out to take advantage of the fine day. Maeve, who now worked as Caroline's lady's maid, had brought food there with her mother and siblings, and their shouts of laughter as they raced around the old stones rang out on the breeze. Far beyond, Caroline could see the fishing boats tied up in port, and the men at work mending their nets and cleaning their vessels. The island was coming back to life.

In the other direction, work went on to finish the

new manor house where the old castle once stood. It would be a smaller dwelling than the sprawling castle, with no frightening towers and crumbling walkways waiting to make the unwary fall. The walls were of sturdy gray stone and the windows were thick to withstand storms. But the rooms would be large and airy, full of light, and there would be the finest library in all Ireland.

There would be a fine nursery, too. And hopefully it would be all done and decorated by the autumn, before their new arrival made an appearance. The small cottage where they had spent the cozy winter, with all their books in crates around them, would never do for three.

"Never fear, little one," Caroline whispered as she pressed her hand over the great swell of her abdomen beneath her apron. "Your lovely new home will be all ready for you."

As if in agreement, she—for Caroline was sure it was another stubborn Blacknall woman—kicked out and made Caroline laugh. The baby had been so active lately, as if she was also glad the summer had arrived.

Caroline turned to reach for her pencil box, which sat atop a stack of new books. They had just arrived mysteriously aboard one of the fishing boats, along with a letter from Mademoiselle Victorine. The books had been her father's, she wrote in her message. Sadly, the Vicomte had died at Christmas, but he wished for Caroline to have these volumes for her studies. Victorine herself had no need of "dusty books," because she had just married a high-ranking officer in Napoleon's army and was busy cutting a dash in Paris. There had also been a letter from Anna, saying she and the children would be on the island for a long visit before the baby was born, so she could make sure the new house was properly decorated. Caroline's stepdaughter Mary was also expecting a child in the winter, and all was quiet in Dublin.

So everything seemed settled in the world now. Caroline knew better than to believe it would last, but for now, life was wonderfully sweet.

As she turned back to her sketch, she glimpsed her husband striding up the hill. Grant had been surveying the fields that morning, and he wore an old tweed coat and mud-splattered buckskin breeches and high boots. His hair was even longer now, and tied back at the nape of his neck, but the wind tugged loose bronze-brown strands that brushed against his shoulders.

Even after months of marriage, her heart lifted at the sight of him, and she felt a heated surge of desire and happiness. She could hardly believe he was hers and that they had built this life together. That they belonged to each other. She waved to him, and closed up her sketchbook to run down to meet him.

"I was about to start our meal without you," she said. He kissed her, once, twice, and gently caressed the swell of her stomach where the baby rested. The baby responded to her father's touch with another fierce kick.

Grant gave a delighted laugh. "I'm sorry I kept the two of you from your luncheon. Someone seems quite demandingly hungry."

"We both are. Cook's lemon tarts have been calling to us from the basket. But we've been quite busy with our work as well." Caroline took his hand

and led him back up the hill to where their meal waited. "Tell me about your day, Husband."

"Dirty, and full of dull things like barley and potatoes and sheep. But it just got much, much better the minute I saw you." He kissed her again, and in that kiss, Caroline could feel all she had ever wanted and all the dreams that bad finally come true. She was at home at last and forever. "In fact, Wife, I would say this is the most perfect day so far..."

AUTHOR'S NOTE

Lady of Seduction is the last of my "Daughters of Erin" trilogy, and I'm very sad to say good-bye to the Blacknall sisters and their heroes! I've had so much fun spending time in their world of romance, danger, and the beauties of Ireland (though I'm also very glad the "danger" part was only experienced in the safety of my desk chair). I've been looking forward to seeing Caroline's story ever since I finished writing the first book, *Countess of Scandal*. I hope you've enjoyed Caroline and Grant's story as much as I have.

The Rising of 1803 was not nearly as widespread as the rebellion of 1798 and was plagued by bad luck and poor timing, though at first it seemed to have many advantages. Its charismatic leader was Robert Emmet, only twenty-five in 1803. In 1798, when he was a student at Trinity College, he became secretary to a United Irish group, and was expelled from the school, and a warrant was issued for his arrest. He fled to France, and then worked to secure French military aid for another rising. He wasn't successful in this, but he returned to Ireland in October 1802 to begin plans for his own rebellion.

At first things seemed to go well. He was able to set up secret arms depots around Dublin to make firearms and ammunitions and produce his own invention, a folding pike that could be easily concealed. He made contact with his old comrades, United Irish officers who bad gone into hiding after 1798 or melted into private life. He thought he could reassemble the old armies of rebels, because anger over the last rebellion still ran high. But the government had suspicions, and after the explosion at the secret Patrick Street armory, their defensive preparations increased. Emmet was forced to advance the planned date of the rising before he had secured French aid or the support of the rural United Irish. The rising saw fierce fighting in Dublin, mainly in the Thomas Street area, with explosive-packed beams, barricades, snipers, and hand-to-hand skirmishes in the street. Lord Kilwarden, Lord Chief Justice of Ireland, was dragged from his carriage and killed, igniting the fires of revenge in the government forces.

Sporadic clashes went on through the night, but the army had quelled the rising by morning. There were estimated to be twenty army and fifty rebel fatalities. Emmet fled into hiding, but was captured on August 25 and executed on September 20. He is famous for his impassioned speech from the dock, which concluded:

"Let no man write my epitaph; for as no man who knows my motives dare not vindicate them, let not prejudice or ignorance, asperse them. Let them and me rest in obscurity and peace, and my tomb remain uninscribed, and my memory in oblivion, until other times and other men can do justice to my character. When my country takes her place among the nations of the Earth, then, and not till then, let my epitaph be written. I have done."

A few sources I used when working on *Lady of Seduction* were:

The Islands of Ireland, Thames & Hudson, 2005 (Excellent source for constructing the fictional Muirin Inish)

FS Bourke, *The Rebellion of 1803, An Essay in Bibliography*, 1933

Marianne Elliott, *Partners in Revolution: The United Irish and France*, 1988

Patrick Geoghegan, Robert Emmet, A Life, 2002

Ruan O'Donnell, *Robert Emmet and the Rising of 1803*, Irish Academic Press, 2003

Visit my website at http://ammandamccabe.com for more information. *Slan go foill!*

ALSO BY AMANDA MCCABE

Kate Haywood Elizabethan Mysteries

Murder at the Princess' Palace

Murder at Westminster Abbey

Murder in the Queen's Garden

Murder at the Queen's Masquerade

Murder at Whitehall

Murder at the Royal Chateau

Daughters of Erin

Countess of Scandal

Duchess of Sin

Lady of Seduction

Scandalous St. Claires

One Naughty Night

Two Sinful Secrets

Flora Flowerdew Victorian Mysteries

Flora Flowerdew & the Mystery of the Duke's Diamonds

Regency Rebels

Because of Miss Everdean

The Earl's Misplaced Bride

Delighting the Duke

The Earl's Second Chance

ABOUT THE AUTHOR

Amanda McCabe wrote her first romance at the age of sixteen--a vast historical epic starring all her friends as the characters, written secretly during algebra class (and her parents wondered why math was not her strongest subject...)

She's never since used algebra, but her books (set in a variety of time periods--Regency, Victorian, Tudor, Renaissance, and 1920s) have been nominated for many awards, including the RITA Award, the Romantic Times BOOKReviews Reviewers' Choice Award, the Booksellers Best, the National Readers Choice Award, and the Holt Medallion. She lives in New Mexico with her lovely husband, along with far too many books and a spoiled rescue dog.

When not writing or reading, she loves yoga, collecting cheesy travel souvenirs, and watching the Food Network--even though she doesn't cook. She also writes as Laurel McKee. historical Elizabethan mysteries as Amanda Carmack., and Eliza Casey...

Please visit her at http://ammandamccabe.com

9 781648 393686